Prai

THE DOG WALKER

A *Marie Claire* must-read

"A clever, fresh slant on infatuation and love . . . made even better by lots and lots of dogs."
—Lauren Weisberger, author of *The Devil Wears Prada*

"It's a great pleasure to meet a dog-walking heroine who loves to snoop. . . . Sweet."
—*The New York Post*

"Delightful."
—*Us Weekly*

"Laugh-out-loud funny, poignant, and brilliantly observed. Schnur is a true original. Some day, readers of other authors will say, 'It's good, but it's no Schnur!'"
—Al Franken, author of
Lies and the Lying Liars Who Tell Them

"*The Dog Walker* will delight and entertain both dog lovers and romance readers. . . . [A] page-turner, which moves toward a satisfying conclusion."
—*Library Journal*

"A perceptive comedy of errors."
—*The Mirror*

"Imagine Julia Roberts in the movie walking eleven dogs on leashes (it could happen), and learn all about her love life. The book is a trip; it's breezy, it's wacky."
—Elmore Leonard, author of *Mr. Paradise*

"What a delightful, witty, warm, wise, funny and stylish debut! [A] winner."
—Harlan Coben, author of *Just One Look*

THE
Dog Walker

A NOVEL

Leslie Schnur

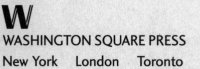

WASHINGTON SQUARE PRESS
New York   London   Toronto   Sydney

Washington Square Press
1230 Avenue of the Americas
New York, NY 10020

Copyright © 2004 by Leslie Schnur

First Washington Square Press paperback edition June 2005

10 9 8 7 6 5 4 3 2 1

Library of Congress Cataloging-in-Publication Data

Schnur, Leslie
    The dog walker : a novel/Leslie Schnur.—1st Atria Books hardcover ed.
        p. cm.
    ISBN   0-7434-8207-7
    ISBN 978-0-7434-8208-0 (Pbk)
    ISBN   0-7434-8208-5 (Pbk)
        1. Dog Walking—Fiction. 2. New York (N.Y.)—Fiction. I. Title.

    PS3619.C449D64 2004
    813'.6—dc22

                                                    2004040981

WASHINGTON SQUARE PRESS and colophon are registered trademarks
of Simon & Schuster, Inc.

Manufactured in the United States of America

For information regarding special discounts for bulk purchases,
please contact Simon & Schuster Special Sales at 1-800-456-6798
or business@simonandschuster.com

For Miriam and Gabe,
my wonderful and unusual children
(who wrote their own dedication)
and
For Charlie, the best dog in the world
(who didn't, but would certainly have agreed)

Charlie
1988–2004

THE
Dog Walker

1

Nina Shepard was in love with a man she'd never met. Perfect, she thought, as she relaxed in the bath she was taking on this sweltering afternoon. The notion made her laugh out loud with that throaty gust of hers. Normally, she couldn't care less about the irony-is-dead-or-not-dead argument, but now at least she knew which side she was on.

It was funny how she could know more about a man she'd never met than all the men she had met put together. She knew that he read books. Okay, so it was that trendy kind of real-life adventure-tragedy-on-Everest-in-Antarctica-in-Krakatoa-with-sharks-with-fire stuff. Sure, it was Dick Lit (a term Nina had coined in response to Chick Lit), but they were books, for god's sake, and not just the sports or business pages that many men considered "reading." She knew he listened to Mozart as well as Lenny Kravitz, neither her favorite, Mozart being totally overrated, and Lenny being just plain derivative and white-bread, but she appreciated the scope. That he periodically went to hear live jazz and even see a Broadway play now and then. She knew he had what seemed to be a nice relationship with his mom and dad. That he had a lovely dog, if she could excuse the fact—and she could, but on this issue, it took some consideration—that he hadn't gotten him at a shelter, but had bought him for who knows how much through a breeder. That he'd gone to Penn, that he worked for a high-powered corporate law firm, which gave her pause, the lawyer thing, but they paid him pretty goddamn good for a guy just turning thirty-two. That he liked to ski, to watch baseball on TV, to play poker every Wednesday night in a coed game. That he ran in Central Park five days a week and that his next vacation would be spent river-rafting down the Bio Bio in South America. That all that exercise gave him an outdoorsy look that was so appealing and sexy and masculine. That he had a singular nose. That he was a Democrat, and contributed generously to a variety of good, liberal causes from the ACLU to Coalition for the Homeless. That he was a non-practicing Catholic, though Christmas was important to him. Christ, he would begin his shopping in September, if he was to repeat what he did last year. He was that organized and thoughtful. He was her wish list, with only a couple minor infractions, personified.

Now, if only she could meet him.

It had been one of those hot and muggy New York City summer days that cooks the garbage, making a stink so profound that Nina promised herself yet again that next sum-

mer, no matter how poor or rich she was, how much work
she had, or didn't have, who she was involved with—she
should be so lucky—or not, no matter what, she'd be sitting
on some beach in California, breathing the cool fresh ocean
air, drinking a Corona out of the bottle. With lime. And it
was only June, for god sakes. August was going to be like the
Mojave, without the dry heat. She was feeling sorry for herself and very disgusted with feeling sorry for herself.

As usual with Nina, it was no win, no win.

So she felt as deserving as she could of this luxuriant
bath, fragrant with bubbles, that she was now so decadently
taking on a Tuesday afternoon at four. She'd finished her
morning and afternoon walks, taken the last dog home and
finally had some time for herself. As her head rested against
the tub, she let her mind drift along with her hair, which,
like a mermaid's, flowed through the water, this way and
that, softly. Had she only fins instead of legs she could swim
to that distant California shore, free, easy, and dogless,
where she'd meet a dangerous pirate who would somehow
turn her into a real woman and fuck her brains out and read
her poetry and gently stroke her face with his beautiful
hands and they'd live happily ever after in a shack, which
they'd chosen because they could live anywhere since they
were filthy rich from his booty, which had been stolen from
a mean dictator whose demise meant freedom for all the
people in the land, so it was okay.

After thirty-five years, she liked her legs. A year of dog
walking and they were still short, but in good shape,
strong and lean and brown. She took the loofah that was
sitting in a wooden slatted Japanese box and brushed

them, feeling life there in those limbs. She brushed her hips, her arms, her neck, and shoulders, easing her strained muscles and scrubbing her skin just as she was told to do by that bitch at Bloomingdale's who had asked her, all incredulous, "You don't exfoliate?" The things she didn't know.

Just yesterday she had gone into the Town Shop on Broadway, which her best friend, Claire, had sworn by, to buy a new bra for these breasts of hers that now, as the water lifted and separated them, looked pert and lovely as they poked out of the bubbles. Nina had a body she was told men loved, but having large breasts required a serious bra. Claire wore a size 34B and that sexy push-up smoothie kind. Bra shopping was easy for her. And she'd always get a thong to match, because that's how women like Claire dress. Or don't dress, depending on your point of view. Nina wouldn't wear a thong on principle. The principle being that one wears underpants to cover one's butt, not to simulate a wedgie.

"But you don't see the panty line," Claire had argued.

"I want to see the panty line," Nina countered. "I want to know I have panties on. And I want everyone else to know I have panties on. The thought comforts me. And god knows it comforts my mother. If you don't want a panty line, why wear panties at all? Thongs make you feel like something—or someone—is up your butt."

"They're sexy."

"They're stupid." She didn't mention that she'd kill herself before getting one of those Brazilian bikini waxes that seemed to have become a prerequisite to thong-wearing.

When did women her age decide that being totally hairless, except for one narrow vertical strip, was a cultural requirement? Was it that facing forty made them want to look like four?

At the Town Shop Nina had been met by a trim and orange-haired fifty-something-year-old African-American woman, her one-inch nails painted red, and topped with gold and black butterfly decals. A jangly bracelet of keys hung on her wrist.

"Hi. I'd like a new bra," Nina explained.

"Come with me." Letting the bracelet fall into the palm of her hand, the woman sifted through the keys to find the right one and unlocked a dressing room door. There were tags on the floor, a couple of bras lying on the old wooden chair, and a mirror that could've used a nice shpritz of Windex. "Take off your top."

Nina waited for the woman to close the door behind her, but she just stood there. So Nina did as she was told. There is no modesty in the Town Shop.

"Honey, you got the wrong size bra. What is that, a 36B? My lord, look at that gap. It doesn't fit you!" She pulled on the sides and tugged at the back.

"I've worn a 36B all my life," said Nina.

"And you been wrong, too, baby. Take that off. I'll get you something."

Nina took off her bra and waited topless until the saleslady returned with a dozen bras, hanging by their straps from her arm, the one with the jangly wrist.

"Try this one." She pulled off a black number, all lacy and seamed, just the way Nina hated them. It got caught for a second in the keys to The Brassiere Kingdom.

"Not my style," Nina said. "Something simpler, smoother."

"Okay, baby. Try this one."

And she handed Nina a plain beige one, seamless and soft. As she tried it on, the woman took the keys off her wrist, put them in her pocket, and dug her hands with those nails down the sides of Nina's breasts and lifted each one into its cup.

"Bend over."

Nina bent.

"Shake."

Nina shook.

"Now stand up and let's take a look."

Nina stood.

"Now that bra fits you, child."

And it did.

"What size is this?" Nina asked.

"A 34C. That's your size. Would you like a thong to match?"

And it was. And she didn't. Nina tried on the other bras and picked three and left the store marveling at how little she knew, especially about herself. When, at the age of thirty-five, you find out you've been wearing the wrong-sized bra for how many years, you realize one thing: you don't know much about anything.

All she knew was this moment, now, in this bathroom, in this tub, washing herself with this loofah. With vigor, she sloughed her heels, the sides of her feet, the calluses on her toes. Her feet that gave her so many problems, these feet with arches as high as the Empire State Building, as wide as the Atlantic, these used and abused dog-walking feet that over the course of the past year had caused her as much embarrassment as pain.

Last month at the podiatrist, she'd gotten the ultimate lesson in how little she knew about anything. There he was, so handsome, so masculine, yet so gentle in his touch. He had pulled up his little doctor stool on wheels, and taken her bare foot in his beautiful hands. He had looked at her foot with his bright blue eyes, then up at her face. Then at her foot again. The Prince had found his Cinderella, Nina thought. Maybe he'll ask for her hand in marriage right then and there. She took a deep breath and smiled.

Then he gazed into her eyes and said, "These are the closest things to club feet I have ever seen." And flashed a brilliant smile right back at her.

Nina knew he was kidding, sort of. But she felt totally humiliated just for thinking what she had been thinking. And still, weeks later, after shelling out $400 for leather orthotics to support her arches and soothe her Morton's neuroma, the thought of what she'd been thinking made her face flush with embarrassment. How could she have believed that these feet would inspire romantic love? She looked at them and noticed that she could use a pedicure. Even these piggies deserved positive attention. She laughed again, remembering the time, a few years before, when Michael, her cinematographer-libertarian-vegetarian-qigong-expert ex-husband, had recommended a chiropractor for her aching feet. Maybe she just needed an adjustment, he'd said—an understatement. She had delayed and delayed going, knowing the kind of alternative medicine he was into. So when this so-called doctor had recommended a high colonic, she simply replied "No thank you" and "No fucking way," to Michael. It was her feet that needed help, not her digestive tract. It turned out to be her heart as well.

But she didn't want to think about this stuff. What was it about a bath, anyway? Her broken heart, her bad feet, her legs, her breasts, her ex, her next, love, sex, and colonics: all this going through her mind while she stared at the hand-painted faux oxidized copper ceiling while drowning the bubbles under palmfuls of water. She was supposed to be relaxing, her mind clearing itself of life's daily detritus. But here she was, getting nuts. Baths! You soak in your own filth, the water goes from hot to lukewarm, the bubbles become a thin soapy film on the water's surface, and your mind goes to places you can't control.

And yet . . . She put the loofah back in its cradle, and scooped up a handful of what bubbles remained. They still glistened in the afternoon light that wafted in through the small glazed window, the only one in the apartment that didn't look out onto Central Park. That was something she couldn't fail to appreciate, nor everything else about this bathroom, with its rich cherry wood, its walls and floor of stone, its copper fixtures, its yin-yang feel of modern and ancient, of hard, cold and sensuous. The sepia Chinese photographs that lined the wall over the toilet, the bidet. A bidet. The height of luxury, until you think about what it's for. Even Sid, the languorous weimaraner lying on the cool floor next to the tub, seemed a study in feng shui–ness.

She ran the water and stroked her 34C breasts, her stomach, between her legs, and let the water flow there, remembering that this was how she learned, in college, to come.

Ah, those were the days. Having the time and inclination to teach oneself—via vibrator, cucumber, brush handle, and running water, sometimes with help from a joint or a glass of wine—the art of the orgasm. A nineteen-year-old boy wasn't going to take the time. So if you weren't for yourself who would be for you? And if not then, when? Since Nina was someone who went at things earnestly, this was a task she took to with devotion. And learn she did. She could feel it now, the old lessons taking effect, the flow of blood through her limbs, the ache in her thighs, her breath shortening, her neck elongating as her chin reached for the ceiling.

She thought of Daniel, the keeper of her heart. His light hair cut short, his rugged face with its incongruous boyish smile, his shoulders, his back, his chest with just the right amount of hair, his graceful hands and legs, his perfect ass.

She thought of being with him on the beach, laying in the sun, feeling its warmth on her skin, his touch all sweaty and salted and sublimely gritty with sand. She thought of him in the car, his hand around her neck, pulling her toward him with unmistakable urgency. She thought of him in her bed, kissing her belly, licking inside her thighs, then on top of her and finding his way inside.

Daniel, Daniel, this man she knew more intimately than any other in her way-too-long life, this man who'd made her come over and over again, as thinking of him made her come at this moment.

All this from going through his stuff. His mail, his drawers, his closets, his books, CD's, e-mail, photos. His pockets. And even, on those very rare occasions, she was loathe to admit, his garbage. Obviously, she knew that it was wrong. To violate the dog walkers' code of ethics: get in, get the dog, get out. But once she took that first step down that forbidden hall, once she took that first look inside that unauthorized kitchen cabinet, once she opened that first off-limits drawer, she was hooked. When had she first let herself snoop? She remembered babysitting when she was a kid, and looking through stuff for who knows what. And when she found something she shouldn't—hidden jewelry, a diaphragm, a dildo, a dirty magazine—how she felt both satisfied and ashamed. And still she couldn't stop herself.

What was to stop her? An overeater looks at an obese person and thinks that could be me. A person who drinks one too many too many times empathizes with an alcoholic: there but for the grace of god. You recognize yourself in another who has crossed the line because you realize how easy it would be for you to go there. But in the matter of the snoop, Nina had easily gone over her backyard fence and out of her neighborhood into regions unknown. Because, out of context, without relativity, without something with which to compare, boundaries are much more ambiguous. It all comes down to how well one's moral compass is working, doesn't it? Are the earth's magnetic forces strong enough to keep you heading north when you want to be going east? And how bad would it be to go east? If only once? Or twice? Would you get lost just by going off the beaten track, into a bedroom or a bathroom, for only a moment or two?

And then there's the question of bad behavior. She saw it every day in so many ways in almost every apartment she entered. Dogs ignored, dogs treated better than a child, dogs treated worse than, well, a dog. This did provide Nina with a kind of relativity. How bad was she when the owners of the dogs were so onerous? Does deviance in others provide adequate justification for being deviant yourself? It occurred to Nina as she soaked in her bath that maybe she was becoming worse than the crazy fucks whose dogs she walked.

Then she heard the front door. Oh my god, she thought. As she quickly sat up, the force of her body caused the water to slosh violently toward the front of the tub and back, almost onto the floor. She tried to still it by patting its surface, ridiculously. The dog's tail started thumping against the floor. He'd heard it too.

"Sid, ssshhh," Nina whispered. She pulled the plug and stood up, tearing a towel off the rack, putting her ear against the wall, as if she could hear better this way, through the wall, across the master bedroom, and down the hall to the foyer. The dog began to pace. Tub to wall, wall to tub, his nails tap tap tapping on the stone floors, his head cocked as he passed the door as if to hear what was happening, his whining as if a cry for help. "Ssshhh. Please, Sid, stop. Stay. Sit, for god's sake." She grabbed her clothes and began to dress.

Keys thrown on the entry table. Footsteps down the hallway.

Oh shit, thought Nina. What time is it? She found her watch on the sink and realized it was almost five. Oh god. She'd stayed too long. Her heart was beating so loudly, she was sure the intruder would hear it.

A drawer opened and closed. Coins on the chest of drawers. The computer turned on.

He was in the bedroom.

Sid was wild now, his paws up on the door, scratching. Nina jumped on top of him, pinning him firmly, one hand across his back and under his chest, so he couldn't move, as if in position to begin a wrestling match, the other holding tight across his muzzle to keep his mouth closed. A whine still crept out now and then, and all she could do was hope to god that it couldn't be heard through the solid cherry door, which seemed unlikely since she could hear everything out there.

A body sitting on the bed, shoes clunking on the floor. The rustling of clothing. Steps. The *click click click* of the computer keypad.

A yelp from Sid.

Daniel must have had heard it, because he'd stopped typing. Nina held her breath, trying to read the quiet.

"Sid?" Daniel asked.

A beat. Then.

"Hey. Where's my boy?" Daniel yelled. "Sid! Siddhartha!"

And then the damn dog was up, whining and scratching at the floor, trying to break free of Nina's clutches.

"Sid, please," Nina pleaded.

"Sid? You in there, boy?" Daniel was at the bathroom door.

Oh god, thought Nina. This is how I'm going to meet him?

"Please," she whispered. And as she opened the door a crack to let Sid out, it was pushed open from the other side.

"Wha—who are you?"

"Hi." Was it just that she'd never seen him in the flesh or did he look particularly good standing there in those boxers?

"Do I know you?"

"I was just leaving," she said.

"You Nina?"

"It was just so hot outside, I drank so much water, I really had to pee. Use the bathroom, I mean. I hope it's okay."

She saw him look at her and hoped to god her hair wasn't dripping and that she'd remembered to pull up her shorts, pull down her T-shirt, and dry her face.

She stuck out her hand. "Nice to meet you." She picked up her backpack.

Daniel squinted at her, disbelieving. His eyes were much darker than she'd thought they would be. They were eyes that made her knees melt, eyes underlined with dark shadows as if they were tired and worn, as if they'd seen much more than their owner would ever reveal.

"Sure, it's all right, I guess. But there's one at the front of the apartment, off the foyer. The one for guests. Okay?" His hair was lighter than in his pictures. His shoulders broader. It was as if his pictures had dulled and miniaturized him. Here, alive, he was vital and huge and light and dark and accentuated. He had a scar on his chin. He had a dimple on his left cheek when he smiled.

"Sure. Okay. Sorry. I just . . ." And she edged past him, smelling him, faintly, deliciously. She eyed the bed, the comforter disheveled and wrinkled where he had sat. Oh, were I that comforter, she thought.

But Daniel raised his hand. "Your hair." He reached out, taking a few wet strands between his fingers, which she couldn't help notice were long and knuckly.

Nina laughed. "Yeah. The humidity." His eyes were on her and she let out a sigh. "It really does a number on me."

He looked at her fully, suspiciously. She looked back, trying not to swoon, shook her head, and looked at her watch.

"Gee. Um, I gotta go," she said. And with one lingering look at his face, at that scar, at those eyes, at his mouth, at that place where his neck met his shoulders, she also said very slowly, "I love . . . your dog."

Before he could respond, she turned and was through the bedroom and halfway down the hall. It was only then that Daniel noticed the towel on the floor.

He called after her. "Hey, Nina!"

But the door slammed and she was out. She didn't have to wait for the elevator and once it hit the lobby, she sprinted past the Persian rugs, the antique benches and chairs, under the chandeliers, and right up to the octogenarian doorman.

"Pete, what happened?"

"I didn't have time," he answered.

"Oh god, Pete."

"Mrs. Gold had packages, the mailman was here, those Butler twins climbing on the—I'm sorry, Nina. You know I'd do anything in the world for you."

Nina smiled. "For me? Or for these?" She dug into her backpack and handed Pete a box of Goobers, as she had each and every day she had walked Siddhartha in the past month and spent a little extra time upstairs. "See you tomorrow?"

"But not so long next time." said Pete.

"I know."

Once she got outside, she could breathe again. The sky was pale orange and lavender as the sun prepared for its descent, sending shadows deep across this most extraordinary day. That was a close one, Nina thought as she made her way home, but oh god, it was worth it.

2

By the time she opened the door to her apartment, Nina was hyperventilating. Not only because she had just come face-to-face with Daniel, or because she had almost gotten caught bathing in his tub and now look what a mess she was in, or because, perhaps, of her own sloppiness, she had lost him forever, but also because she lived on the top floor of a five-floor walk-up. No matter how many times a day she did it, no matter how fit she was, it was one hell of a climb.

Sam, the best dog in the world, jumped up on Nina the minute she was in. She scratched his head and bent down mouth to muzzle. She kissed him. He licked her. He stayed by her heels as she threw her backpack, the mail she had just picked up in the lobby and her keys on the table, and opened the fridge to pour herself a glass of wine. White, ice cold, anything but Chardonnay, which was so thick and syrupy it got stuck in her teeth.

As he sat, panting, waiting for her to make a move, she sipped her drink and put on the original Broadway cast production of *South Pacific*. She was cynical, sometimes, yes. She could be curt when she grew impatient with people, which was often. But she was romantic, always. And though she knew it was anachronistic to love old Broadway musicals so—Rodgers and Hammerstein, Lerner and Loewe, even Sondheim, but never ever the pop schmaltz shit of Andrew Lloyd Webber—she couldn't help it. They spoke to her. They moved her and made her cry. (Not that making her cry was difficult. A TV commercial could do that.) But how could you not be thrilled by Ezio Pinza singing "Some Enchanted Evening"?

Then she sat at her dining table/desk/work space/drafting table at the center of her tiny apartment, and turned on her clamp-on fluorescent magnifier lamp, for those hard-to-see holes. This was where she worked hours each and every day—whenever she wasn't walking the dogs or on a date or having coffee with a friend, or taking a stupid bath—on these goddamned ridiculous structures (as opposed to sculptures, which she felt was too pretentious to call them) made from stuff she found on New York City streets. Tiny objects, the smaller the better. Beads were best: they already had holes. Little buttons were good too. Pieces of glass, of plastic, even stones worked if she could bore through them with her Black & Decker drill with its hardened steel carbide tip drill bits. Only the $\frac{1}{32}$nd size worked for the glass, which she'd learned from painful and messy experimentation. (Her cheek had taken two weeks to heal from that flying shard.) She would string them with wire that she shaped and twisted and knotted, making hangings up to eight feet tall (the height of her ceilings) containing thousands of itty-bitty broken, cut, and found pieces. Two of these masterpieces hung around her now (which she'd store in her closet to make room for her next), looking like funky crazy Calders or the stuff she saw made by mad people at the Outsider Art Fair at the Puck building in Soho. There, people from prisons and insane asylums sold their art for thousands and thousands of dollars. Someday, maybe, she sighed, as she picked a bead from the red bucket sitting on the table and strung it on the only available wire left on this piece. Sell a structure, that is. Not go to prison. Or an insane asylum.

This room, a barely-enough-space-for-a-bed bedroom, a tiny kitchen and bath, made up her apartment. Except for one other thing. She had a 750-square-foot terrace. With a park view. It was what, besides old Sam, kept her alive. And sane. So to speak.

How she got this apartment with this miracle outdoor space involved a macabre set of circumstances and a really cute cop. In a nutshell: right after her divorce she lived in the apartment directly below, and upstairs in what was now her apartment lived a guy she had seen maybe once or twice in the elevator. He dressed only in black, was covered in tattoos of the scary black warlock variety, had pins in his ears, his eyebrows, his lips and god knows where else, and played "Sympathy for the Devil" by the Stones every night so loud that her walls shook. The bass, which must have been turned to its highest possible decibel level, caused Sam to run round and round chasing his tail in some hyperkinetic energy freak-out, and forced Nina to lie awake in her bed, staring at her ceiling, unable to sleep, too afraid to move. Until she was too tired to be afraid. Then, she'd bang with a broom handle on the ceiling, and complain to the super and the landlord. But the devil kept spinning his disc.

So one night, about a month after all this started, after Nina knew the song backwards and forwards and could mouth the words along with Mick (imagining his lips, those lips) Nina got out of bed, went upstairs, and banged on the devil's door. *Please allow me to introduce myself.* No answer. How the hell could he hear her even if he wanted to? Back to her apartment she went, where she inscribed this note:

Dear Neighbor,
  You are very inconsiderate to play your music so loud. I cannot sleep and though I have asked you many times to lower it, you have ignored me completely. Please please lower your music or I will be forced to call the cops.
                                              Your Neighbor Below

She took it upstairs and slipped it under his door. Not five minutes later, she received this missive in return:

Dear Bitch,
  Satan sleeps for no one. Death to the nonbeliever. Do you think You shall be spared? Do You think Satan does not know who You are? Don't fuck with ME.
                                              Satanic Messenger

She called the cops. They found two ounces of hash in his freezer, and he was arrested. Nina got his apartment, but only with the help of the cute cop, the one with the tight ass and the mustache, which she forgave for a while because he was a cop and what did he know from right and wrong, and only after paying five grand in key money to the landlord. That cute cop had licked the backs of her knees and kissed the inside of her elbows and made love to her on the bricks of her new terrace until he could no longer stand her refusal to get involved with him. To *talk* to him. For Nina, it was the perfect post-divorce fling: at her place, on her terms, no talk, lots of sex. And she knew it would end the minute the mustache mattered. It took a surprising two months.

Nina tied a knot in the wire and stood, taking a step back to look. It's getting there, she thought. She'd name it "Walking the Dogs," she thought, because that's how she got most of its material. Yes, that was perfect. She turned off the lamp, picked up her glass of wine, and headed to the terrace. Sam padded along right behind her, but as they reached the glass door, he could take it no longer, his patience up to his fuzzy brown brow, and he pushed her out of the way, nearly tripping her to get out. The sky was black, starless. But the stellar landscape of the New York skyline, bright and glistening on this summer night, made her feel as if she were looking at the Milky Way. Music from inside made its way out. *Younger than springtime are you.* She flung herself down in a chaise, old, teak, and splintered from years of sun and rain and snow. She'd been meaning to get new outdoor furniture, but on this night, she didn't care. She looked around and felt the same mad rush she had the first time she saw this place. How lucky could a girl get? So what if she was obsessed with a stranger who thought she was just a crazy old dog walker, which, she had to admit, she had become. What had she been thinking to overstay her welcome? Not that there was a welcome, really. She just stayed too damn long, that's all. So her apartment is the size and shape of a shoebox. So she has no boyfriend, no potential sex, even, and probably never would again, now that she destroyed what chances she had with Daniel, the man of her dreams. *Angel and lover, heaven and earth, am I with you.* Exactly. But all she had was this. This space, this sky, this view, this dog, this glass of wine.

Be here now, she tried to tell herself ten times a day, every day. *Be here now.*

It didn't work.

She stood, rousing Sam from his snooze, and took one last look across the park to the east, marveling at the lights of the wealthy apartments on Fifth and past to the bridge beyond and wondered what kind of dinner parties were going on across this great, wonderful city tonight. It was her understanding that every evening people were having and attending dinner parties. Full of yummy food, good music, warm lighting. The talk was fun and furious and intellectually stimulating. People were making new friends and contacts, showing off what they knew about the Middle East, the recent discovery of that other solar system, the Schnabel retrospective at the Whitney. They talked about their trips to Spain, they talked about sex. They laughed, they argued, they formed new alliances and reaffirmed old friendships.

Nina hadn't been to a dinner party in years. Or more.

And she didn't know anybody who gave dinner parties. Unless they gave them but didn't invite her.

All of Nina's desires, everything in her that made her feel as if she were caving in on herself, all that she felt that was missing in her life—someone to love, someone to love her and appreciate her, to *cherish* her—were represented by the dinner parties she wasn't invited to. That life other people led, they led because they were loved and lovable.

She let out a sigh and walked back inside and took off her clothes, putting on a huge UCLA T-shirt that Claire had sent her. She brushed and flossed her teeth, she washed and moisturized her face, which she did every night even though she knew it didn't do a goddamn thing, that heredity and the weather and how she smiled—wrinkles, dimples and lines and all—would determine her facial future, and crawled under her covers.

She couldn't get comfortable. Christ, was it going to be one of those nights? Sam was in his usual position at the bottom of the bed where her feet should be, sending her body diagonally across it. And her head was full of all kinds of lists—from groceries she needed, to errands she had to run, to places she wanted to go, to men she had slept with.

This was a list she liked making because the number always varied. There was always a name on the tip of her tongue, an experience on the edge of her mind, or, embarrassingly, not in her mind at all, having forgotten it completely. Clearly, some things you want to forget. Like that Columbia poli sci professor she'd met at a democratic fundraiser, who said he'd left his wallet at home, so he took her there, sat her on the couch while he went into his bedroom to search, and came out stark naked. She, in some horny, craven stupidity, had laughed. And went to bed with him. Only to find out later that he'd used the same trick on what he called other "naïve democrat babes." And just yesterday she'd read a piece by him on the op-ed page of the *New York Times* embracing the conservative Supreme Court nominee and justifying his own move to the right. And the other day, while watching King, a dog in need of Ritalin if there ever was one, trying to hump Sadie, the basset hound, whose ears either drag on the ground or fly like sails, depending on the wind, a face and a name popped into her head: Dick, that dentist, who had been married three times before, each time to a *dentist*. He was someone she'd forgotten she'd ever dated, until for some mysterious reason she thought of him at that particular moment. Maybe it was his preference for that same position, she couldn't be sure.

But she never forgot, not for a day, not a detail, the one man, besides her ex, with whom she thought she was in love. It lasted six weeks. It was in college. His name was Jack Schreiber and he was an artist and so so very intoxicating. It was hot and it was intense. Lots of sex and lots of marijuana, lots of philosophizing and laughing and dreaming and that feeling that you know you're lost. Then, one night, his eyes didn't look into hers, his face turned away when she spoke and he went back to his girlfriend and Nina went back to being alone. And it was over with a thud. How could something so fine and so passionate end so abruptly and finally? How could the necking up against a brick wall in the darkness of a quiet street just stop as if there had been no momentum at all? As if the earth could stop its spinning on a dime, with no force behind it to slow it down steadily, so all its inhabitants could prepare themselves for the end. Nina hadn't been prepared, so off the earth she flew, landing hard and hurt on her ass.

It was Claire who had to tell her the truth: no one said the hottest or even the deepest relationships were the ones meant to last.

Well, what the hell does that mean, thought Nina, sitting up in her bed, throwing her covers off. Sam raised his head, looked at her, and went back to sleep. Claire's theory is totally opposed to anything Nina knew about love, which wasn't too much. Hell, if love ain't deep, what is it? She'd had her share of shallow. Her ex a case in point. Their life together consisted of movie premieres and parties, arguments about politics, about art, novels, and music, and the pros and cons of eating tempeh raw. Michael was nothing if not passionate—when it came to his own interests. And he was brilliant. He had told her so. But his and Nina's emotional life was nonexistent. He hardly looked at her, as if acknowledging her existence was beneath his Mensa mind, their sexual life was by-the-book, literally, for he consulted sex manuals to be sure he could give himself an A, and their relationship about as deep as a puddle. She'd thought she loved him, and her reasons weren't totally stupid: she loved his head, his curiosity, and what he *represented*—a cinematographer! an *artiste!* an intellectual! a lovely-to-look-at alt-lifestyle junkie! But there was no connection between them—that thing that you take for granted when you have it and can't live without when you don't.

Love, like in the songs, like when Maria sings to Tony, *Only you, you're the only thing I see forever,* soaring and magical, that is inexplicable, that comes from some deep, unknown place inside oneself, was all she wanted.

At least she wasn't desperate like so many single women her age seemed. She'd been married. She'd walked down that aisle. She didn't have to feel embarrassed that no one had loved her enough, at least in his way, to take that giant step. And she wasn't lonely in that I-hate-being-alone kind of way. It was a larger angst she felt, that perhaps a love like the one she dreamed of was not in the cards for her.

Eventually Nina fell asleep and dreamed one of her transportation dreams where she's not sure where she's going, but it's crowded, she's late, and she has a gnawing sense that she's left something important on the platform back at the station.

3

Right as Nina fell asleep, a guy from Wilton, Connecticut was opening beer bottles with his bellybutton. And William Francis Maguire, Billy to his family and friends, and Sid, the dog, were watching him on the Stupid Human Tricks segment on Letterman, confirming Billy's theory that Connecticut had to be the most overrated state in the union. The inns are too precious, and when he went away for a weekend, which was almost never, the last thing he wanted was to be forced to eat breakfast and share small talk with a yuppie couple from Boston. The rustic charm of the villages had long ago been lost to artsy-craftsy "shoppes" selling candles, paperweights, and itchy, ugly, hand-loomed mittens. The historical interest of the covered bridges, and the Revolutionary War sights couldn't beat what you could find just walking down one little side street in Greenwich Village. And one could see the leaves turn in any northeast state in America. Besides, don't these people have better things to do with their time than practice stuff like this? How many times had the last guy, also from Connecticut, the one who drank milk and made it come out of his eyes, try that before he perfected it? Once was disgusting. Over and over again was just plain stupid. The Letterman writers should've just titled the segment Stupid Humans from Connecticut, and left it at that. But what were his choices? There was Leno, the equivalent of corned beef on white with mayo, and the History Channel had yet another show about the air battles of World War II. Anything but World War II, the war Spielberg made trendy, and he'd be there.

But tonight it really didn't matter what he and Sid watched, because his mind was elsewhere. He'd had a bad day and he was in a pissy mood. His boss had griped again about how long it was taking to get a handle on Constance Chandler. How long? Ten whole days, that's how long. Couldn't he just barge in there, and see for himself what was going on? That's why they'd brought him in, wasn't it? He was the best, the top IRS agent in the North Atlantic Region. Nobody solved more cases and collected more money in the entire agency. But Billy, William at work, had argued that one had to finesse these things, that he had his own method, his own sense of timing, and it wasn't time. He agreed with those who came before him, and there were many, that something was up with her to the tune of hundreds of thousands, maybe millions. But exactly what and how and how much, he didn't know. You have to be very careful about these kinds of cases, or all the evidence can be hidden or spent or laundered in the blink of an eye. Not to worry. He had a plan, he had a deadline. The plan: well, he'd improvise. The deadline: a month or two. But both were his own and he didn't have to explain or justify himself to anybody, not after ten years of getting the bad guys and bringing home, he didn't know, maybe billions of dollars. The job was difficult enough without having a boss to answer to.

And what had that dog walker, Nina, been doing in his— or rather, this—bathroom? Was it possible she was actually taking a bath? He knew from his work that people were strange, to put it mildly. But to actually take a bath in someone else's apartment, without being invited—now, that's bordering on psychotic. He thought of how her hair was just wet enough that one lone drop found its way from her brow to the corner of her mouth, and how she ignored it, as if stubbornly refusing to acknowledge its existence, until her tongue took an unconscious swipe at it. She looked pretty cute there, all flustered, he had to admit.

Yes, he'd give her another chance, because he didn't want to have to break in a new dog walker. He looked at Sid, who sat staring at the TV, as if he got the jokes, which he probably did. Billy would set down the rules for Nina and maybe give Pete ten bucks to keep his eye on her. Time her if he had to. She should be able to get in and up, get the dog, and go down and out within five minutes. And that was generous, figuring the elevator could be up when she wanted it down and vice versa. He rubbed the tip of his right index finger into his left palm, as if squashing a bug, his left palm swiveling right to left and back—a little memory trick he'd learned from his brother Daniel, probably the only thing of value that jackass had taught him—to remind himself to time the entry and departure, to talk to Pete, and give Nina a warning.

But to give credit where it was due, Billy wouldn't be so close to nabbing Mrs. Chandler if Daniel hadn't let him use his apartment, which was, fortuitously, across the street from Mrs. Chandler's place. It was only for a couple months, so Billy could be closer to his prey. He didn't expect the transaction to go so simply, but Daniel was ready for a little R&R, as he put it, so instead of taking Billy's tiny place on West Forty-ninth Street, he went hiking in Nepal for a couple of months. And one night Daniel left with a backpack and a couple hours later Billy came in with a garment bag and a laptop and a black case, and the doorman didn't blink.

That Daniel and Billy were twins helped. Nobody noticed the change. Not the doorman, not the mailman, not the crazy dog walker, not anybody. They were monozygotic, identical twins. But not exactly. They were one of the twenty-five percent of identical twins who were mirror images of each other. Daniel's hair whorl was on the left, Billy's on the right. Daniel's right eyebrow was arched higher than his other, as was the left one on Billy, whose overbite as a kid was on his left and Daniel's was on the right, making the orthodontist have to fit them for opposite braces, which confused the heck out of the entire practice.

You had to look pretty close to see their opposite aspects, except when it came to personality. From about the age of twelve, they were opposite everything. Billy had always believed the family mythology that Daniel was the leader, Type-A, the star, while Billy was always, and would always be, number two. Born Baby B, as labeled by the hospital because Daniel was lower in his mother's belly, taking up all the room and therefore, delivered first, Billy was forced to live those nine months squished like a frog, his knees up by his ears, his entire body folded into a tiny space right under his mother's ribcage. Breach, bothered, and bewildered, Billy was delivered second, destined forever to follow in his brother's amniotic footsteps.

Daniel was always an A student, an athlete, outgoing and popular. From an early age, Billy had learned to let Daniel win, whether it was a race, a game of Sorry, a spelling bee. He even let Daniel tell the jokes, be the clown, the life of the party. Otherwise Daniel would get angry. And Billy felt, what the hell, if it was so important to his brother to be first, so be it. It wasn't as if Billy didn't have friends, excel in school, run a pretty fast five-K, or get a blue ribbon at a science fair. It's just that he always had to be on guard, protecting his brother and insuring his place at the top. While Daniel wasn't comfortable with being anything but the leader, Billy wasn't comfortable with being anything but not. Therefore, he grew up to be the more sensitive of the two, caring more for other people's feelings. His mom always said he was "the sweet one."

The price Billy paid for being kind was difficult to pinpoint. But he knew pretty early on he was never going to become President of the United States or of anything, for that matter.

I hate Letterman. He's gotten mean and he's not funny, Billy thought, as he got up and walked to the kitchen, Sid leaping way ahead and beating him there. It had been maybe ten hours since he'd eaten and that was a bowl of his favorite wonton with roasted chicken soup from the Korean salad bar deli around the corner from his office. But his cupboards were bare. And his fridge, well, he'd make some eggs. If you can't have soup, eggs come in a close second.

Three over-easy with a little salt, heavy pepper, hastily eaten standing in the kitchen, staring at the floor, later, Billy turned off the TV. He slumped in the black leather sofa, Sid curled on the floor at his feet, and took a good look at his surroundings. This apartment had Daniel written all over it. Slick, expensive, and devoid of personality. Looked like a hotel room. The only things that were specific and individual were a few books (right off the bestseller list, of course, which he read so he could talk about them; never for the enjoyment of reading) and the photos he'd put of himself everywhere. Daniel in Gstaad skiing. Daniel sky-diving in the south of France. Daniel hiking in Yosemite, Daniel at a Yankee game. Daniel shaking hands with the mayor. It was as if he were an artist who painted his muse over and over, in different scenes or perhaps different styles—here she is in his blue period, now in his cubist, now abstract—but with Daniel, the artist's muse was the artist himself.

And speaking of women, well, Billy didn't want to. What happened in San Francisco was dead and done. He didn't want to think about Daniel and women versus Billy and women. That train pulled out long ago and there was too much blood on those tracks to survive further scrutiny.

Disgusted, Billy got up and turned on his computer. As he waited for it to boot, he stared at the screen and tapped his middle three fingers on the desk, first all together and then one at a time like the *da-da-da* of the *William Tell*

Overture. He opened his e-mail. Tons of spam, stuff he couldn't believe. Pornography that you didn't have to open up to see. This time, what looked like a woman giving a horse a blow job. Couldn't be, could it? Without thinking, he turned to look for Sid, who was now fast asleep in a roll on his own bed. Good. Not that he was a prude, far from it, but he wouldn't even want the dog to see this! Imagine if he had a kid sitting on his lap, talking about his school day, laughing about some joke he'd heard, or something, as this came up on the screen. Billy rubbed his index finger into his palm. What he was going to do, he didn't know, but this just wasn't *right*.

He had a thing about right. Like not cutting in line at the movies, like saying "excuse me" if you bump into someone, like letting someone come out of a doorway before you go in, like driving considerately and never driving a Hummer, a gas guzzling military vehicle that had no place—because of the environment, because of its size, its symbolism—in personal ownership. (What's next, an F-16 in the neighbor's backyard?) Like honoring your commitments to your family, like paying your taxes because it's your duty as a citizen. Doing the right thing because that's what makes a person different from a duck.

Just like his thing about language. When he heard kids on the street using the f-word, when he heard his colleagues at work using all kinds of four-letter words, when his so-called brother used the c-word that once at Thanksgiving dinner, he cringed. Again, it wasn't because he was a prude, or that he wasn't open to street talk, in principle, or that he had such a good vocabulary. He just thought that if you had a brain, and sensitivity to those around you, you used real language. It just showed how uneducated or how sloppy or unthinking a person was when he or she resorted to words that offended.

He had to face it: this is why people thought he was a nerd. And he supposed he was. An ethical, nonswearing, trombone-playing, History Channel watching, language-respecting, scuba-diving (even that, which others did for the adventure of it, he did once or twice a year because of his love for fish, for sponges, for coral and anemones and any living underwater creature, which he catalogued diligently after each and every sighting), U.S. Department of Treasury nerd.

He had a hundred e-mails from work. Drafts of new laws, new rules, changes to old rules, new meetings, changes to those meetings, a different date, a different time. Stupid, boring stuff. If he didn't love his work so much, didn't feel how important it was, this stuff would make him sick. But then he'd read in the paper about some public school that'd had its budget cut, wiping out special reading programs, extra music classes, and he'd get inspired. Sometimes he hated his job, but he loved what he believed it could do.

More e-mail: a joke from his dad, a sentimental poem from his mom, family photos from his California cousin. News from Scuba International and upcoming trips to Cozumel, New Zealand, Belize. His buddy Jim's libertarian ravings, which this time included an article from the *Spectator.* When had it become cool to "diss" liberals? And forget people, but to disparage liberal, socially conscious thinking? I like Jim, he thought, I've known him almost my whole life. We're almost like brothers. And then he laughed out loud with one big "ha!" Closer than brothers. It was amazing, he thought, as he closed out of e-mail and turned off the computer, how friendship, and therefore, love (he guessed), the kind that lasts years, that builds history, can transcend the fact that Jim is really a narrow-minded, vitriolic . . . jerk.

And then he went to the closet, waking Sid, who followed slowly, as if wanting Billy to just settle down already. Billy turned on the light and reached inside, leaning in, searching past his two suits—one gray, one dark blue—past his shoes, past the astounding amount and variety of Daniel's clothes, behind the plastic storage boxes in the back, for the big black case hidden deep behind everything.

He took it into the living room and opened it. He removed a piece of a shiny brass trombone, fitting it gently but firmly to the next piece and the next. He affixed the mouthpiece, cleaning it first with a cloth he kept in the case, then wetting it with his tongue. And then he blew some notes, his arm stretching on the slide as far as it could go and bringing it up again, practicing the scales, feeling the weight of the instrument, the deep tones of its sound.

Sid was used to this by now and instead of cowering in the bathroom and covering his ears with his paws the way he did in the beginning, he rolled on his back on the floor, back and forth, right to left, his feet in the air, as if doing some crazy limbo dance.

And then Billy put on a Max Roach CD—the classic one with Duke Ellington and Charlie Mingus—and he began to play to it. Quietly at first, stiffly, as he listened to the music, getting the rhythm, the key. And then, as if the medicine had kicked in, the patient got up and walked. Billy played that horn boldly and unselfconsciously. He let loose for an hour that night, he and Max, just as they did almost every night, playing that trombone, accompanying it on the drums, Billy dreaming of a day when he might meet the man himself, the percussive wonder, the Shakespeare of the snare, the Newton of the cymbal. And then, not thinking about anything, but feeling his lips vibrating, his chest letting go and then sucking in air, his head, his heart, in the music.

4

The next morning was hot again and Nina dressed appropriately in bicycle shorts, a Sorbonne T-shirt, black hiking boots and socks, her hair in a ponytail, and her ever-present L. L. Bean fishing hat, which she wore dog walking, rain or shine, down over her face to her eyelids. First she took Sam out. The sky was tan, thick with air, the sooty, smelly, New York summer kind. They went to the park and walked around the reservoir to the doggie run near the tennis courts, where Nina picked up three shards of green glass and a pink button, and Sam got to jump and play and smell all the doggie butts he wanted. Humans stood around in clusters of threes and fours, talking news, the heat, and the adorable things their dogs did and other bullshit, which Nina hated to join, which is why she wore the hat. It kept people away.

Sam was tired and out of breath when they got home,

so she sat with him for a minute and stroked his belly. His brown eyes stared into hers as she scratched his ears, smoothed the fur on the side of his face, kissed his nose, all cold and wet. She felt as she did every morning when she would leave him to walk other dogs. As if she were the one committing adultery. She thought of taking him with her, but she didn't want to subject him to the ordeal of sharing her. And he understood, as he always did. He licked her face.

"Sam, my man, you are my pookie. My one and only. It's you and it'll always be you. Don't even think about it."

She left, closing the door gently, with one last smile at Sam, as he walked round and round scratching at her rug until he finally settled into a ball, exactly where she would find him when she returned in a couple of hours. She put on her nylon backpack as she descended the four flights. It was filled with all the essentials: instructions, plastic bags, sunglasses, wallet, and apartment key. And hanging from the outside zipper were the keys to her salvation or undoing, depending on your point of view.

It took over an hour to round up her charges: ten dogs of all ages, colors, breeds, makes, and models. She was adept at holding tight to all those leashes, her outstretched arm in front of her, pulled by labs and spaniels and collies and pugs and mutts. Individually, each was simply a dog—one nice, another not. One peppy, full of spunk, another a lumbering galoot. But together, they were a cellular structure, a family, a community, a country. The individual gave way to the whole and the whole became the thing itself. And the whole was damn cute, Nina knew, for people stared, cars honked their horns in applause, and the world smiled on this only-in-New-York sight.

Her hat did its job and kept the sun and the rain away but once in a while a harsh element of the human variety would seep through. Today it was in the form of two upper East Side-y women, about sixty, her mom's age, but instead of the leggings and sweater, one wore a Chanel suit, Chanel pumps, a traitorous Tod's bag. And the other, one of those knit jobs from St. John, with a pair of those two-toned Ferragamos. These two living clichés were at the corner of Eighty-ninth and Central Park West and Nina couldn't help wondering what were they doing on the West Side, anyway.

As Nina walked past them, trying to keep her dogs together and undistracted, she overheard the one in Chanel say, "I wonder what's it like to do that. You think it's interesting work?"

To which Madame St. John replied, "You thinking of a new career, Judy?"

"She could have a regular job, couldn't she? I bet she even went to college."

"She does look like a fairly normal young woman, except for that silly hat."

"If you think wearing bicycle shorts with those Nazi stormtrooper boots is normal."

Nina raised her chin and looked out from under her denigrated brim and couldn't help herself.

"Ladies," she addressed them.

"Don't do it, baby. Don't give it away!"

A voice from behind, that voice, with that distinctive high-pitched yawp, made Nina and the two older women turn. And there stood Isaiah, a six-foot-three, one-hundred-and-seventy-five-pound Rasta, with dreadlocks down to his booty, as he called it, surrounded by eight dogs that he held by their leashes. Isaiah was Nina's colleague and competition, an ex-con, but only for personal drug use, he'd explained, the drugs purchased with money that he acquired from breaking and entering of the illegal variety, he said. After three years inside, he was back on the streets, rehabilitated and a college grad, now entering people's homes with their permission.

Nina looked at Isaiah as their dogs sniffed and snuggled and checked each other out like singles in an East Side bar on a Friday night. The two women were waiting eagerly for whatever it was Nina was going to say.

"I walk about sixteen different dogs a week, on the average twice a day, every day, five days a week. If you multiply sixteen times two times five, you get one-sixty. Multiply that by fourteen dollars, because that's what I charge per walk, and you get over two thousand dollars. Cash. Per week. Add to that the weekend walks, the boarding I do when the owners go away, at forty-five a night, plus bonuses, gifts, whatever, and I net almost twenty-five hundred a week. Cash."

She smiled.

Isaiah frowned. "Nina, hey, they gonna want your job." And off he went, with his dogs, down Central Park West.

"See you later, huh?" Nina shouted after him.

Madame Rive Droite de Chanel smiled before turning on her little sling-backs, and said, "Entrepreneurial, yes. But is it really satisfying?"

More than you could ever know, thought Nina.

How could she tell them that what these dog owners gave her that was worth more than the money, even more than being around the dogs themselves, were the keys to their apartments? How she would *entrée libre* and pick up their precious pooches while they were, who knows, at work or at lunch, meeting a secret lover at a Midtown hotel or buying a Barbara Kruger at a Soho gallery. Maybe getting a pap smear, a colonoscopy, or plane tickets to Tahiti. Whatever. All Nina knew was that she had their keys and their dogs were hers, if only for an hour or so. For something so New York—where else would people spend thousands on pure-bred dogs, keep them in tiny apartments and then hire someone to walk them—the entire enterprise was based on a spirit of trust that was so not New York.

And take them Nina did. Down the stairs or down the elevator, out the glass doors, the brass doors, the old wooden carved doors, past the doorman or past no doorman at all. Onto the busy streets or the quiet side streets, the streets littered with trash, the streets lined with trees. To Ninety-second Street, where the old homeless guy lived out of his cardboard box, or Seventy-eighth Street with the mural of daisies and rainbows and kittens painted by the kids of PS 87. Into the warmth of the sun or the bitter cold, she went on a brisk beautiful morning, on a sweltering humid afternoon, in a tsunami of an evening storm. She took them. And they peed and pooped for her, thank you very much.

As one did right now, on the sidewalk, almost on top of those upper-class aspirant two-tones. Luca was taking a dump. The two women turned away in disgust, leaving Nina to her own self-satisfying devices and a plastic bag to tote the offensive offering away.

Nina took Webster and Cody and King and Luca and Sadie and Safire and Lucy and Zardoz home, leaving only Edward and Wallis, the dachshund duo owned by Celeste and George Crutchfield. She had planned it this way because it had been weeks since she was really inside the Crutchfield apartment. And what an apartment it was. So overstuffed and chintzed she felt she might have an allergy attack. The walls were an insipid yellow, the pillows and rugs red, gold, and pale green. Florals mixed with stripes, and antiques were festooned with bric-a-brac and vases filled with peonies. Every nook was filled, every cranny jammed. No books, art—landscapes and still-lifes only—like Muzak: looks familiar, you may've seen it before, whatever original-ity had been there originally now transformed into wallpa-per. It was an apartment out of *Architectural Digest*: traditional, expensive, and completely dull. Except that Nina knew where the good stuff was buried.

She took the service elevator, and entered through the back door, as she was supposed to do. She unlocked it with her key and let the two dogs off their leashes, allowing them to scamper past the laundry room, the maid's room, and into the kitchen for a drink out of their Italian ceramic hand-painted bowls, then past the foyer and into the living room, where they jumped onto a nineteenth-century wing chair, almost colliding mid-air in the process. After turning round and round a few times, muzzle-to-tails like doggie donuts, they found that perfect spot and collapsed into it, side by side. On the other wing chair were two small embroidered pillows with the likenesses of Edward and Wallis, with their names and birthdates below.

Nina first checked to be sure the place was empty.

"Hello? Anybody here?" She waited. Nothing. "Christina? You home?" Christina was the live-in maid. Nina was pretty sure she'd seen her leaving the building with her shopping cart as she entered. But she called her name again, just to be sure. "Christina?"

When there was, again, no answer, Nina went inside. She planned to just look a little at the bedroom, with its lush bedding. Nina could care less about the furniture, the flat-screen TV on the wall, the stuff. But the bedding. This is what dreams are made of, she thought. Everything was silver and cream and off-white and vanilla. This was why they called it linen: the sheets were actually made of it. Not the rough, wrinkly cheap summer clothing kind that Nina hated because it made its wearer look like the potatoes inside a burlap sack, but the softest imaginable, embroidered with tiny silky flowers in the same cream color. And this is luxury: on top was a silk duvet covering a one-billion-loft European goose-down comforter and, then, on top of that a bedspread hand-woven in France, with shams to match. And more silk pillows of velvet and satin. She just stood there for a moment, looking, wondering what it would be like to sleep in such a bed every night. To have someone wrap his arms around you when you got in. To have someone stroke your hair and hold your face and kiss you softly at first, then with passion, and then slide one hand down your side, lightly caressing the side of your breast. To have him make love to you under all those perfect sheets and blankets, slowly, deliberately. Nina sighed. What would that be like?

Well, she certainly wasn't going to climb into the bed to see. Not after what happened yesterday at Daniel's. No, today, she was going to be good. She turned to leave but then she turned back and perused the room. She'd just do a simple snoop, something minor, to see what she could find out. About them. Celeste the art historian. George the banker. She turned and went to Celeste's bed-side table. Celeste slept on the left, if you're looking at the bed; on the right if you're in it. Her table had a *People* and a *Town and Country* in its drawer, along with two pens, a pad of paper, a couple of pennies, a paper clip, a recipe torn out from *Gourmet* magazine, a receipt from Bergdorf's. And, behind and under everything, a letter. Nina smiled. She'd hit the snooper's mother lode. She sat down, or up, more accurately, since the bed was so high with its thick mattress and box spring and duvets and blankets and all.

Dear Celeste, the letter began. Nina held her breath. And just like she did with novels, she read the last line first. *With love, Tommy.* "Ooh la la," she said out loud, to herself. "Okay!"

And she began.

> Dear Celeste,
>   I am so sick of your guilt trips.

Whoops. Nina stopped reading and looked up. This was not what she'd expected. But she went on.

So I didn't call you after 9/11. It's so you to make that tragedy into your problem, not to mention it was a long time ago. Have you asked yourself why you expect me to call every time there is some kind of disaster in New York? Life would be so much easier for you if you didn't have so many rules. If you don't expect, you don't get disappointed when it doesn't happen. Don't expect me to follow your rules. Rules were meant to be broken. And I love breaking rules. So, screw you for laying your stupid guilt trips on me. Move out of New York if you think it's so dangerous and you need family contact every time something happens. Life happens. Shit happens. It's not always about you.

With love,
Tommy

Yow, thought Nina, as she gritted her teeth in embarrassment for Celeste. She had expected a love letter. You see why you have to read the whole thing and not just the beginning and end? she thought to herself. Tommy, obviously Celeste's brother, is one mean asshole. Whatever Celeste demanded of him, was it too much for her to want contact with family when something bad happens? And to expect the family far from the trouble to contact the family nearest the trouble? Family is about love, and love means concern, and concern means contact.

Or it should, Nina thought to herself, reminded of her dad. She knew he loved her, in his way, but then, why didn't she ever know how to reach him? He never left an address or a phone number, and would show up once or twice a year. The last time she had asked him how she could contact him if something bad happened, if she needed him. He looked at her then, his eyes lit with amusement, as if the thought of her needing him was funny, a joke, and he said to her: "That's why I don't leave a number! You think I want to hear the bad news?" And he had laughed and pinched her arm, playfully.

"But you're my *dad*," Nina had pleaded, with a smile.

"And I'm very proud of you," he answered.

The hurt people carried with them, Nina thought, as she put the letter back in its place. You'd never know it most of the time, but people, even the Celeste Crutchfields of the world, with their layers of warm and protective bedding, were vulnerable.

When Nina got home she called her mother in Santa Fe.

"Mom. It's Nina, your daughter."

"Honey, you are the only person who calls me 'Mom.' Though I'm certainly referred to as a real mother from time to time."

Nina laughed. She couldn't deny that her mom had a good sense of humor.

"How are you?"

"I'm okay," Nina said. "You?"

A long beat.

"Mom?"

"I saw the new Grisham in the bookstore yesterday. You wrote his cover copy, didn't you?"

"The flaps."

"It's been almost a year."

"Mom."

"You could get your job back, couldn't you?"

"I don't know. I don't want it back."

"Of course you want it back, sweetheart. You had a desk. An office. Your own assistant."

"Half of one."

"Your name was in books. People acknowledged you." A frustrated sigh.

"Oh yeah. Thanks for writing my flap copy. For distilling a year or two or three of hard work into three paragraphs in the hopes that people do buy books for their covers."

"Sometimes four, I think, no?"

"Years or paragraphs?"

"What?"

"Did you mean four years of hard work or four paragraphs of copy?"

"Nina! Look, if I were independently wealthy, I'd give it all to you, but I'm not."

"I know." Nina hadn't been depressed when she picked up the phone only a minute ago. "I just called to say hi, Mom."

"That's nice, dear."

"Have you seen any good movies?"

"Not really."

"Still seeing Morty?"

"No. It was getting to be too much too fast," she said. "I like being on my own. I like my apartment, I like having my own fr—"

"That's right. Why have a nice boyfriend to go to dinner with, to movies with, travel with, not to mention have sex with? It's only been seventeen years since you and Dad . . ."

"Okay. Well, it was nice of you to call. Bye bye, honey." And she hung up.

"Shit," Nina said, slamming down the phone. Why is it so hard with her? she thought.

Nina's mom never really had a career. As a young girl she had dreamed of being a photographer, but in order to make a living, she became a secretary in a bank. Then, when Nina was born, she gave it up, since, as she always told Nina, there was nothing to give up. "Do whatever you love, but become *something,*" was her mantra.

So when Nina left her job in publishing, which her mom was very proud of, to be a *dog walker,* which she wasn't, her mom was devastated. And things had not been the same between them since. She so wanted Nina to be happy, and assumed that meant to have an important job, a serious career. Likewise, Nina wanted her mom to be happy, and assumed that meant to fall madly in love and live happily ever after.

Both wanted for the other what they feared they'd never have for themselves. And neither could imagine seeing the other's life through any eyes but her own.

"Huh, Sam?" She stroked his face and then, as he rolled onto his back, scratched his belly. "What's up with that? Huh, boy? You like that, don't you, my pookie." He looked at her with the full knowledge of human existence. And she responded with the words she could say only to him: "I love you, Sam. I love you."

5

Mrs. Constance Chandler was listening to the radio when the doorbell rang that afternoon. She listened to the radio every day, all day. Everything from 1010 WINS, You Give Us Twenty-two Minutes, We Give You The World, Imus in the Morning, to NPR, or National Palestinian Radio as she referred to it, to classical, jazz, and Broadway musicals. Radio was her company, giving her someone to argue and sing with, to learn from, to dismiss as ridiculous. She listened while she worked, as she was doing now, she listened while she bathed, while she watched TV, while she cooked steamed halibut for lunch or tofu with Asian vegetables for dinner, and while she ate. The only times she didn't listen to the radio was while she was getting her hair done each morning at the John Barrett Salon at Bergdorf's (one hour) and when she went to the Mark for drinks every afternoon at five. (One to eight hours, depending on who was there on a particular day.)

When the doorbell rang, her dog Safire, a one-foot-tall, fifty-pound bulldog (the kind everyone said is so ugly it's cute, but she thought is so ugly it's ugly), lifted his head from his front paws, snorted, and looked at his mistress.

His mistress looked at the Tiffany clock on the mantel. "It's too early for—"

The doorbell rang again.

Safire barked.

"Who, in God's name . . ." said Mrs. Chandler, as she put down her Montblanc pen, a gift from the Bellagio in Vegas, onto the pad of yellow lined paper, which sat on a T. Anthony green leather writing tablet. She was, perhaps, the only living writer who still worked in longhand. On paper. She pushed her early nineteenth-century wooden chair back and rose with an irritated sigh and walked to the intercom. "They're not back to torture me, are they, Safire? Say it isn't so."

The dog just looked at her, his bulging, drooping red eyes with their black centers answering in the affirmative.

She pushed the top button.

"Yes? Hello."

She let go of the button to listen.

"Mrs. Chandler?" A man's voice.

"And with whom do I have the pleasure of speaking?"

"Mrs. Chandler, it's Daniel Maguire."

Two, three seconds of silence.

"Daniel Maguire, your neighbor? We met at the Kayes' wine party? I guess I should've phoned first."

Mrs. Chandler's face fell, annoyed. Still, she let out an enormous sigh of relief. She turned to Safire. His tongue fell out of his mouth.

"My feelings precisely."

And she buzzed Daniel Maguire in. Then she turned to the mirror across the hallway and straightened her low-cut black cashmere sweater, that showed just the right amount of cleavage, over her slim black knit wool pants, adjusted a diamond brooch that sat squarely on her right collarbone, put two hands up to her hair and gently ran her fingers through it, careful not to undo what had been done that morning, and waited for the knock at her door. Not bad for a woman of fifty-ni . . . fifty-four, she thought.

He must've sprinted up the stairs.

"Mr. Maguire, how lovely. And unexpected."

"For you. And it's Daniel." He handed her a box of See's candy.

"You're cruel." She smiled.

"I was in Los Angeles."

"So there is a reason that city deserves to exist. How very kind of you. Come in, please."

She recalled the party in question and the heated argument over chocolate, the snobby appeal of Teuscher and Godiva, her low-brow love of Hershey, and his adamancy for middle-class See's, a box of which he had brought as a gift for the hostess. He had quite charmingly walked around, selecting a piece for each guest. And with one bite of that milk chocolate caramel nut cluster, she was a goner, a convert, forever in thrall to the best chocolate in the world in its simple black-and-white packaging. And she had had the best. With friends in Belgium, Paris, and Frankfurt, she had been sent the most expensive truffles, the loveliest bonbons, the richest drops and creams. But none compared to See's nuts and chews.

She led him to her sitting room, which doubled as her office. He sat on the quilted red leather sofa, she on the embroidered wing chair.

She opened the box, and held it before him.

"Not for me. Thanks."

"Shame on you. Don't make me eat this entire box alone."

He smiled. "All right. One."

He picked a nutty dark chocolate piece and put it in his mouth. He smiled as he chewed. And with a lift of his chin, he urged her on.

How handsome he is, she thought. He had to be at least twenty years younger than she. Such eyes, which she hadn't remembered. And quite tall, really. But there was something about him. What was it? She hadn't noticed it before, at the Kayes'. In fact, there he had seemed extremely self-assured, a young turk. But now she couldn't help but notice a certain rigidity. An awkwardness. Still sexy, but something of a nerd, she thought. He could learn a thing or to from an older, experienced woman. She selected a milk chocolate square, certainly a caramel, she hoped. She took a petite bite and yes, oh god, a caramel.

They sat, chewing in silence for at least a minute, until they had finished their pieces.

"That painting," Daniel said. "The Hudson School?" He stood and walked over to it.

She smiled. Hmmm, and intelligent, she thought.

"Yes," she responded. "Nineteenth century, George Inness. One of my favorites."

"Yes," he said. "I can see why."

She looked at him standing there, in her study, admiring

her painting, and it reminded her of a time not so long ago when a young man like this might have regarded her with a similar degree of admiration. And, with both palms on her thighs, her back straight, her torso leaning ever so slightly forward: "Let me get you something to drink. What would you like?"

He turned to her. "Water's fine, thank you."

"Well, I'm having a vodka. Are you certain you wouldn't like something stronger?"

"Thanks, no."

She got up and left the room, Safire padding along at her heels. Billy listened as her footsteps receded down the hall and into the kitchen. When he knew it was safe, he went to her desk. He bent over her pages and admired her penmanship. Lovely, old-fashioned flourishes, but neat and readable. Nobody writes like this anymore, he thought. No one writes anymore, he chuckled to himself. He had become so accustomed to a computer keyboard that on those rare occasions he did actually write—a check, a birthday card—he noticed that his writing had become barely legible.

He heard ice cubes clinking into glasses from the kitchen and forced himself to get to the business at hand. He hated this part of his job. Snooping around. Lying about why he was there. Pretending he had been at the party when it was Daniel who Mrs. Chandler had met over chocolates. But he forced himself to stay focused. It's for the benefit of others. And, often, it was the only way to really learn about someone. If this lady isn't paying her taxes, if she's hiding, like they suspected, millions of dollars, he'd get her, and this all would have been worth it. And so he read. Mrs. Chandler was writing about Prague. He assumed it was one of her articles that would appear in one of the many magazines she wrote for: *Travel and Leisure, Departures, Town and Country.* Recently she'd written on the best hotels in Venice for *Food and Wine.* It was a terrific piece, making him long for the kind of money that would allow him to stay in one of those places. And it wasn't just about the room, or the service, or its location. She described eating breakfast on the terrace at the Gritti Palace, the rising sun's light sifting through the thick morning haze. He remembered how she rendered the freshly squeezed blood orange juice as nectar of the gods. He had closed his eyes and joined her there in Venice, on that terrace that morning, sipping that thick, sweet pink nectar. He had watched, under his closed lids, the morning rush hour pass under their feet. Garbage boats, water taxis, boats carrying lumber, food, books, and plumbing supplies. The bells of the Santa Maria della Salute chiming across the Grand Canal. She had taken him there. She took him to the Cipriani, the perfect place, she so lucidly argued, to take kids. Kids! At over $800 a night. Kids in the pool, kids playing baci on the lawn, kids roaming the beaches for odd pieces of colored glass. After a morning visiting the Doges' Palace in Piazza San Marco, what better place to return to for an afternoon of fun and frolic.

His folks had taken them to the Grand Canyon once in a funky old camper. That, to his experience, was how you traveled with kids. Now he dreamed of taking his own children one day to the Cipriani in Venice. Hell, he dreamed of just having a kid, and if he did, of taking him or her to a ball game. His dreams were simple, he told himself.

Back to his task: he opened a desk drawer. Only paper clips, stamps, and rubber bands, neatly organized. He opened a silver box on the desk, engraved with her initials. Pennies. He quickly went to the tall wooden file cabinet and quietly opened the top drawer. Files perfectly labeled on every aspect of travel, and about every place in the world from Bali to Zanzibar.

He heard the hallway's old wooden floor creak under her weight as she walked on the Oriental runner that covered it. He closed the drawer and dove onto the couch. And then, there she was, in the doorway, carrying a silver tray with two glasses, a bowl of almonds and a plate of cookies, which she put before him on the coffee table. She handed him his glass of water and then sat, taking her vodka and mixing it with a swizzle stick.

"Thank you."

"You're welcome." She lifted her glass. "Cheers."

"Yes." He drank. "You know, I really just stopped by to give you the chocolates."

She raised her brows.

"Of course, it's always nice to see you," he added.

"Of course." A long silence. "Tell me, Daniel. If I may ask you a personal question, what did you think about Roger Clemens in yesterday's game?"

He laughed. "That's not so personal."

"It is to me." And she smiled. "You have no idea what can be learned about a person when it comes to his or her attitudes about sports."

"Okay then. I didn't see yesterday's game. But, I can tell you that whatever Clemens does is okay by me, since he may be the last baseball player who plays for the love of it. Who gives everything . . ."

"His *all* to each and every game. I completely agree." She smiled again in that waifish, benign way of hers.

Billy blushed. There was something formal and old-fashioned, yet youthful, about her. It made him feel at home. And uneasy.

"Unlike that waste of a human form, Barry Bonds," she added.

"I'm with you." And he laughed. "You're a real fan."

"Baseball, especially. Football too. Ask me anything about last season's Jets."

"Anything?"

She just smiled. "Want to compare stats pre- and post-Herman Edwards?"

"Unusual for a woman, if I may be so politically incorrect."

"Incorrect is the only way to be when it comes to politics. And religion."

Billy laughed again. He looked at her and took a shot.

"You bet on the games?"

She looked back at him.

"Now that's personal."

"But you do spend a lot of time in Vegas."

She eyed him warily.

"You must be referring to those old pieces of mine in *Esquire*. That was a lifetime ago, wasn't it? Now I write about traveling in lieu of travel."

He was silent for a moment, not sure how far to take this first meeting. Then the front door opened and slammed shut.

Safire barked and ran, or rather, lumbered, down the hallway, barking the entire way there and the entire way back.

"Safire!" She shook a finger at him. "Inappropriate behavior!"

"Sapphire? Like the stone?"

"Like the columnist, the great William."

Before Billy could respond, the dog ran back down the hall and reappeared a couple seconds later, his tongue to the floor, his body swaying left to right with each step. A human followed in his footsteps. Billy looked up. It was Nina, his dog walker. In her T-shirt (had she actually gone to the Sorbonne?), shorts, and army boots. She looked like a kid.

"Hey, Mrs. Chandler. How you doing today? Boy, it's beautiful out—" She extended her hand to the older woman.

"My dear. Do you know—" she gestured toward Billy— "Daniel Maguire?"

Nina turned to see him standing right there, only a bulldog and a coffee table away. She seemed startled, and it took her a few seconds to recover.

"You know each other." Mrs. Chandler looked from one to the other, then back.

"Yes. She . . ." Billy started to explain.

"Sure," she interrupted, with a hand to her hair. "I walk his dog, Sid. Uh, hi."

"Sid? For Sidney? That's a funny . . ."

"For Siddhartha," interrupted Daniel.

"Siddhartha." Mrs. Chandler laughed.

Nina joined her. "Yeah, right? But that's nothing. I walk a Zardoz, a King, an Edward and Wallis, a Stanley and Oliver . . ."

"Those rank high, I admit, but a Siddhartha! Now, we aren't laughing at you, Daniel. We're laughing . . ."

"At me." And he laughed too, embarrassed.

"It's just that you don't strike me as the pretentious type. Nor a Hermann Hesse acolyte."

"Well, I'm not the one who named the dog." Christ, he just stepped in it.

"Really?" asked Nina, interested. "Then who did?"

"My brother." Shoot. He didn't want to mention him. To let anyone know that he had one. There was something about this Nina person that put him off guard, made him careless.

"You have a brother?" asked Nina.

Why would she be surprised if he did? "My sister, I mean."

"Your brother or your sister? Or is it your brother and your sister?" Then she slapped her own face, left to right and back. "My brother, my sister, my brother, my sister."

She made him laugh. And she laughed too.

"Well," said Mrs. Chandler, impatiently bringing everyone back to matters at hand. "I am sure Safire would be delighted to take his walk."

"I'll head out with you," said Billy. "I was just leaving."

Nina looked down at her boots. Then up at Billy, her eyes

straight into his for a second, then away. She gathered her-self and said, "Come on, Safire. Time to go." She bent down to attach his leash to his collar. "Nice to see you, Mrs. Chan-dler."

"It's always a pleasure, Nina. And Daniel, it was lovely of you to visit. And thank you again for the chocolates." She headed down the dark hallway toward the front door, with Nina, Safire, and Billy behind her.

At the door, Daniel put out his hand. "It was nice to see you."

Mrs. Chandler took it. "Come again, Daniel, " she said, immediately wanting to shoot herself for saying this, know-ing that he was probably the kind of person who does as he's told.

"See you in an hour or so," said Nina.

"Lovely, dear."

As Daniel opened the door, the whoosh of heat and the stinging glare of the sun that bounced off a car's windshield into Mrs. Chandler's eyes forced her to take a step back. But, squinting, she watched them as they walked down the town-house's front steps toward the pack of dogs waiting on the sidewalk below.

Mrs. Chandler closed the door behind them, leaning against it, breathing in the cool darkness of her hallway, and said, "He's one of them. They're back."

Outside, a dog barked.

"My feelings exactly," she answered.

6

"The bathroom girl," said Daniel from two steps below.

Hello. The Bathroom Girl? thought Nina as the dogs waiting for her on the sidewalk stood up. She untied their leashes from the post that held the sign that said DON'T YOU EVEN *THINK* ABOUT PARKING HERE. Shit! Shit, shit, shit, she thought. It's worse than The Dog Walker! Though he did call her a girl. That, she liked. Once she had fought so hard for people to think of her and refer to her as a *woman*, particularly because of her petite size. Now, she thought it was youthful and sexy to be called a *girl*.

"I know. It's a problem. Drink and pee, drink and pee. I have a bladder the size of a dime. I got two twenty-four-ounce bottles of water in here," she said, gesturing with a cock of her head to her backpack, "and I'll drink them both in the next two hours."

He just looked at her. The dogs did too, expectantly, standing on the sidewalk, waiting to get going.

"I know every public bathroom on the Upper West Side. I just couldn't get to one yesterday. I'm sorry, okay?"

"And the bath?"

"What do you mean by that? You think I need a bath?" She feigned outrage. "Hey, I take . . ."

The dogs, in unison, sat back down, their tongues sticking out, their breath heavy, panting from the heat. All canine eyes were on Nina, eager to be in the park already.

"No, no. I . . . you took a bath in my apartment yesterday, didn't you." He phrased it as a matter of fact.

She heard it, but pretended it didn't register. "I mean, of course I bathe, usually in a shower. But I don't bathe in a shower. I shower in a shower. In fact, every day." Then, realizing what he had said, she looked at him funny: "Wait a minute. Did you think I was actually bathing in your bathroom yesterday?" She let her mouth open wide, in total astonishment. "No. Why would I do that?"

"I have not a clue."

"Listen, you," she said smiling, flirting, her finger pointing at him. "Okay, so I used your potty. But I sure as hell—"

Daniel raised his eyebrows, a small, skeptical smile interrupting her defense.

"I didn't. And, by the way, in America, we say, 'I don't have a clue.' 'I have not a clue.' What's that? They don't use contractions on Uranus?" She smiled to show she was teasing.

"Hey, can we not discuss my rear end? I hardly know you."

That made her laugh.

"Dumb joke," he said, apologetically.

"But cute," she answered.

And they looked at each other for a moment, self-consciously, but the dogs were antsy, getting up and sitting back down. Turning around, then sitting. Yelping, whining, standing, sitting.

"I better go," he said and started to walk away. But something was caught and he couldn't.

"Wait," Nina said, pulling their leashes. The next moment seemed like an eternity, when you know something horrible is about to happen and there's nothing you can do about it. It was like the gas station scene in *The Birds*: the trail of gas, the lit match, Tippi Hedren's face, the thrown match, the line of fire, Tippi Hedren's frightened face, the explosion. Here's this version: Nina feels the tug on the line and is pulled back, the dogs are anxious, Nina turns to look, Sadie's leash is around Daniel's ankles, Nina's concerned face, Sadie gets wacky and pulls harder to get free, Nina's face, Daniel's face as he realizes what's happening, Sadie pulls again, the line pulls taut around Daniel's legs, Nina's frightened face and—

"Hey! Ow!" Daniel was down, on his ass on the sidewalk, in the middle of the dozen dogs dying to get going, barking in full force. They were hysterical, as if a dangerous foreign object has been thrown into their midst. So they pulled him three feet before Nina could stop them.

"Whoa there, you dogs!" she cried. "Oh god, oh god. I'm sorry." She knelt to extricate him from the tangle, and help him up. Doing this while trying to control the dozen dogs was not easy.

"It's okay," Daniel said, getting up and brushing off his butt, which Nina imagined was adorable under those baggy khakis he was wearing. Probably bruised. A corner of his left pocket had been ripped in the scuffle, she noticed. "I gotta go," he said.

"Listen, I'm really sorry. Your pants . . ."

"It's okay."

He looked at her as if he had something else to say, his eyes doleful and unsure, but he turned and walked away. Nina watched him as he crossed the street. She felt like calling out to him—hell, she felt like running to him and hugging him and making sure he was okay—but she had another dog to pick up and it was getting late, so she hurried along, not giving herself the time to beat herself up about what just occurred. She'd have plenty of time to do that later.

So, to Central Park West and Eighty-ninth she went, to get Luca, the yellow lab, owned by Jim Osborne, the comedy director. There was nothing funny about Jim. Or how he treated Luca. Sure, he worked on some of the best sitcoms on TV, but that didn't excuse the fact that he didn't allow Luca into the apartment.

Everybody knows that when you get a dog, it becomes part of the family. Even if you don't want it to. It insinuates itself into your life, onto your couch, on the foot of your bed, and deep into your heart. There's no escaping it. Unless you're Jim Osborne and have a heart of lead. In Jim's apartment, Luca, big, brawny, and energetic, is forced to stay in the back office area. So while Jim is eating in the dining room, Luca's locked behind a child gate in the office, on the other side of the kitchen. While Jim is at the TV, howling with laughter at his own clever staging, Luca is locked behind a child gate in the office, on the other side of the kitchen. And when Jim is in bed, Luca's in hers, locked behind the child gate in the office, on the other side of the kitchen.

It stands to reason that, like a person, a dog who is shut out, kept out, locked out, will become a lunatic. And that's what Luca was. A neurotic, crazy dog, who humped every leg in every elevator, who barked and showed her impressive incisors to every dog passing by, who pulled and pulled on her leash with the ferocity of a puma.

So when Nina collected Luca each afternoon, she was careful to love her a little first, before introducing her to the pack downstairs. Sometimes Jim was there, in the office, blocking another hilarious scene. Those times, she had to tiptoe ever so delicately, so as not to interrupt the brilliance spilling forth into his computer. When he wasn't there, she could venture in and cuddle and canoodle with Luca until she was calm and comfortable enough to join the group.

Today, Jim was home, which Nina discovered upon opening the back door to the apartment. She said nothing, having learned not to speak to him until spoken to. Luca came bounding over, rubbing her body up against Nina's, forcing her to hold onto the doorframe for ballast.

"Hey girl," Nina whispered, while scratching Luca's ears, under her chin, her hips. "How you doing, there?"

She attached the leash to Luca's collar and left, slowly, quietly, closing the door behind her, leaving the Emmy Award–winning Director undisturbed. Every day that Nina got in and out of there without a word from him, she was relieved. Nothing much had ever happened, except for that one time when she was still new on the job and she didn't really know the rules and spoke to Jim, causing him to become distracted, losing his train of thought, and therefore turning to her to yell, "Shut the fuck up!" at the top of his lungs. Since that day there'd been only a glare now and then, but she was afraid every time she entered that apartment. It seemed inevitable that one day she wouldn't leave there alive.

But today she had survived. And once Luca was integrated into the pack waiting on the sidewalk below, they headed to Central Park, where one by one they peed, then peed on each other's pee, then sniffed, then pooped, then walked and wagged. They couldn't know how her heart was still racing from her encounter with Daniel. Something about it, or him, or them together, made her fingers tingle, her senses alert. But, she wondered if the dogs noticed the heavy stirring smell of the forsythia, or the toddler who picked up a handful of dirt and stuck it in his mouth, his mother laughing and screaming, "No! No, no, no, Jonathan." Had they seen the remarkably frail old woman covered with a red plaid blanket in the wheelchair being pushed by a nurse in a white uniform? Could they possibly be aware of the couple making out on the blue-and-white checked tablecloth on the grass? The kids playing soccer on the dusty field? The dad riding his bike with one kid in a seat in front, and another kid on a seat behind? The girl in a blue striped bikini on her pink towel reading *War and Peace*? What did dogs notice? They had good eyes and a strong sense of smell, but what did they really see? Some say a dog's brain is about on the level of a two-year-old child. Which means that they must feel love, sadness, joy, and fear. But are they conscious of life around them? Nina was and today it moved her, the life in this park. Tears welled in her eyes. You live, you screw up, like she just had again with Daniel, *you live*. Here was the proof, all around her. The dogs, the grass, the green, the heat, the kids, the bikes, the shit, the lovers, the life. Such a place! Only in New York, only in this park, and only if you let yourself see.

7

That night Nina had a date. She hated dates but she hated not going on dates. She particularly hated the idea of going on a date on the very day of her newest run-in with Daniel. But what the hell. She had to remain open to the unlikely possibility that this date, or any date, could turn into a fun and wild affair, if not true love. Besides, a commitment's a commitment. So she forced herself to go and put on her favorite—and only—summer dress. It was sleeveless, it was black, and it fit close, but comfortably, to her body. Nina knew by now that if she had to even think about what she was wearing, if she had to be concerned about whether it was riding up or showing too much or too little, or if she couldn't get into a taxi easily or run from danger, she would have a terrible time doing whatever she was doing. Mindless dressing, Nina's motto.

She wore black strappy sandals, kept her tan legs bare,

and put her hair into a ponytail high on her head. No jewelry except for the minuscule diamond studs that were a gift
from her father. As she turned her head to try to catch the
light in them, to see them sparkle, which she could do if she
slowly, carefully looked left and then brought her ear down
toward her shoulder, she was reminded of the night he gave
them to her.

It was her eighteenth birthday and her dad had looked
her straight in her eyes, which was unusual for him. He'd
always seemed to be uninterested in her, which wasn't
exactly true. He was a gypsy at heart, wanting only to be on
the go, even if it meant, she would soon learn, leaving his
wife, his responsibilities, her. She so wanted to be his
princess (figuratively speaking of course, since nobody she
knew had a lot of money), the way her friends were to their
dads. But he so wanted not to be the king. Yet on that night,
he was right there and in his hand was a little black velvet
drawstring pouch.

"Soon you will graduate from high school. I am very
proud of you. Whatever you choose to do now—learn to
type, get married, or maybe even go to college—I will always
be proud of you."

He looked at her, perhaps waiting for a response. But the
only thing she was thinking was, *Learn to type*? Did her
father have no idea who she was? Or that she'd spent the
last year filling out college applications? Was he the only
Jewish father in the world who didn't insist on an advanced
degree? Or two?

"These are for you. I love you, honey."

She opened the pouch to find the exact same diamond

stud earrings that he'd given her two years before. She felt a little woozy like she was either having an acute sense of déjà vu or she was going crazy. She looked at him, her eyebrows pinching together in disbelief and disappointment. Not only did he expect so little of her—*maybe even go to college?*—but he thought so little of her that he'd forgotten that he had engaged in this ritual on her sixteenth birthday.

Of course, someone else might have viewed this in exactly the opposite way: her father, forgetful though he was, loved her so much that he gave her the same gift twice in an attempt to express his feelings for her.

But then, that person would be an idiot.

Though even she had to admit that for him this was a special father-daughter moment. And she wasn't going to mess it up. She thought she might cry if she said anything so she just took in the moment and put the earrings on. "Beautiful," her father had said, as he stood behind her, his hands on her shoulders as he looked at her in the mirror.

Now, as she dressed for her date, she looked at herself in the mirror, wondering where the seventeen years had gone. Where, actually, her father had gone. One day, soon after that Night of the Second Pair of Earrings, he left. She saw him after and since, but no more times than she could count on two hands. She raised one hand now as if she had her other on the Bible and were swearing to tell the truth, the whole truth, and nothing but the truth, and, standing straight and as tall as she could, she said out loud, "Nope. I am not going to go there. I have a date."

Sam, sitting next to her right leg, looked up at her in real life, then at her in the mirror and back and forth, unsure which Nina would be the one to hear his plea for a snack. *Gimme a snack. Gimme a snack. Gimme a snack. Please! Come on. A biscuit. A chew. Something, for god's sake. Anything. I'm starving!*

She looked again at herself in the mirror. Smoothing her dress, a hand to her hair, a side view, now full frontal and a smile. Her skin was golden from the summer sun, her brown hair streaked with blond highlights by its rays, her cheeks pink from its touch. A little lipstick, and there. She was ready for this date, if not to love and be loved without fear of departures or betrayals. Carrying a flat black wallet (her apartment key tucked safely in the coin compartment), the fake Prada kind that closed with a zipper wrapping around three sides, she bent down and kissed Sam's head.

"You, mister, I love fully, totally, and madly," she said to him, thinking to herself, without an iota of fear.

He whined: *the snack! the snack!*

And she was out the door.

It was so humid, even now, that she could hardly breathe. Like soup, she thought to herself. Her claustrophobia kicked in at times like these, and she had to stop and breathe slowly to prove she could. She made her way to the subway, caught the B to the F to the shuttle to the 4 and got out at Lafayette Street in Soho, where she was meeting her date, Ziggy Wallerstein, for dinner and a movie.

Ziggy was a radiologist she had met in a coffee place near Tower Records by Lincoln Center. It was a couple of weeks ago. She had finished her afternoon walk and desperately needed a caffeine drink of the cold, icy variety and so found herself swiveling on a stool at this little dive on Columbus.

Sipping from her iced skim mocha latte, she noticed this guy
come in, order a something or other, and then look her way
and smile. She turned away. Eventually she turned back, but
he had gone. Thank god, she thought. After a few minutes
she left and headed for Tower, where she was going to buy
the original Broadway recording of *The Pajama Game*.

But as soon as she was out the door, this guy, the one
from the coffee shop, was walking by her side.

"Hi," he said.

"Hi," she replied.

"Where you going? Can I walk with you?" he asked.

"Okay, I guess," she said.

"Where you going?"

"Tower."

"I love your T-shirt."

She looked down. She was wearing her torn University of
Hard Knocks. She had a UNIVERSITY OF T-shirt collection that
included 116 real-life institutions, silly jokes, like this one,
and samples from all fifty states, twenty countries, and all
seven continents. She was proud of it, though it was beginning to take up more room than her apartment had to spare.

"I can't stop looking at you."

She couldn't respond. He'd had a nose job, she noticed.

They'd arrived at Broadway and were waiting for the
light.

"What are you going to get at Tower?"

"*The Pajama Game*."

"I love *The Pajama Game!*" he said too loudly, with too
much enthusiasm. "It's a musical, right?"

They entered the store.

"I'm buying it for you, " he offered.

She opened her mouth to decline.

"Don't say no. Let me do this for you."

And with those words, "Let me do this for you," she could ignore the nose, the fact that it was 3:30 in the afternoon and he wasn't at work, and the little edgy quality that made her think he was a coke dealer. Let me do this for you, she said to herself and smiled.

They found the CD way back in Broadway Musicals, and he bought one for himself too. They left the store together, each with Steam Heat in a little yellow bag.

She turned to say goodbye and thanks, but he beat her to it.

"Can I take you out sometime?" he asked.

"Listen, thank you for the gift."

"How about next weekend? This weekend I'm working but next, I'd like to take you to dinner, maybe a movie, on Saturday night. Okay?"

She felt the weight of the bag in her hand. How could she say no? "Okay. That sounds good. What work do you do?"

"I'm a radiologist but I'm on a sort of sabbatical. I work at Roosevelt only part-time while I'm exploring other things."

Like the cocaine trade in South America? she wondered to herself.

"Oh, and my name's Ziggy Wallerstein."

Oy, she thought, not to be anti-Semitic, but Ziggy Wallerstein? "Nina Shephard," she said as she offered her hand.

They shook hands and exchanged phone numbers and said goodbyes and she turned uptown and he down.

"Love that T-shirt," he yelled, almost a block away.

She grimaced and looked at her CD-in-a-bag and wondered what the hell she had just done.

And there he was, standing in front of the Angelika movie theater, as planned. With a big stupid grin on that face of his with its way-too-small nose.

"Hey," she said, mustering a smile.

"You look good," he answered. "Let's go. The movie's about to start."

It was one of those totally forgettable independent movies full of drugs and nudity and a whiney voiceover by a character you hate and don't give a shit what she thinks about anything. But at least it was air-conditioned inside. That's what kept Nina awake.

That, and the fact that Ziggy was *holding her hand.* What was he thinking? They had said hello, gotten some popcorn and Diet Cokes, found two seats toward the front but way over to the side because the place was jammed, and spent a minute discussing their week. ("Busy." "Pretty good.") But they were basically strangers. Nothing intimate or warm or sexy happened between them that would have been the natural precursor to this. What made him think that as soon as the lights were out, he could—and that it would be welcomed—take her hand and hold it?

She didn't want to hurt his feelings, so she left her hand in his. But she got fidgety and uncomfortable and hot and it was so crowded and they weren't sitting on an aisle, so maybe it was her claustrophobia. But then he started to move his thumb back and forth across the top of her hand and her thumb. Oh god, she hated when guys did that.

What's with the stroking? It reminded her of her ex, who rarely showed her much affection, but whenever they went to a party there he was, his hand on her back, stroking it up and down and left and right, as if to remind her: *You belong to me. Do not forget that I am here and you are mine.* Boy, did Nina hate that. It was distracting, it tickled, it made her feel like a dog, owned and petted, as this thumb thing did now. She pulled her hand away. He turned his head to look at her, but she kept her face forward, feigning interest in the movie. He soon looked forward as well. It felt like a hundred hours. But eventually the movie ended and they left.

There was more to come. Dinner at Blue Ribbon Sushi on Sullivan. Too crowded, too trendy, and too close—as in little air, tiny tables, and too much Ziggy. But the spicy tuna rolls, with their fresh sprouts and arugula, their mixture of hot and sweet, crunchy and chewy, were almost worth it.

Ziggy spent a lot of time telling her very little about his suspiciously vague life. He was a radiologist. Sort of. He was close to his plastic surgeon (ha!) dad. Sometimes. He had an idea of what he really wanted to do with his life. But not exactly. He traveled a lot to places unmentioned. He had a lot of money that he clearly didn't spend on clothes. And when he returned from a visit to the men's room, he was sniffing and rubbing his nose.

Nina left quickly after that, having made the standard it's-late-and-I-have-to-get-up-early-to-walk-a-pug excuse, hopped in a cab, and was home in twenty minutes.

Someone was standing on her stoop. As Nina got out of the cab, that someone began jumping up and down and flailing his or her arms, madly.

"Ni-NAH! It's me!"

It was Claire. But she was supposed to be in California!

"Oh my god," Nina squealed. "What are you doing here?"

The two women embraced, which isn't so easy, Claire being almost a foot taller than Nina, but they lingered in each other's arms. Claire pulled away first, looked at Nina, then hugged her again, rocking her left and right, laughing.

Until Nina pushed her away, almost down the steps. "You're home. Goddammit!"

"Very nice. Give me those," said Claire as she took the keys from Nina's hands, unlocked the front door, and walked into the building. "It's reassuring to know you haven't changed one bit in the time I've been gone. You're still you. But as they say in Hollywood, it's all good."

"You're going to want your job back."

But Claire didn't hear her. She had begun her trek up the mountain of stairs into the thin altitude of the apartment five stories above. Nina caught up to her and together, breathing heavily, steps in sync, they reached the summit. Nina grabbed her keys from Claire and unlocked the door.

"You're going to want to walk the dogs, aren't you?"

But Claire was staring at Nina's structures, her hands touching the beads, the broken glass, examining the knots from top to bottom. She moved slowly from one to the other, through and around each one, really looking, as a true friend would.

"Nina, these are amazing." And she turned to her. "Did you make them?"

"What. It's a bunch of shit I've picked up off the ground, for god's sake."

"Wow, these are wild." Claire said. "Really wonderful." Then she turned to look at Nina, who was scowling. Leaning down to get into Nina's face, she again asked, "What's the matter with you? Tell me."

Nina just looked at her.

"Come on. It's not like you want to be a dog walker for the rest of your life," Claire argued.

Nina raised her brows.

"You don't."

"No, of course not!" She wasn't sure. "But I sure as hell don't want a job."

"You have to have a job. Unless, of course, since I've been gone, you've become independently wealthy." Claire said.

Nina smirked. "But not a job-job. Never again. To have to go to an office, to have a boss, to have to be nice."

"That I understand. Being nice consistently is certainly not something you'd want to do on a daily basis." Claire smiled. She went to the fridge and poured herself a Diet Coke.

"Besides, I met him today, I mean yesterday. Then again, today." Nina said.

"Who? What?"

"Guess."

"Daniel?"

Nina nodded.

"And?" Claire smiled. A beat. "AND?"

"And? And? I was taking a bath in his goddamned tub."

"Hey, don't yell at me. I didn't—you what?"

Nina couldn't bring herself to say it again.

"And then you show up. What are you doing home anyway? You didn't call, you didn't write. You didn't give me any warning."

"Wait a minute. Not so fast, little girl."

This time, the girl thing was meant to infantilize. Not sexy in the least.

"You took a bath in his bathroom?" Claire continued. "In his apartment? With his soap? Was he there at the time? Did he know you were there? Did he say, 'Why not just take a bath here?'" She took a breath. "Stop. Shut up. And tell me everything."

"It was hot. I was sweaty and tired. Nobody was home. So."

Claire shook her head, her golden hair swinging side to side. "Ni-nah."

Claire had this way of saying Nina that sounded French, with its emphasis on the *Na*. As if there were an *accent aigu* over the *a*.

"You want your job back, don't you?"

"No. Not yet. Soon. A couple of weeks, maybe a month. I'm glad I was written off the show, but it's going to take me a little while to get back into life here. So do you mind doing it for a little while longer?"

Nina shrugged.

"But no funny business. You're going to get into trouble, you!"

A couple weeks. A month even. Not enough time, by far, but it would have to do. Nina hugged her. "I am so glad you're here. How about a glass of wine?"

"Me too. I have no one else like you."

"I know. Me neither."

"I'm BAACK!"

"You're BAACK!" And they both screamed, hugging and jumping.

Finally, they'd had enough and quieted down. Nina got a bottle of white from the fridge, and Claire studied the sculptures. "These are really good." And she turned to look at Nina as if she'd never seen her before.

"Come," said Nina, as she led Claire out onto the terrace, two glasses and the bottle in her hands. And the two old friends took up right where they left·off, as if three thousand miles for almost twelve months hadn't happened at all.

8

ere's the thing: everything at three in the morning takes on the blue cast of the moon. What would seem doable in the light of day becomes insurmountable, rocky and craggy, full of pitfalls and danger, a million miles away. Nina had no choice but to get out of bed, her heart racing.

Sam, of course, watched her every move from his red plaid doggie bed, picking up his head until he decided she'd be okay and then rested it back on his front paws. Instantly, as only a dog or a child can, he fell back to sleep.

Nina went out on the terrace and looked over the park to the city below and beyond. The moon was full, its light making the leaves of the trees glow like the stars above. She brushed some dirt off the top of the four-foot-high brick wall that prevented her from crashing to her death on the sidewalk a hundred feet below. Two days ago Nina had met

Daniel. Tonight, Claire had come home. And all in all, what a fool she'd made of herself. So what else is new, she thought. I am an idiot. Taking a bath in his apartment! When had a little looking here, a little checking something out there, as if that wasn't bad enough, become personal household usage? She'd stop this terrible—not to mention risky— behavior right now. He was a lawyer, for Christ's sake! He could have her arrested. Worse, he could sue her. So she would have to see him under more normal circumstances. But how and when? He was never there when she went to get Sid for a walk. To get his attention, to get him to see her as a regular person, to get him to want to know her, using legal and ethical means—this was the challenge before her.

And Claire would be taking her job back in two weeks, a month, who knows. But soon! This was Nina's life as she now knew it. Who'd-a-thunk she'd call herself a Dog Walker. It seemed like just yesterday that she was writing flap copy for Random House, haggling over *the* or *a* with the authors, being treated like shit by the arrogant editors. It was enough to keep her from jumping out the window, she was so god-damn bored and disgusted.

Claire had called at the very moment Nina needed it most. A best friend knows these things. And Nina's life changed. And there was no returning to what was. Not that she wanted to be doing this forever, but, as with everything, it was so hard to consider the future and much easier to obsess about the past. So that's exactly what she did.

It certainly wasn't her love of dogs that made Nina the most popular dog walker on the Upper West Side of New York City. Not that she didn't love dogs. But she didn't know it until she was thirty-three years old, the year her marriage came to an end. Two years ago and she could remember the day clearly. There she was, walking down Columbus Avenue with her soon-to-be-ex, who was lecturing her about the sublime romanticism of Luis Buñuel, whose films you have to be of a certain intelligence to really appreciate, which he, needless to say, as a card-carrying cinematographer and member of Mensa, had (and she, needless to say, had not), when a little brown-and-white beagle, his tiny pink tongue hanging out of his mouth, pulled his owner right out of his shoes to get close enough to her to reach his front paws up to her knees. He sniffed, he nuzzled, he licked and panted his way under her skin as if he knew how much she needed the attention. And maybe in total rebellion against the whole Dada surrealism thing or to prove her anti-intellectual bent, her unremitting down-to-earthness, she sat down right there on the sidewalk, crossing her legs to let Scoop sit in her lap, lick her face, and yelp as she scratched his ears and stroked his head. And she loved it, desperately. It was as if she had just learned that she was a lesbian, it was that momentous. How do you live thirty-three years and not know you love dogs?

Maybe it was that discovery that gave Nina the courage to dump her husband. She knew he could easily be replaced with a much more sensitive, human creature. Just by going to the ASPCA.

Signing the divorce papers was one of those rare moments in life that knocked the wind out of Nina. She was now a bona fide failure at love. It was in the genes, she figured. First her parents' divorce, then her own. Twice now she was so hurt that she aged beyond her years, and could feel herself wizening into a cynical woman with dreams of love but no real hope of finding it. Breathing in again would take almost a year.

Like her backpack filled with crap, Nina carried her disappointments with her. They were heavy, and she probably would have been better off to leave them at home, but she was used to their weight and would feel naked without them. Hell, in some ways she was proud of them. To have survived gave her more self-respect than had she never suffered at all. And it was impressive to others, to boot.

So thank god for Sam. On an ice-cold day in December, Nina found herself at the pound over on East Ninety-third. And on that day she fell in love, unconditionally and permanently, with an eleven-month-old mutt of questionable heritage, though she thought he was of the lab and spaniel persuasion. With Sam it was love at first sight, and it's only been up from there. Okay, so he is a dog. But after loving anything that way, you are spoiled forever. How full and deep human-to-human love must be in order to stand up to it.

Then Claire, the Perspiring Actress, which her friends called her because of her proclivity to flop sweat during auditions, got a short-term gig on a long-running sitcom that would take her to L.A. for about four weeks. Claire was the most beautiful of Nina's friends. Tall, blond, and a brilliant actress, to boot. Nina would've wanted to kill her if she wasn't like everyone else Nina liked: neurotic, self-doubting, and funny. Apparently, the sitcom had a call out for a character just like Claire: a babe who could sweat on cue. So talented yet so afflicted, Claire had lost many a part she was born to play—Ophelia, Nora, Emma, Ally McBeal—so it was ironic that she would find herself and ultimately, fame, on prime-time TV.

But before Claire could leave, she had to get her life in order, and that meant finding a sub for the dog walking she did to make ends meet. Who did she know who wasn't really committed to her career, who could take four weeks off, who might welcome this change, and who wouldn't be too bored or feel too big to do this smallest of jobs? This menial, service kind of job that required no brain to speak of, just timeliness and regularity, two able legs and the willingness to pick up dog shit in a plastic sandwich bag?

That would be Nina. Good old reliable Nina.

Especially since Nina was about to commit murder at her office and would need to find another way to make a living. That spring, everyone at Random House was preparing for the publication of the biggest, most important, most exciting, lyrical, exquisite, sprawling, accomplished— and every other superlative one could find in Roget's Thesaurus—novel to be published in the twenty-first century. Nobody, except Nina, had the guts to acknowledge that it had been only a couple years into the new century, making this not such an amazing feat after all. And when she did, in one of their weekly "positioning" meetings, she was met with a roomful of dropped jaws, as if what she had just said was sacrilegious. The writer was a handsome Brit and the book a pretty good, romantic novel about an eighteenth-century painter in love with a twenty-first-century woman (don't ask). They'd paid about eight million dollars for the thing so it was pretty tense in the hallways and the boardrooms.

And Nina could not get the flap copy approved.

Now Nina had been on an executive trajectory, everyone looking to her to replace her boss (nice, sweet, pretty dumb) when he retired in six months. She wrote well, she spoke well, if at times a little too harshly and opinionatedly, she had savvy opinions about the positioning and marketing of books.

But she could not get the flap copy approved.

If the author liked it, the editor hated it. If the editor liked it, the publisher and the author hated it. Then the agent had to like it, the author's wife, the head of sales, the head of sales' dog. So Nina tweaked, she rewrote, she invented and embellished.

And still, it was not approved. Nina asked different people to try to write it—her assistant, her boss's assistant, the editor, the author, the receptionist—but to no avail.

How many times does it take to write flap copy, the words on hardcover book jackets that tell potential readers what the book is about? Oh, about a million. It was as if the company's entire eight-million-dollar investment rested on the goddamned flaps. Nina knew the failure of the book would be blamed on her. Its success, credited to anybody but.

And Nina knew this was not the life for her. Yeah, it paid the rent, but so could driving a taxi or . . . dog walking, for chrissakes.

Then, finally, she did it. She wrote the flaps that got approved. The cover went to press and all sighed a sigh of relief, especially Nina, who for the first time in weeks got a good night's sleep.

Until that fateful day when the proof—an early jacket sent from the printer for all to review before five million were printed—arrived and was hand-delivered to the publisher's office.

Nina, whose office was down the hall and around the corner and down that hall, could hear the scream. She could hear the heavy footsteps get louder and louder as they came her way. She could see the publisher in her doorway and how his head had become huge and red like a tomato and that smoke was coming out of his ears and eyes and mouth.

He stood there and threw the offensive jacket at her and said, "This is the biggest piece of shit I have ever seen. You, Nina Shephard, are going to bring this house down!" He had obviously forgotten he had approved the copy weeks before, or changed his mind, or both, as hysterical executives are wont to do.

That was almost a year ago, thought Nina, as she watched a helicopter make its rounds over Central Park, back and forth, forth and back, its lights flickering brightly against the navy blue sky as it hovered like a mama bird protecting her nest. She wondered what that helicopter could possibly hope to see down in the darkness of the park below. What danger lurked there that Nina couldn't even imagine? The dangers she could imagine were enough. But the unimaginable, the unthinkable—now, that was a whole category of dangers she could worry about without even knowing what it was, exactly, she was worrying about. To worry about the unknown, to be afraid of things that haven't happened, to make oneself unhappy about things that might never happen: this gave Nina much to think about.

Nina remembered the Thursday evening in early September last year, when she went to pick up keys and instructions from Claire, who was leaving the following Monday for L.A.

"Here's the weekly schedule. The owners have your cell and home number in case of an emergency. Always carry your cell."

Nina gave her a look.

"This is important, Ni-*nah*. The dogs and their owners count on you."

She was being so serious. This made Ni-*nah* want to giggle. When Claire handed Nina about twenty envelopes in a Bonwit Teller bag, Nina lost it.

"I remember Bonwits." Nina was laughing.

"Ni-nah, this is important."

"Bonwit Teller closed how long ago? And you still have a bag." Nina's eyes narrowed, she smiled wickedly and stretched her neck toward Claire. "I bet you save everything. I bet your closets are a nightmare, stacked to the gills with *stuff.* Stuff you can't stand to throw away. It's your WASP upbringing."

Claire grabbed Nina's sleeve and pulled her down the hall to a closet door and opened it. What Nina saw would stay with her forever. This was unlike anything she had ever seen before. The planning, the obsession with order, the maniacal attention to detail. This was the closet of a serial killer. Each shelf was eerily labeled with words like QUEEN FLAT SHEETS and GUEST TOWELS and SHOPPING BAGS (where the Bonwit bag must have been stored, no doubt) and even

PICNIC BLANKETS (as distinguished from bedding, she supposed). As Nina thought, Do we really ever know anybody, she turned to look at crazy-assed Claire.

"This," Claire said, her arms folded, her head held high in what looked like pride, "is my WASP upbringing. Now pay attention."

And she did. It's like that old joke: What do you do with a 2,000 pound gorilla? Anything he wants.

"Each envelope has the name of a dog on it. In each envelope you will find the dog's address and phone number, and instructions. For example, at Cody's building—god, you will love Cody; he's so adorable—there is no key. One of the doormen brings the dog down and takes him up. So when you pick up Cody, you ask the doorman for him and then you give Cody back to the same doorman when you're done. Be sure never to leave Cody with a different doorman than the one who gave him to you. Because Cody will freak out. He'll get scared if he's not returned to the same guy. This is really really important. And look."

As she opened an envelope with the name Webster on it, she looked at Nina to be sure she was attentive.

"Webster is very special. He can only be walked with two or three other dogs at a time and never ever with Sadie, who lives in his building. I don't know what it is, but those two dogs hate each other."

"An old family feud, perhaps."

"Stop it, Nina. This is serious. You want those two dogs to kill each other? Then don't listen to me."

"Claire—"

"Now besides the key or instructions about the key there

are other instructions about taking care of the dog. Like, where he or she likes to be walked, if you need to feed him or her, what to feed him or her, his or her pooping hab—"

"Would you stop with the gender modifiers, for chris-sakes? Come on. These are dogs. Dogs who need to be walked so they don't take a shit on their owners' sarouks. Owners who love their dogs so much they take them to dog-gie shrinks, but are too busy to walk them."

"You have a lot to learn, Nina. Dogs are people too."

"What?" Nina started to laugh.

"What what?"

"Forget it." Still laughing.

"I hate it when you do that, you know," Claire said.

"What?"

"That higher-than-thou smirk."

"Come on, I'm listening. You're just so *serious*. Dogs are people too?" She couldn't stop laughing.

"Ni-nah. This is serious business. These dogs count on you. Their owners count on you. If I lose one client while I'm gone, I'll—"

"You won't. I promise. I take this seriously. I do."

Claire handed Nina the Bonwit Teller bag filled with its envelopes that contained all the information she would need to know to get her started in a life of crime.

That night, sitting on her terrace with Sam, under an enormous white full moon that sent light into her lap, she studied Claire's notes and instructions. Up until now, Nina considered her relationship with her dog, Sam, normal. She fed, walked, and petted him a couple times every day. She often played ball with him, let him sleep on the foot of her bed, swam with him in the summer and, on weekends, hiked with him outside the city. She had him groomed about four times a year. Okay, so she shared her ice cream with him. From the same spoon. Okay, so she let him kiss her by licking her lips. Okay, so she talked to him. It's just that he listened *so well*.

Claire's clients are insane, thought Nina, and I am living in a nightmare. She had started to read. First, a letter from Claire on her monogrammed stationery.

Dear Nina,

Hi. Thank you for coming to my aid. I really really appreciate your help. It's important to follow these instructions to the {sic} teeth. Please do exactly as you are told. I will be home soon and I'll want my job back without losing one client!!!

In this bag are a few things. First, keys to apartments. The keys on the ring are labeled (cute, don't you think?) with the names of each dog and his or her address. (Many keys are kept by the doormen; some owners are in the apartments and don't provide keys at all.) Second, dog-by-dog instructions, in separate envelopes, which you are to follow verbatim. Word for word! Exactly as I have written them! And third, a calendar of the month is also inside this bag for you to follow as if it were the Bible. (As if you were religious! Hahahahahahahaha)

Now, raise your right hand and promise me this: you have agreed to walk my dogs as per the enclosed schedule for the four weeks I am gone. If you cannot do a walk, you still have to. You are allowed no sick days, no vacation days, no personal days. Only in the event of hospitalization or death can you call my cousin David at 326-2209. (You met him at my birthday party. He was the one you hated because of his shoes.) But being in the hospital, or being dead, are your only excuses. The dogs count on you, their owners count on you, we are all counting on you.

You may not diverge in any way from these instructions. Just follow them and all will be well. I will see you in a month. Again, I am totally grateful to you for covering for me. I love you!

Your soon-to-be famous (hahahaha) actress friend,

xxoxoxoxoxox

Claire

What did Nina expect from a woman who labeled her linen closet, she asked herself as she drank some wine. Sam was chasing a moth. She opened an envelope marked KING.

NAME: KING
ADDRESS: 32 West 88th Street Apt. #2
PHONE: 212-262-3390
TYPE OF DOG: Dalmatian
WALKING SCHEDULE: Five days a week; three times a day—morning, mid-day, and evening (see calendar)
OWNER: Theresa and Matthew Quint
ABOUT THE OWNERS: Very successful lawyer/stockbroker couple. King is their "baby."
KEY: On ring.
PAYMENT: Cash left every Monday for entire week on piano in entry.

SPECIAL INSTRUCTIONS: If the temperature outside is below 63 degrees, the dog must wear his sweater, which you'll find in a box in the front closet labeled KING'S THINGS. Leash is always on hook inside front hall closet door. Feed this dog every night the organic beef that's in the freezer in a bag marked KING'S DINNER. Put the entire bag in the microwave for one minute on defrost and one minute on cook. Pour into his food bowl, replace water. Bag goes into blue recycling bin under sink.

OTHER: Should Theresa and Matthew go away for a few days, they will call you to bring King over to your place—

Whoa there girl. Strange dogs sleeping at my apartment? thought Nina. With Sam? Oh god. Oh god. What had she gotten herself into? A sweater? Organic beef? Sleeping over? This King was a fucking prince! She picked up the phone and dialed.

"Hello-oo." It was Claire's sing-song voice.

"You didn't say anything about strange dogs at my place. With Sam? Sleeping over? No way. Sorr—"

"They're not strange—"

"Okay. Stran*gers*. Dogs unbeknownst to me. To Sam. You did *not* tell me this."

"Come on. Ni-nah—"

"And these notes. 'Anal' doesn't do them justice. I don't think I'm the pers—"

"Ni-*nah*. You *promised*," whined Claire. "I'm packing. My flight leaves in the morning. You're it."

"To dream the impossible dream."

Claire laughed. "I know you love that Broadway stuff, but you really need to update your musical references."

"I'm not kidding." There was a long silence. "You better bring me a nice gift from L.A. That little shop on Melrose—"

"I love you. I'll miss you. It's only four weeks."

A click and she was gone.

Nina was drinking way too much wine, but envelope number two awaited. It was marked LUCA. She liked the name.

NAME: Luca

ADDRESS: 317 Central Park West Apt. 22A

PHONE: 262-5784

WALKING SCHEDULE: Twice a day—morning and evening (expect many special requests for other times)

TYPE OF DOG: Yellow lab

OWNER: Jim Osborne

ABOUT THE OWNER: Jim is a sitcom director, so he's mean. Do not (and this was underlined four times) talk to him if he's working. This is not easy, since you have to walk through his office to get the dog.

KEY: With doorman.

PAYMENT: Cash left every Monday in envelope on hook where leash is hung.

SPECIAL INSTRUCTIONS: Enter always through the rear service door. You have to walk through Jim's office to get to the dog who is always in the laundry room behind the kitchen and prevented by a gate to walk around the rest of the apartment. Do not feed this dog, unless specifically asked to do so.

OTHER: Luca is very sweet but very neurotic. She may jump on you and—

A neurotic, lonely, starved-for-attention, starved-for-food dog. Poor Luca. *Poor me*, Nina was thinking.

NAME: Edward and Wallis

Oh please. Anglophiles with dogs, thought Nina.

ADDRESS: 278 Central Park West #8F
PHONE: 262-7118
WALKING SCHEDULE: Twice daily, Monday through Friday—morning and afternoon
TYPE OF DOG: Dachshunds
OWNER: Celeste and George Crutchfield
ABOUT THE OWNERS: Celeste is an art historian at Sotheby's and George is a banker. Both are Anglophiles.

Hello.

KEY: On ring.
PAYMENT: Daily cash left on entry table.
LEASH: Dogs will bring them to you. The owners hide them each morning and insist the dogs find them. It's a game.

Sounds fun.

SPECIAL INSTRUCTIONS: The dogs prefer a British accent
and will respond better to orders said with one—

Edward and Wallis, as in the Royal Family, as in the Royal
scandal, as in a royal pain in the ass. And, as if topping on
the royal pudding, to whom you must speak in a British
accent. Not if they want a fucking walk, she thought. For the
first time Nina understood why people owned cats.

NAME: Siddhartha

You're kidding, right?

But I call him Sid.

Now I feel so much better.

ADDRESS: 14 West 91st St. Apt. 12A
PHONE NUMBER: 267-8833
WALKING SCHEDULE: Monday through Friday, mid-day,
     and mornings and evenings when requested
TYPE OF DOG: Weimaraner

Sieg Heil! Hasn't anybody heard of getting a mutt from
the pound?

OWNER: Daniel Maguire
ABOUT THE OWNER: Totally cute! A lawyer! Single! But
     I never see him because I only walk Sid when he can't.

Such is life.

KEY: On ring.
LEASH: On table in front hall.
PAYMENT: Every Friday on same table.
SPECIAL INSTRUCTIONS: None, really. Sid is sweet and
    well-behaved. Daniel will call if he needs extra walks.

But that was then and this is now. Four weeks had turned
into four months, then six, then nine. And now, Claire was
home. Nina was thrilled. Claire was her only friend with
whom she could speak in shorthand. On the other hand,
Claire was home. Nina was disconsolate. If she had to give
Claire her job back, what would she do? The clamoring in
Nina's head was so loud, and yet tonight, out on the terrace,
the city was silent. Not a beep, not the *wop-wop-wop* of a
helicopter, not a scream nor a siren to be heard. Only Nina's
pulse banging like tom-toms in her ears. She had so screwed
up. She had damaged, perhaps irreparably, any chance she
might've had to get to know Daniel, or rather, get *him* to
know *her*, and then, with luck, well, she'd never say such a
foolish thing, but she could think it, fall in love with her.

And yet. There had to be a way. She could make one of a
million excuses to call him or go see him, but she'd still be
the Dog Walker to his Master, the help, the hired hand. No,
she had to meet him outside the context of dog walking.
Maybe even outside the context of *her*.

And then she heard it. A saxophone. No, a trombone, she
thought. Yes, now unmistakable. A trombone being played,
melancholy, sweet. Live, in someone's apartment, the sounds

of the big brass horn made its way past the vertical blinds of its room, out the open windows down three flights of the stone apartment building two blocks away, around two corners and up five flights, over her brick wall, onto her terrace, and straight into her head and her heart. And, then, What is that? she wondered. She listened, her eyes on the moon, imagining she could see it in its three dimensionality, instead of the flat disk that hung before her. They were drums, played as if they were a violin, with care, drums played with precision and attenuation, with lyricism and melody. She had never heard such a thing. And there was a piano, yes, beautiful. But only the trombone was live, speaking directly to her through the New York night air.

9

There are many bad things about being a dog walker. You have no colleagues per se, except other dog walkers who, for the most part, are a pretty weird bunch. And your clients aren't good conversationalists, though they do respond to a "sit" or "stay" now and then. And you have to pick up dog shit, which, in the case of an eighty-pound lab, is a handful, so to speak. Sometimes you get treated like dog shit, and Nina didn't know which was worse: the picking up or the being put down. Plus, it's not a really impressive profession. Nobody actually *aspires* to be a dog walker.

But the one really terrible thing, the thing that's the hardest to get accustomed to, the thing that is a fight day in and day out, is that you have to get out of bed early in the morning, no matter what, each and every day, unless by some miracle, you have no morning walks, which never, ever happens. That's the point. The dog walker walks dogs when no one else wants to.

Rain or shine. Seven days a week. Hung over or sick or depressed or just plain tired. Or else you have to contend with cranky dogs and pissed off owners and potential loss of business. It sucks, thought Nina the next morning when she was just too . . . too *something* to get up. Maybe it was the shitty date the night before (when would she learn to trust her instincts and never date a man who'd had a nose job?), or some bad sushi she had eaten (she imagined a worm making its way from her stomach to her intestines—and back), or the lack of sleep (she had read that you can actually die from that), or the fact that it was pouring outside (and already ninety degrees). Maybe it was running into Daniel at Mrs. Chandler's. Maybe it was his falling on his ass. Maybe it was the ass she made of herself. One of the above. All of the above.

From her bed she could see sky out the window if she laid on the far left on her back and let her head fall off the mattress, allowing her neck to stretch over and down, her chin pointing to the ceiling, her head almost hitting the floor. In this way, at this angle, she could see up past the wall of the building next door to the sky above. And this morning, at 5:45, it was a golden brown, the rising sun finding its way out from behind the clouds, filtering through the smog and rain.

Nina threw herself back onto the center of the mattress and stared at the ceiling. Shit, she thought to herself, I have to get up and I am in one hell of a bad mood.

As if reading her mind, Sam hopped up on the bed and

snuggled tight against Nina's body. She barely responded, except to adjust her leg, so he'd fit. He put his paw on her shoulder. She took it off. He licked her cheek. She wiped it. He nudged her head with his muzzle. She ignored him, still stared at the ceiling. He waited a couple seconds, and then, as if fed up with her attitude, he slowly got up to jump off the bed, putting his tailed butt in her face. But, he faked her out and did a complete one-eighty and jumped on her in one surprising, nimble move. Sam was a circus dog at heart.

Nina wrestled the growling mutt, held tight to his muzzle, and kissed the side of his face. Then, with a huge sigh, as if willing away the happy moment, preferring to return to her misery, she sat up, pushed him off the bed, and went directly to the shower.

Everything this morning was hard. Washing her hair, shaving her legs, choosing which white socks. Each decision, every movement took tremendous effort. It was as if the thick smoggy air outside had inhabited her insides. Lugubrious was how she felt. Logy was how she moved. Lethargically was how she finally got dressed and made some coffee and a slice of toast. The eight-grain-from-a-bakery-kind, not that she was a health nut, but it sure beat the shit out of packaged "whole" (yeah, and Nina was Marilyn Monroe) wheat. She took a bite. She chewed. She noticed that her apartment needed painting. She was sick of her furniture, what there was of it. She took another bite. She hated the structure she was working on and told herself that she had to throw it away a.s.a.p. She took another bite. She had to do something about her anti-bedroom. Like get

some color or a rug or something in there. She was so intim-
idated by fabric selection, she had only a rolling shade, no
pretty bedspread, no nothing. It was like a jail cell in there.
She swallowed. She looked at the clock. And, oh shit. All that
dilly-dallying in the bed, in the shower, dressing, hating
everything, had made her late. Now she had no time to take
Sam out first for his walk. She'd have to take him with the
morning pack.

She threw her coffee in the sink, swallowed the remain-
ing toast, put on her backpack, attached Sam's leash to his
collar, and they were out the door.

The wet heat hit her like a ton of bricks. It had stopped
raining, but at a humid ninety-two degrees you wouldn't
know it. You get just as drenched. As she tried to take a
breath, Sam pulled her down the stairs and toward the park.
Air got caught in her throat, mingling with a piece of left-
over toast, and she coughed. And then, she couldn't stop
coughing. That tickle in the back of her throat, that insidi-
ous tickle that sometimes came to her at the worst possible
moments—in meetings, at the doctor, in the library, on an
airplane—that tickle that made her gag and eyes tear and
her face redden attacked her now.

So she was gagging and hacking and turning crimson
on Central Park West, folded over with air blockage, her
dog mad with concern. He jumped up on her, his paws on
her chest, almost knocking her down, not helping at all.
She threw down her pack, while holding tight to Sam's
leash, and fought the buckles and got a bottle of Poland
Spring out and drank, the air passage opening to allow a
wheeze.

A construction worker carrying a load of lumber asked, "You okay there, honey?"

Physically unable to reply "Don't call me honey, fuck-face," she struggled in a high breathy voice, "Yeah, I'm okay."

Now that some air was able to make its way, she got on her way. First stop, Luca. Oh god, Nina thought, let's hope Jim is still asleep. She left Sam with the doorman and climbed up the few flights. She knocked on the back door. No answer. So she ever so quietly, literally on tiptoes, let herself in. Jim wasn't in his office. Luca was lying on her bed in the tiny room off the office behind the door guard.

Why do people have dogs if they don't want them to be part of the family? Nina marveled every time she came to get Luca. There should be a goddamn law, thought Nina, that made people go through a series of tests to first prove they'd be good dog owners, and maybe even to determine what dog they'd be best suited for.

Luca had a Booda Bone, a tied-up rope toy that dogs use to play tug-of-war with, that was Nina's bellwether with which she measured Luca's happiness. If it was in the same spot that she had left it since she was here the last time, she knew Jim hadn't played with her.

And there it was, in exactly the same spot she'd left it in yesterday. Nina knew there was no Booda-Boning going on in this household.

As soon as Luca saw Nina, she raised her head. Then, her hind legs rose as she rested her weight on her front legs. She looked like a camel the way she was getting up. Finally, she was up in front, she shook, and came galumphing over to Nina, her tail wagging furiously.

"One minute, girl." She couldn't open the gate. "Damn these things."

Luca was getting impatient and put her front paws on top of it. Nina pushed her off, and continued to wrestle with the latch. Until the gate toppled over. And Nina knew what was next.

"Hey. What the fuck—" Jim, who had apparently arisen from his slumber, yelled from the bedroom at the opposite end of the apartment. "Shut the fuck up out there."

"Hurry, girl," Nina said to Luca. And to Jim: "Sorry." And to Luca: "Let's go." And she opened the door and Luca jumped out and bounded down the stairs. Nina had yet to put her leash on.

In the lobby, Luca almost tripped an old lady with a cane, ran literal circles around a stupid standard poodle, getting the leash tangled in her feet, annoying the owner, a rotund man who looked like walking a block would kill him—so wrong, of course, for a standard poodle, who needs much romp and run. Nina handed him her card, which she adroitly took out of her back pocket, then put Luca on her leash, grabbed Sam from the doorman, and with a "Thanks," was gone.

Now with Sam and Luca, Nina went to pick up King, the spoiled Dalmatian of the Quints. She left Sam and Luca tied up in front of the building under the watchful eye of the doorman.

What, everyone was still in bed this morning? Everyone but Nina? She knew the Quints were there because she could hear them making love. When she walked in, King was going crazy, running back and forth from the front door to the closed door of his master and mistress's bedroom. Obviously he, too, could hear them. You'd have to be as deaf as Bono's old beagle, Che, to not hear the screams. Though he probably couldn't decipher the actual meaning of "Oh god, fuck me baby," King certainly got the gist of it.

When King joined Luca and Sam, it was like a Woofstock. Too much energy in too little space. It took a few minutes, and some amount of dexterity from Nina, before the dogs calmed down.

Now with King, Luca, and Sam, Nina went to pick up Edward and Wallis from the Crutchfields. Even these two well-trained little dogs were acting scary. It was as if some alien being, some sinister anticanine force, had gotten inside each mongrel and was punching at its insides to get free. Okay, so if an alien being wasn't about to pop through their collective skins, then something else was making them wacky. Was it the weather? Was it the full moon that was safely camouflaged in the cloudy sky? Or were the dogs, those intuitive ciphers, simply reacting to Nina's edgy, unnerving mood?

Whatever it was, no one could be sure. But by the time Nina got the other six dogs that morning, for a total of eleven dogs, it was if the entire pack had woken up on the wrong side of the doggie bed. Each dog was cranky, unsettled, and impatient. Those who witnessed the dog fight were certain that something otherworldly had taken over the bodies of the beasts.

The fight began like this:

Nina knew, as any experienced, competent dog walker would, that placement is everything. Like seating assignments at the dinner parties she didn't attend can make for either fascinating or exceedingly dull conversation, for intelligent political discussions or the kind of ridiculous arguments that can only occur between a knee-jerk liberal and a neo-con, walking placements of the dogs is serious business. Putting the right dogs together can mean the difference between a peaceful walk and a walk of mayhem and destruction, which is exactly what happened that morning.

In Nina's stupor, in her haze, in her lousy, uncompromising mood, she screwed up. Simple as that. She put Luca next to King (a no-no) and Edward on her left, away from Wallis on her far right. She mixed it all up, as if she'd thrown the dogs in the air, and where they fell was the bold new order.

The subjects rebelled.

Edward used every tiny muscle in his body to get close to Wallis. Luca did everything she could to get away from King, who tried to out-yelp, out-growl, out-pounce Luca.

But it was the little Lhasa Apso who crossed their path that did it. Oh sure, one might think a Lhasa is cute. But those in the know know they are Dogs From Hell. One must not be fooled by their peanut size, their little black eyes and noses, their little pink tongues, their fuzzy white fur, their adorable cartoonish walk. They are devil dogs incarnate. And their owners are, ninety-nine percent of the time, the devil's workers. There is no more adorable dog than theirs, none more deserving, more important, smarter, cuter, better. Like parents who think their child is perfect, Lhasa owners think it's funny when their little evil ones climb up and scratch you, or run between your legs, entangling you in their leashes, or nip at your hand when you pet them, or, as happened that morning, run uncontrollably through a group of dogs yipping and yapping, with Nina yelling to get him or her, or it, to stop. The owner, laughing in delight at her perfect little beast.

The dogs went nuts. Luca was on King, Edward nipped at Sam, Wallis jumped on Luca and even grabbed his hackles with his teeth and pulled, making Luca lunge at Safire. It would have turned bloody had Nina not been yanked to her senses by Sam, who pulled the entire entourage away from the offensive Lhasa Apso. Then Nina put the brood in appropriate order, made them sit, bribed them with biscuits, and gave them each a two-minute time-out for their misbehavior.

10

And after all that, Nina still had one more stop: Che on Eighty-fifth between Central Park West and Columbus. Picking up Che with a pack of dogs was always worrisome, because Che lived in a huge, five-story townhouse, so there was no doorman, forcing Nina to leave the dogs tied up alone on the street while she went inside. But today, what with the mood of the mutts, it became a logistical nightmare. She separated King and Luca, making two groups of dogs, each tied to its own tree. Careful not to tangle the leashes, she made a slip-knot in each and one by one, she unleashed each dog, wrapped the leash around the tree, and reattached it to the dog's collar.

Then Nina turned and headed to Che's house. By this time of day, Bono would normally be at school but since it was summer, he'd be doing nothing. His dad would be at work and his mom who knows where. Here was a family she couldn't fathom. Richer than god, the parents were not precisely neglectful, it's just that they had their priorities. And their number one priority was number one. The dad, Richard Armstrong, was a community activist and lobbyist. He shuttled back and forth from Harlem, where most of his organizations were located, to Washington, D.C., where the money and power was. He was a superb example of the new millennium liberal. He worked on behalf of the poor and disenfranchised, while wearing Armani. He partied with the trendsetters and the power brokers, while trying to get decent low-cost housing and jobs for the unemployed. He drove a BMW, but he had no time to play baseball with his son.

The mother was Phyllis Batterman Armstrong, aka insane U2 groupie. One doesn't usually think of a married mom approaching fifty as a groupie, but here she existed, nevertheless. She not only went to every U2 concert, but she went to rehearsals, to rehearsals of rehearsals, as well as to award shows and every single charity gig Bono did across America and Europe. (She'd have followed Bono to Africa and South America, but that's where Richard put his foot down because she was a mother, after all, he implored her.) Nina would never forget the story Phyllis told her of the recent Grammy Awards show, where Phyllis finagled a seat-filler job, and somehow actually filled Bono's seat when he was performing, though, of course, only literally because it was impossible on a theoretical level, and how he was still backstage when the award for Best Album was announced. When he didn't win, she had stood up and cried, "We were robbed, Bono! We were robbed!"

And with a flip of her hair, with one hand on her Diesel-clad hip and the other on her Miu Miu adorned chest, she breathlessly told Nina how she and Bono had made eye contact. "He looked right at me. And I knew how important it was for him to see that he had fans who wore Prada."

Bono Van Batterman-Armstrong was their only child. Bono after guess who, Van after Morrison, Batterman after his mother and Armstrong after his father. Che, their only dog, was named after the Latin American revolutionary from the sixties. And their cat, Einstein, was named after, well, if one couldn't figure that out, one sure ain't one.

Each and every day Bono would come home right after school and watch movies on TV. Noir mysteries, screwball comedies, musicals, and romances. Action adventure and sci-fi. Anything and everything. Even a kids' movie now and then. And now that school was out for the summer, he had all day every day to sit around vegging out in front of the screen. He was probably the only kid of his income level in New York City who wasn't at camp or taking tennis lessons or trekking in the Italian Alps. For some reason Bono was free to be all summer long.

It's not as if his parents left him alone. They were older parents, yes, who had had Bono when they were already in their forties. And so changing their lifestyle to meet the needs of a kid wasn't on the top of their agenda. So he had Melissa, a babysitter who read all afternoon—usually *Us* or *Vogue* and once in a while a shlocky novel or her psychology textbook from her classes at Columbia—and who couldn't be bothered with playing chess or taking a walk or going to the playground or even talking with an eight-year-old boy.

Having successfully tied the dogs to the trees, Nina found her key to the Armstrong townhouse. She climbed the outdoor steps and unlocked the huge red door. She stepped into the vestibule and yelled, "Hello? Hell-oo! Che?"

There was no dog in sight. No pitter-patter of beagle feet. No bark, no whimper. Che, at fifteen years old, was practically stone deaf, so Nina didn't expect him to respond to her hello, but she usually found him asleep on the parquet floors of the entry hall.

"Che, where the hell are you?"

When there was no answer, she wandered into the living room, with its Persian rugs, floor-to-ceiling bookshelves, copies of the *Nation* and the *New Republic* and *Harpers* covering the coffee table, and paintings by Ben Shahn decorating the walls. She took another few steps toward the grand piano and opened the seat. Interesting: among the Chopin etudes and Bach sonatas, there was a copy of Danielle Steel's latest bestseller. Ha! Vivid proof of the dumbing-down of America, Richard would've admonished his wife had he found her reading it, vivid proof of his ignorance. A letter from the White House sat on the grand piano. She put her hand on it and was about to pick it up when Bono jumped out from behind the French doors. He was holding Che, who let out a wild yelp.

After Nina landed, she said to Bono, "Not funny. You scared the hell out of me." She composed herself, her right hand covering her heart.

"You pledge allegiance to the flag," recited Bono, as he put the dog onto the floor. Che slowly spun around a couple times before stopping, his little beagle face with its little pink beagle tongue and black beady beagle eyes looking up at Nina, grateful to be going out. Bono's eyes went from Nina's to the letter on the piano and back.

"You don't have to say the pledge to read a letter from the President, you know."

"Shut up, you," responded Nina with a laugh. "And I wasn't reading the letter."

Ignoring her denial, he said, "Here, I'll read it to you."

Now she ignored him. "What are you doing home anyway? Don't you have camp or somewhere to go?"

Just then Melissa came out of the kitchen, carrying a book in one hand and a plate in the other.

"Hi Nina." She sat on the sofa.

"Hey." There was something about Melissa—how self-possessed she was, especially for a college student, her sense of entitlement, her Hermès bag—that made Nina want to slap her.

"Can you believe this kid? He's not feeling good, so I have to come at eight. In the morning!"

"Eight! Oh my god, that's outrageous. They cannot be paying you enough," said Nina.

"Lucky I didn't have a class today." She turned to Bono, and shook her book at him like a Baptist minister shaking his Bible. Nina could see that the book was *The Nanny Diaries.* "Lucky for you, you have a nanny like me."

"Holy Mother, Mary of God! You're a *nanny?* And I thought, I thought, all this time, you were my . . . my . . . mommy!" He pretended to cry.

With a loud *tsk,* Melissa opened her book.

"What's the matter with you, anyway?" Nina asked, cracking up.

"I have a cold. Bad one too. Want to see my boogers?" He held a finger to his right nostril.

"No, I don't want to see your boogers. That's disgusting. Don't your parents teach you anything?"

"I don't know nothin' about birthin', Miss Scarlett."

Nina let out a laugh. "Okay, so you've seen *Gone With the Wind.*"

"You looking at me?"

She laughed again.

"You looking at *me?*"

" Christ, *Taxi Driver?* You're only eight!"

"And a half."

"Come on, you," said Nina. "Enough TV. No more movies. Let's show you some real life. You're not so sick that you can't take a walk. It's nice out." They both turned their heads to the window, then back at each other, knowing she was lying.

But Bono put on his sneakers and put the leash on Che and they walked out, leaving Melissa alone, sitting on her fat ass (that wasn't so fat, really, but deserved to be) reading a book that would make her feel *justified.*

As Bono, Che, and Nina approached the pack waiting for her, they could see that the dogs were in a state of unrest. To put it mildly. The dogs were howling, barking, growling, turning, spinning, chasing their own tails, sniffing at others', yipping and yapping, baring teeth, hairs on their necks raised straight up, eyes red. Ready for another fight.

Then, when Che joined this nefarious group, all hell

broke loose. They pulled as if they were in the Iditarod. Two by two, they dragged Bono and Nina as if their lives depended on it, toward Central Park.

As they crossed Central Park West, a bright yellow Hummer almost mowed them down. "Butthead in a Hummer!" Bono yelled.

Nina looked at him, laughing. "Be careful. His car is bigger than yours."

"Only a butthead would drive a car like that. I ain't afraid of no ghosts!"

Nina laughed again.

"*Ghostbusters!*"

"I knew that! I can't believe you thought I didn't know that," said Nina, cracking him up.

And then they reached they park, the dogs tugging like there was a steak in it for them at the end.

"Hey! Six miles an hour in the parking lot, buddy!" yelled Bono.

Nina looked at him, as she tripped over Sam's hind legs.

"*Inspector Gadget!*" he yelled again.

The dog run was south of the reservoir on about Eighty-fourth Street. That part of the park was sunken, far below Central Park West. The only way down was a concrete path that led to hundreds of stairs. Normally, the pack took this in stride.

Today they seemed to leap from stair one all the way to the bottom, their ears blowing behind them, Nina and Bono flying to keep up with them, Nina struggling to hold on to their leashes, Bono yelling, "Mush!" Nina looked over at him, his light-brown hair with its goofy cut flat against his head from the humidity, his T-shirt so big, you could hardly see his skinny arms, his big baggy shorts that went down past his knees, his high-top Nikes, his face part fear, part pure joy. And her throat got full and her chest sunk. A kid. How she'd love to have a kid. And not a perfect kid, god, far from it, but a kid like this. Offbeat, original, bright. A nut. She'd love him. She'd stroke his hair. He'd tell her jokes. She'd take him to see *The Music Man*.

"Puppies and babies," Claire once had said. "All I want is puppies and babies. A house in New Jersey."

"And what about your career?" Nina had replied. "You're full of shit."

"And what about you? You'd never admit it, but you want puppies and babies too. You pretend to be tough, but you're a fake." She squinted her eyes and pointed a finger at her. "I know you."

And now look at her: her entire life is puppies, she thought. A baby, a kid, wouldn't be so objectionable. But, so far, not in the cards for her. So far, nothing in the cards for her. Except this morning's mongrel madness.

Down in the park, the first order of business was the pooping. One after another the dogs pooped, first sniffing for the perfect spot, then turning around it three, five times. Then the squat, then the poop. And all this done politely, the dogs having exhausted themselves from the earlier fight and wanting to prevent another time-out, within their leash line space, careful not to trip over another dog's leash. Picture it: from Nina, an axis of leashes, stretching out like wedges of pizza. Each dog within its wedge space finding its poop place and pooping. Thoughtful, considerate dog behavior. They could teach a man a thing or two about putting a toilet seat down or leaving underwear on the floor, Nina marveled. Even on this day, the park so thick with overgrowth and no-see-ums and bees and mosquitos, even after the fight, the dogs had excellent and refined behavior. And then it was her turn to do her part: the picking up, which she did, each and every time, which she felt was her duty as a citizen. It made her crazy to step in poop, to almost step in poop, to see old poop, to witness a human not pick up his dog's fresh poop. "Pig!" she'd often say under her breath.

Then it was time for the doggie run. The dogs loved the run. For them, it was a place to run unfettered and free, without the constraints of a leash or a human, a veritable doggie playground. Surrounded by a wire fence, it was about a block long, a half block wide. Inside there were a few benches along the perimeter and some tree stumps where humans sat waiting.

Nina hated coming to the run. Even if she chose, which she always did, to not engage in stupid dog-owner conversations about breed, age, maladies, and insipidly cute dog tales, this peaceful enclave for the dogs had become the site of an ongoing war. And not between the dogs, but between their idiot humans: those opposed to the run (the dogless) and those for it (the dog owners). Apparently the barking and yelping, the stench of the dogs and the poop and the wood chips that lined the run, the fun the dogs were having running wild, and the resentment that engendered from some close-minded humans, like runners, had become such an intrusion to many in the neighborhood, to environmental groups, and others that the run had become the number one issue at the local community board meetings. Animal rights, freedom of expression, ownership of public spaces, class differences (dogs of privilege versus the streetwise dogs of the working classes), and bathroom behavior all played out in the dog run. This haven for the four-footed— not counting Shmooey, the shepherd/collie mix who lost a leg the year before to cancer, about which Nina had to hear every grueling detail—had become a hotbed of urban contention. New York in a nutshell. And it made Nina sick. How could something so simple, so inoffensive, so over-the-top sweet (a playground! for dogs!) become divisive? If the dogs didn't enjoy it so much, Nina would never have stepped foot near it again.

But there was Bono standing on top of a tree trunk, grinning like a monkey in response to the dog shenanigans. And there were the dogs: all happy and a-humpin' and a-runnin' and a-sniffin' and a-playin'. For some, joy was simple.

Then, out of the corner of her eye, something outrageous got her attention. She turned, and yes, there it was. Oh my god, she thought. You pig!

There, not twenty feet outside the run, was a pug who had just pooped and whose owner had left the poop on the ground. He had left it there and walked away. A *pig* with a pug!

"Keep your eye on the dogs," she said to Bono. She ran to catch up with them before they got away.

She tapped him on the back. "Excuse me. Sir, excuse me."

He turned. He was wearing one of those insipid blue-and-white seersucker suits with brown loafers that looked soft and expensive and a brown belt to match. What kind of man wears seersucker? thought Nina.

"Hi," he said, smiling, glancing at Nina's breasts, then legs, and, finally, as if an afterthought, looking at her face.

"You didn't pick up your dog's poop." She ignored his smile, which was altogether way too goofy. He was wearing a gold wedding band.

"What?" It took him a moment to get with Nina's program. "Well, we're in the park. It's part of nature, isn't it, after all?"

"Park or no park, it smells, it carries disease, and it's the law."

"Why, aren't you the concerned citizen," he replied. His condescension oozed through his stripes.

"That's right. People in New York City need to pick up after their dogs, or the city will become a dog-doo wasteland. I step in it every day, for god's sakes. Here's a bag." She handed him a plastic bag, which he merely looked at.

"If it's of such concern to you, pick it up yourself," he said, as he turned to head up the hill.

"Whoa, whoa there. Where you going?" She ran in front of him, stopping him in his tracks. From there she could see Bono at the doggie run, watching her, giving her a high five. "You really need to pick up your dog's poop. It's the right thing to do."

"The right thing to do, is it? Who the hell are you—the ethics police?" His voice had gotten louder, and she could see his pasty face begin to rise in color.

"No, I'm actually the Poop Police. Yeah, I'm the Captain, in fact. I'm sick and tired of people like you leaving their dog's shit all over for everyone to step in. Let me ask you: Where do you get that sense of entitlement? What makes you better than everyone else? Don't you believe others should pick up their dogs' poop?"

"Not in the park. We're talking dirt here. Nature. Dust to dust."

"That refers to death. And if you don't want it to be yours, you'll pick up that poop or I'm making a citizen's arrest."

"Listen. I'm going to work. You want to pick up the shit, be my guest. But I have more important things to do."

Something about this day, the heat, her mood, made her unwilling to let this go. She grabbed his puckered sleeve.

"What the—?" He tried to shake her off and in doing so, she stepped back onto a stick or rock or something, felt her ankle give way, felt herself lose her balance, and fell.

"Hey! You! Mister! Cut it out! Hey!"

Oh god. It couldn't be, thought Nina. But it was. It was Daniel. He had Sid's leash in one hand and the guy's lapel in the other.

"Nina, you okay?"

Nina looked up at him. There was that feeling again. Of her heart, hell, of all her internal organs slipping from their perches, muscles giving way, arteries letting loose, her entire interior self shifting. Was it his eyes? His anger? How his hands held Sid's leash, over the wrist and through his fist? Yes, yes, and yes. But, goddamn it, why, why, why did something always weird happen when she ran into Daniel, which was happening with bizarre frequency in recent days, after a year of never seeing him. Life was funny that way.

And now he was holding her elbow, then taking her hand in his, and she was feeling the fool.

"You okay? Nina?"

"I'm fine. This guy, he—"

"Nina! You okay?" It was Bono, now at her side and out-of-breath from running like the wind when he saw her.

"You're supposed to be watching the dogs."

"They're okay. Were you hurt?"

"Listen, mister," Bono said to Seersucker Man, "Why would you push her like that?"

"Look, I didn't mean to hurt her, I only meant to get *away* from her. She was insisting that I pick up my dog's poop. Here, in the park!"

"*Ohhhh!* Why didn't you tell me?" And Daniel looked at Bono and then at Nina like they were insane and then back at the Poop Prince, and said, "So pick it up."

The man gave him a look.

"Listen, if everyone let their dog poop and didn't pick it up, this park would be a sewer. It's already got rats the size of your dog. And I hold you personally responsible. Now do the right thing. And pick up the poop."

"That's the second time I've heard 'do the right thing' this morning. As if you both are the legitimate proprietors of right and wrong. If that's so, I'm in Ethical Hell. Call the police, you assholes."

"Excuse me, but there's a young boy present," said Daniel. "I'm Daniel, by the way," he said to Bono, putting out his hand for the shaking.

"Bono," Bono answered shaking Daniel's hand. "And I'm a big ass mother and I don't take no crap from nobody," said Bono directly at Seersucker Man.

All three adults turned to look at the little boy.

Bono cocked his head and shrugged.

And Nina couldn't help but notice Daniel smile. And what a smile it was: warm and genuine. It wasn't something he did very often, Nina thought. In the photos of himself in his apartment, wasn't he always smiling? But in person, he seemed much more reserved, as if he were taking everything in and learning something from even the most inane exchanges. Like this one.

But the man had started to walk away with his pug.

"Come on, Zeus. Let's go. Enough of these *mere mortals.*"

"Zeus." Nina laughed.

"He should have named him Poopititus—the God of Dumps," Bono yelled after him, and let out a squeal of laughter, cracking them all up, except Seersucker Man, of course.

"Let him go," said Daniel. "It's not worth it."

"Oooooh, people like that make me nuts," she said.

"Yeah. Me too."

"Me too," said Bono.

"You?" yelled Nina with phony anger. "You were supposed to be watching the dogs."

"They're fine. They're great. Look at them."

And all three humans turned to look down at the doggie run, and at least one of them marveled why it is that dogs can get along in a small space so much better than humans.

Then Daniel said to Nina, "I'm glad I ran into you."

She smiled at him. "Really? Me too."

Then Daniel said, "Yeah, I need you to walk Sid tomorrow morning."

Then Nina, trying desperately not to show her disappointment, said, "Oh, um, sure, no problem."

Then Daniel said, "Good."

Then Nina said in a pissy tone of voice, "When?"

Then Daniel said, "In the morning."

"Yeah, I know. But when exactly would you like my services?" Her disappointment had turned to anger.

"Oh right. Um, let me think." And he did, for well over a minute as if he were trying to figure something out that was very complicated and deserved this kind of attention.

"About nine A.M. Okay?"

"No problem. I have nothing better to do. I'm just a dog walker, you know—"

"If it's a problem, just—"

She realized how she was sounding and got a hold of herself. Besides, it gave her yet another opportunity to be inside his place. "No, no, no. It's my job."

"Good. Thanks. So, um, glad you're okay."

Nina thanked him for his gallantry. She thought she saw him blush. Then she and Bono said goodbye to Daniel and Sid, who walked up and out of the park.

And Bono said, "Weird guy."

"Yeah, I know," she said.

"Sort of dorky."

"Yeah, he is, right?"

"Like he's uncomfortable or worried or something."

Nina looked at Bono. "What are you, eight? What do you know from uncomfortable and worried?"

He shrugged and put his hands in his pockets. She smiled sadly and scruffed his neck. He laughed.

As Nina and the kid walked down the hill toward the run to gather their dogs, Daniel stopped and watched them the entire way. This Nina knew because when she reached the run, she looked back up at him and his eyes were on hers.

11

Nina was on a mission. With focus, determination, and a little of her loopy kind of thinking, Nina was going in. Her reveille, the radio alarm, woke her early and she quickly showered, dried her hair, brushed her teeth. Next, she suited up in shorts (comfortable) and a Harvard T-shirt (impressive) and of course, her black boots (enabling a run or a climb or a hide), with black socks (cute). Then she chowed a nourishing breakfast, which she had done since childhood, when she was taught it is the most important meal of the day by the same Mom who told her that if she crossed her eyes too many times they would stick. And finally, she marched out with Sam, brought him home, gave him a biscuit, scratched the sides of his face, kissed him, and left to face the enemy.

She was ready. She picked up the morning's clientele one by one, using her key, borrowing the doorman's key, or being buzzed in and up by the owner. She walked them and returned them to their rightful homes. Then she went to get Sid and was surprised to hear the shower running and Daniel scat singing as if he were a horn of some kind, at the top of his lungs. *Bum bum, bumbumbumbum,* sounding a little like Bing Crosby. Perhaps he was running late, or could it be that in her excitement, she was early? Now she looked at her watch, and yes, it was only eight-thirty.

She stopped in his foyer and listened, trying to discern the melody, as she swayed ever so slightly to the music, her weight shifting from left foot to right and back again. There was something familiar about the tune, but she could not place it. It was on the tip of her tongue, the edge of her mind. This was the kind of thing, she knew, that would come to her in the middle of the night, waking her up with a "that's it!" So she decided to not let it make her crazy, but to trust in her powers of recall.

She would've stayed for the entire concert, or forever, but Sid was more than ready. He did what he always did, in that preternaturally energetic way of his. He loped, he pranced, he danced for her, and wouldn't take "later" or "soon" for an answer. So she took Sid's leash from its perch on the table, hoping that Daniel would be gone by the time she got back.

Her first stop, before Daniel's closet, his clothes, and his bed, his desk drawers, his computer, not necessarily in that order, was the bodega on Columbus and Eighty-ninth to pick up Pete's box of Goobers. She left Sid outside, tied to a parking meter. Some places allowed a dog inside. Not here. But she could see Sid from inside the store, so if anyone tried to mess with him, she'd be there in a second. Not that dog theft was rampant in the city, but Nina always imagined the worst. If one dog was going to be stolen to be used as a live dog biscuit in a dog fight in a dark alley, it was sure to be hers. If one dog was going to be stolen for any goddamn reason, it would be hers. It wasn't about odds or likelihood. Hell, she didn't understand odds. Was 3–2 better or worse than 5–3 or even 2–1? She must've missed that day at school, she often joked. She always lost Claire's Oscar pool, simply because she couldn't decipher which star had the greatest odds. Even when the odds were specified, as they were in *Entertainment Weekly. Especially* when they were. Thank god she didn't bet on the horses.

But if Nina couldn't rely on the odds, she wasn't so sure about fate. On one hand she thought you made your fate happen, that an individual makes her own life, makes decisions, chooses which road to take in the goddamn yellow wood. But, on the other, things definitely happen to you, as if they were meant to be. Like that guy she read about in the *Times,* who, during a recent electrical storm, went onto the roof of his brownstone to watch. It turned out to be a dumb idea. Because a minute later he was dead, killed by lightning. Nina argued with herself about this one frequently. Okay, it was fate. What are the chances (she didn't have a clue) that he'd get struck by lightning when surrounded by taller buildings in a city full of them? No, it was personal choice. No one forced him to go outside during an electrical storm. Isn't he responsible for his own stupidity that led to his death? Or was it simply bad luck that got him in the end?

Nina didn't believe in luck (if she did, she had none), but she was superstitious. One day while walking the dogs in the park, a dead squirrel fell out of a tree right at her feet. Hello, if that wasn't an omen of some kind, what was? It turned out that nothing bad happened that day or that week, but something could have. If she always walked down Central Park West to get to, say, the Quints' building on West Eighty-eighth, what would happen if, just this once, she decided to walk down Columbus and turn left on Eighty-eighth instead? That would be the day, in Nina's mind, when a car, driven by a shrunken ninety-two year old who could barely see over the wheel and out the window, pressed on the gas instead of the brake, would jump the sidewalk and plow right into the corner of Columbus and Eighty-eighth, right where Nina and Sam happened to be walking *on that day,* killing Sam instantaneously but leaving Nina in a coma for two weeks before she died.

Nina had the nagging sense that if she did something differently, or, she had to face it, something *at all,* she was sure to increase the odds of danger occurring. Tie her dog to a post, it was sure to be her dog that was taken. Go right instead of the usual left, and right would be met by a falling piece of building. Or whatever. She imagined the newspaper article: "Usually Nina Shephard went left, but today, she decided to go right. And a comet fell from the sky right on top of her, killing her instantly."

It wasn't that Nina's cup was half empty. It was that a person could drown in an inch of water. So, every decision Nina made was with the thought that it could be her last.

But, not one to consider herself a wimp, she lived every day as if going forth into the breach. And today Nina had to buy the Goobers. She had to get past Pete with the old "taking Sid home from his morning walk" story (easy) and get up to Daniel's (easy) and have Pete cover for her (hard). But she was driven. A woman obsessed.

So, with Sid tied up outside, Nina went inside. This particular bodega was not a bodega at all, but whatever the Arabic word is for bodega. Al Jazeera was tuned in on the TV that hung from the ceiling and the Palestinians shelved Coca-Cola and Poland Spring water, rang up change, and argued about the soccer game in their native language.

But Nina's appearance got their attention.

"Hello lady," said the cashier, with a thick accent. "Let me guess: Goobers today?"

Nina smiled. "How'd you know?"

"It's not, how do you say, the science of the rocket ship? You've come in here ten, twelve times. And every time, you buy Goobers."

"And bottled water," added the guy working the bottled water detail.

"Yes, that too."

She put a bottle of water and a box of Goobers on the counter.

"That's two-twenty-five, please, lady."

Nina dug into the little pocket on the front of her backpack. She put the money in the cashier's open hand and put the water in her backpack, holding onto the candy.

"Thanks."

"You be careful today," said the cashier, with a piercing look that ran through Nina like a sword.

In Nina's mind, he was warning her of something. Was this deli, with its shelves cluttered with cookies, canned goods, cold cuts, and candy, really a front for Al Qaeda or who the hell knows what? She didn't, that was for sure, but she, of course, could imagine the worst. His look might be interpreted by someone else as a simple friendly goodbye. Yeah, and she was the Queen of England. To her, it was as if he knew she was up to no good. She pocketed her change, smiled as best she could, and walked out.

Billy took one last look at his computer screen before sending in his report to his boss, saving the file and closing his laptop. He sat in his boxers at his desk and his hair, still wet from his shower, dripped a little down his back, as he thought about Mrs. Chandler. Where the heck did she get all that cash? Maybe she was a drug dealer, as many people at the agency suspected. Yeah, and he was the Prince of Wales.

And she didn't fit the profile of a gambler: male, male, and male. She wasn't dealing in stolen goods and had no real connection with the mob, other than lunch once a year with Tommy Rozzano in Frankfurt. Where was it coming from? And where did she keep it? Some, and that meant a lot, in the bank, according to her statements. But there had to be more, because he had long ago learned that where there's smoke, there's fire. It wasn't in overseas accounts, unless she had other aliases than the ones they were aware of. Could it be under her mattress? The thought made Billy laugh out loud. With all he had seen in his years with the IRS—the ruses, the ploys, the extravagant lies—nothing would surprise him, except that. Cash under a mattress. A cliché, simple and brilliant.

He got up and got dressed. Where the heck was Sid, who usually hung in the bedroom while he was there?

"Sid? Sid!" he called. But there was no answer. He tip-toed down the hall and saw that his leash was gone. Nina must've come to get Sid while he was in the shower. He checked the clock on the kitchen wall. It was only nine. She'd come early and must've heard him singing like a maniac in the shower. His face flushed with embarrassment at the thought.

She had seen him fall, and now she heard him singing in the shower. But he had seen her fall too. To see her in his bath, now that would be interesting. He let his mind go there for a moment, seeing her naked, her hair fanned out over the water, her spirited self relaxing in the hot water, but quickly pulled the image back as if it were tied to his finger like a yo-yo. He'd never bathe in someone else's tub without asking first. It's ridiculous behavior. But maybe that's why he was so predictable and she was so out there, so unrestrained and free.

Billy looked at himself in the mirror by the front door, disgusted. He could use a better haircut, he thought. And this suit. He needed a new one. Actually he was sick of the whole conservative suit thing that was part of the IRS culture. Dress professionally was one of the rules. Why couldn't they get with the times and allow their agents to dress like normal people? Maybe then they wouldn't be hated so much. Not that clothes would make their jobs less reprehensible, what with their constant harassment of the wrong (read: not wealthy, not criminal) people, but it would make them seem more human. He made a mental note, rubbing his right index finger into his left palm, reminding himself to talk to his boss about this. Though this was tiny compared to the things that were really on his mind: his growing ambivalence about his job because of the constant rule-bending for the affluent and the severe penalties for those with so little they could barely keep afloat, his increasing distrust of his fellow agents who seemed to be in it just to make their quotas, his huge disillusionment with civil service and its ability to keep up with the issues in people's lives.

The IRS was particularly anachronistic. One outdated rule, the breaking of which could mean your badge, was that an agent must always announce himself for who he was. There is no undercover in the IRS, at least at his level. Show your ID immediately upon arrival and never enter unless asked to do so. He had sidestepped those procedures, under pressure to get the goods. Heck, with all the stuff he had witnessed in the agency, this was nothing. Besides, his normal moral compass wasn't always working these days, to tell the truth. He was fed up. He had planned to come clean and tell Mrs. Chandler the truth about who he was, and hope for the best. Or be creative, within the confines of IRS rules. That's how he always got his men—or women—in the past. He'd tell them who he was and get to the truth the right way. Process was, or should be, everything. If you go about anything in a way you know is wrong—if you lie to get to the truth, if you steal to feed the poor—then the truth and philanthropy have no meaning whatsoever. No ends justify the means if the means are illegal, unethical, or just plain wrong. Until now.

Plato did say that telling "noble lies" was sometimes necessary. Of course, he was talking about the rulers for the good of the citizens. Still, it almost worked as justification for what he was about to do. And now it was late. He'd have to hurry to get over to Mrs. Chandler's if he wanted enough time before she got home.

What were they not seeing? The trips to the Bahamas, to Frankfurt, to Vegas they knew about. The gambling, the stock trading they followed. The freelance work for magazines, newspapers, and tourist boards they could document by date, payment, and deposit. So maybe that was it. Maybe their suspicions were unjust. Maybe she was simply a journalist, reporting her income honestly and paying taxes in full and not engaging in an illegal enterprise.

It had been known to happen. How many times— uncountable really—had the agency been sure of someone, been on top of them, breathing down their necks, pressuring, harassing, and searching, only to find that they were of such small potatoes they didn't need to be chopped for the salad.

He put a hand through his hair, picked up his keys, and headed over to Mrs. Chandler's, wanting to do the right thing. Knowing he wouldn't. The rules of the IRS were often out-of-date and just plain wrong, but if she was doing something that hurt someone, anyone, that was wronger still.

•　　　•　　　•

Right as Nina and Sid turned the corner onto Daniel's street, she saw him leaving his building. Oh shit, she thought as she ducked under a brownstone's stairway. And then: What the hell am I doing? It was appropriate that she was on this street. She had every right to be on this street! She had to return Sid, for god's sake. So she ran into him. So what? Why was she being such a dope? It was that guilt thing again. She knew what she was intending to do in his apartment and it *was* something to hide about.

Down there, five steps below the sidewalk, she hid by the door to the brownstone's ground floor. A cat was in an open window, behind the grate, and it meowed aggressively.

"Shut up," Nina replied. She pocketed a piece of brown glass and waited a few more moments before she stuck her head out from around the stairs.

Just as she did, Daniel's leg hit her forehead with a loud *wumph,* sending Nina onto her butt, making Sid bark and the cat mew in a perfect pet duet.

"You okay?" Daniel was bending toward her, offering her his hand. Then to Sid, "Hey boy."

"Ow!" she answered articulately, as she rubbed her head, which was already growing a bump.

"I didn't see you. I'm sorry. You sure you're okay?"

"I was . . . I had . . . I'm not . . ." She was trying to come up with a reason for her being down there, but she was stumped.

He didn't seem to care. He just looked at her. It was odd. It was as if he were at once entranced and distracted. He seemed to be studying her but thinking of something else. Or was he just nervous? It didn't even seem to cross his

mind why she was down there in the first place, she was sure
of it. Hell, she didn't know what he was thinking, but he sure
seemed uncomfortable.

She tilted her head and scrunched her brows and smiled,
trying to figure him out.

Then he looked away. "Well okay," he said, "if you're okay,
I have to go. I'm awfully late already. Be careful, Nina."

There it was again! A warning. It was as if she had a sign
written across her chest, "I am about to go to a stranger's
apartment—*your apartment*—and look through *your*
stuff." Was she so transparent? She was often told how all
her feelings were written on her face, that poker would be
impossible, that she had no ability to hide anything. She
had to work on that, she told herself.

And she watched him head over to Mrs. Chandler's
house. That's twice in as many days. Very interesting, she
thought to herself.

One of them was always picking the other up, Billy thought
as he walked away. What's up with that, as they say? That
Nina, that strange dog walker, was a fixture of the neighborhood and had now become a fixture of his life, it
seemed.

He had tried to not look at her large brown eyes. He had
tried to not see how the part in her hair was crooked, making him want to pick up the errant lock that was going left
when it should've been going right. He had tried so very
hard to not want to feel the softness of her skin, especially at
that place under her collarbone, which was just prominent
enough to make him want to run his fingers across it. He

had tried not to look at her. But—and he knew she had to notice—he couldn't look away.

Nina arrived at Daniel's building, her cheeks flush with both the embarrassment and excitement of her encounter with him.

"Pete," she said.

"Now, where you been, dollface?"

"Aah, the life of a dog walker. We come, we go, we pick up poop—" She rubbed her bump.

"That's enough, thank you very much. I don't need the details. You got the stuff?" he asked while looking over his shoulder.

"This time, payment up front?" she asked. Then she took his hand, held it palm up, and slammed the box of Goobers into it. "I might be awhile. Watch out for me, okay?"

"Don't know how long he's gone, so don't stay forever."

"Please, I beg you, buzz up if he's coming. Okay?"

"I'll do my best, but it gets pretty busy in the mornings."

She walked with Sid into the foyer and heard Pete's voice behind her. "Don't blame me if you get caught!"

And she continued to the elevator.

Billy climbed the flight of stairs to Mrs. Chandler's door. He turned to look at the street below. What a day. Rainy, hot, humid, and Nina. Something about her, maybe how he rammed his knee into her head, yes, that must be it, made him feel anxious. He sighed. Like this narrow street lined with brownstones, flowers in window boxes, flowers surrounding the trees that rose every twenty feet or so right through the

sidewalks, that made him feel that his life was missing something huge. Something important. Not a house, not a *thing*,
but the thing that would make him want a house, think it was
possible for him. Forget it, he told himself. Get on with it.

He rang Mrs. Chandler's bell.

Nina rang Daniel's bell. She had just been clobbered by him
on the street, had seen him go to Mrs. Chandler's, and had
spoken to Pete about him, so she found it impossible to
imagine he was home. But the way things were going lately,
you never knew.

Of course, there was no answer, so she used her key and
went inside, letting Sid off his leash. He bounded to his
water bowl in the kitchen like a duck, well, to water.

But of course, there was no answer, because Mrs. Chandler
would be, right about now, having her nails done and hair
blown dry. It was Tuesday morning and that's what happened every Tuesday morning. So Billy took out the key,
which he had copied after stealing Mrs. Chandler's. It was
like eating one of those See's candies. You know it's bad for
you, but the force to do it, to reach, to eat, is so much
stronger than the force to stop and think and consider the
fat and cholesterol content, or, in this case, weighing the
moral issues. Once it was in his head, he couldn't stop himself. He was en route, he was making headway, he was in
process, up and at 'em, full force, full steam ahead. He wondered what Nina was doing in his apartment when she
dropped off Sid. Would she take a shower this time?

Key in the lock, he opened the door.

• • •

Sid bounded out of the kitchen, and off down the hall, turned and ran back, and then back down the hall and then back again. As if he were saying, *Look at me. Look at me! I can really move! I'm a horse! I'm a tiger!*

Safire was standing and staring straight at the wall. As if he were thinking, *Open the fuck up, would you, so I can get outta here?* He was in the exact spot as the last time Billy had visited Mrs. Chandler. When Billy closed the door behind him, Safire looked up and lumbered over to him. Ugly dog, thought Billy. He had never been a dog person, but he realized, as he scratched Safire's ears and smiled at the ugliest face he'd ever held, that he might be becoming one. But Safire, who appeared to be a loner just like his human, quickly had enough and wobbled back to his staring space. Billy followed him.

Nina went directly into the bedroom, where she first sat on his bed, low and coolly modern. It was neatly made, the gray comforter smooth and sleek to the touch. The room's air conditioning unit blew nearby, and she laid back, her feet still on the shiny wood floors, her face looking up at the ceiling.

There was something about this room, besides the fact that he slept here, and did who knows what else, though she could imagine. Sure, it was stylish, in that Calvin Klein zen chic way, like the bathroom, but it was also cold. There wasn't one homey or surprising or spontaneous item. The pictures on the wall were handsome enough, but they didn't seem purchased out of passion. In fact, the only pictures with life were the ones of him on the desk, over in the corner. Maybe this was typical of all guys, she was thinking when she felt a wet tongue on her knee, and hoping it was Daniel, she realized quickly that it was, in fact, Sid.

Now in the closet, she took a T-shirt from the hook inside the door and put it up to her body. Way big. Nicely big. Perfect big. She smelled it and oh god, she felt like a dope, but wow, how yummy was that? She smelled it again and tried to get that smell inside her memory so she could recall it any time, any place, but especially when she was alone in bed, tonight.

She saw the beautiful suits, the many dress shirts organized by color, the shoes on racks in rows. They looked like they hadn't been touched in the couple weeks since she'd been here. She arched her eyebrow and bit the inside of her cheek, thinking, wondering, hmm, that's interesting. She noticed stuff crammed to the right inside the closet, past the suits, behind the shirts. As she stepped in to get back there, she tripped on a pair of shiny brown lace-ups. Beautiful leather, she thought, as she hit the ground. Sid came running up, barking, jumping.

"Sshh!" she said. And she quickly got up and reached as far as she could. It was a case of some kind. She grabbed it and pulled.

Out came a large black case for a musical instrument. It was heavy. Maybe a sax or a trombone, she thought. She placed it on the floor and opened it. Yes, it was a beautiful, shiny, brass trombone. She carefully, lightly, touched the bell with the tips of her fingers, then the slide. Something was gnawing at the edge of her memory, as if she knew someone who played a trombone, or something, she didn't know. She pulled the mouthpiece from its slot and put her lips in it. It was cold and smooth, and it embraced her lips and held them sweetly in its cone. She wiped it on her shirt, put it back in its place. She loved this case and how specifically molded and slotted each place was for each piece; there was no danger of damaging the pieces by putting them away incorrectly.

She put the case back where she found it, hidden in the back of the closet, behind everything. This was a surprise. Something about Daniel she hadn't discovered before. It excited her. What else about him did she not know?

She felt like Goldilocks. She had tried the bed, the closet, the trombone, and now to the desk with its computer. Would the bears or Daniel be more threatening? she wondered, as she opened the computer. It blinked, waking from its dormant state, and her eyes went to the photos on the desk. God, he looked good, hair all windblown on the beach. Boy, she wished she had been with him there on that mountaintop. Gee, what a night that must have been at that black-tie benefit where he got to shake hands with the president. Shit, he was photogenic, the camera capturing something in him that didn't seem to come across live, in person.

Or maybe it was her. Maybe he was just so preoccupied, or so disinterested, that she never got to see this other side to him, this vitality, this energy, this sexiness. Not that the Daniel she knew wasn't sexy. It just simmered deeply below the surface, like a volcano, unsure of its reach, not quite ready to go. In these photos, he seemed as if he had exploded long before and now was confidently dormant, rock steady with the knowledge of how powerful he was.

Odd: the screensaver had changed. Daniel always had soaring airplanes or snow-peaked mountains. Now there was a scuba diver deep among the fish, anemones, and coral. She opened his most recent file: Project Schopenhauer. He had been there this morning. She opened it. It contained dates, times, and notes about something that was difficult to decipher. The notes were cryptic: Supplier? Contacts? Las Vegas, New Orleans, Frankfurt. Friends with Alvarez? Rozzano Family? Susskind? Hochschober?

She didn't have a clue what she was looking at but it all made her uneasy. And then she saw it: Chandler cash.

This room was perfect, thought Billy, sitting at Mrs. Chandler's desk. He could live here, he thought. The books, the antique desk, the comfortably lived-in leather sofa, the books, the Oriental rug, the perfect lighting for reading and writing, the books. He got up and fingered the spines along the top shelf and found political memoirs, histories, philosophical treatises, art and literary criticism.

She is something, this Constance Chandler. None of the women he knew were as interesting. If only she were younger, he thought. He smirked. Young, schmoung. Age had nothing to do with it. He knew she wasn't for him, but he could appreciate her, couldn't he?

He forced himself to return to the matter at hand. The money. Where it comes from. And where she keeps the rest of it. He thought of her iconoclasm, her sarcasm, her surprisingly fresh response to things, and he knew.

He laughed so loud and hard, Safire actually looked up, snorted, then went back to his wall.

And so, Billy walked down the hall and entered the bedroom of Mrs. Constance Chandler and went straight for the bed. He picked up the brocade coverlet and flung it off the side onto the top, revealing the mattress covered in cream-colored sheets and the box spring, covered in a thick, stiff fabric that fell to the floor. He lifted the mattress. He took a deep breath. There, the "stash" was revealed. It had to be about a million dollars in crisp hundred-dollar bills, sorted and stacked in short packs.

There had to be more.

He thought of all the silly old movies he'd seen, the Lucy shows, the Marx Brothers, all the old farces and physical comedies, and he went to the toilet, opened the top of the mechanism and found a chunk of dough in a plastic bag. Then he went into the living room and searched inside the grand piano, and yes, there too. And he went into the kitchen to the cookie jar, knowing full well Mrs. Chandler would never have a cookie jar except for this reason, and it was filled with cash. And then, finally, he went back into her study, and behind that nineteenth-century Hudson School painting he so admired was a door cut into the wall, unlocked and easy to open. And it was filled. This apartment was worth millions—and it had nothing to do with its antiques and art nor its value as real estate.

Nina closed the laptop. So, Daniel must be either Mrs. Chandler's lawyer or a thief. That's why he was over there all the time. Very interesting that neither had mentioned it.

There seemed to be a lot of covert covering up going on, besides Nina's.

Then she heard a bump and a screech and before she could attribute it to Sid scratching himself on the hardwood floors, she got up and out of there as fast she could, as if the bears were close behind.

When she arrived on the sidewalk in front of his building, she looked right and left to be sure he wasn't coming. When she saw the coast was clear she hoofed it like mad all the way home.

Of all the gambits and takes and cons and schemes, none could beat this. Hilarious, he thought. But it was how she got it—and what, if any, taxes she was paying on it—that worried him, so leaving Safire staring at the wall, Billy went out, locking the door behind him. Mrs. Chandler would enjoy a more responsive dog, a real companion, he was thinking as he descended her front stairs.

The minute Billy opened his front door, Sid was there, jumping and yelping, a warm and frisky hello. A minute later, they were both at Billy's closet door, Billy changing into a T-shirt and jeans, pulling out his trombone, Sid watching every movement with keen, tongue-drooling, tail-wagging interest. Billy set the case on the bed, as he always did, and opened it. Gorgeous, he thought. What a piece of art itself. He took the cloth from inside the flap that held it and rubbed the pieces as he put them together.

It wasn't until he put his lips into the mouthpiece that he knew someone else had been here recently. He looked closely at the mouthpiece, then put his lips in it again, then looked at it again. Definitely. A telltale fingerprint. A smudge. She had been here. She had found it. And she had tried it.

He put his lips again into the mouthpiece and imagined hers there. Had she noticed the perfect depth of the well, how only a genius could've invented it, with its perfect shape and size? Had the coldness of the mouthpiece surprised her as it did him every single time he put his lips to it? Had she blown into it and heard the deep tones that sound at once strong and sweet, brash and sensual?

What was she doing in his bedroom, going through his closet, pulling out his trombone and playing it? What was with her? What was she looking for? Who the heck was she to come in here and snoop?

He lay down on his bed, put the trombone to his lips, the slide pointing to the ceiling, Sid finding his place, as he always did, at the foot of the bed. And there, amidst Billy's questions and confusion, his interest in Mrs. Chandler, his strange attraction to and distrust of Nina, his dislike of his job but his desire to see justice done, all his conflicts and turmoil, he played.

And as he played, he saw Nina again, down on those steps, him having just bashed her head in with his knee, her eyes on him, looking at him. Him never wanting to look away, unable to see anything else but her eyes, that face of hers.

Back home and out of breath, confused by all she had seen and not understood, Nina put on *My Fair Lady* and went to lay on her bed, Sam following at her heels and jumping up on the bed, then doing three doggie circles before scratching at the cover before settling down. Nina was flat on her back, staring at the ceiling.

I have often walked down this street before . . . Daniel and Mrs. Chandler. Daniel being strangely un-Daniel, if she were to trust in her own perceptions of who he was. *But the pavement always stayed beneath my feet before* . . . And how they were running into each other with the kind of strange regularity that if she didn't know better she'd attribute to fate or somebody up there wanting them to get to know each other better.

"Okay!" she said aloud, immediately feeling foolish, and making Sam raise his head. *The overpowering feeling that any moment you may suddenly appear!* "Okay, I'm going to get to the bottom of him."

Safire was at his wall spot when Constance Chandler unlocked the door, her hair newly coiffed, her nails just manicured. He sat, his short hind legs folded on the floor under his sagging belly, his forearms taut to hold him up, his tongue protruding, his eyes watering.

"Baby love. Mama's home," said Constance.

Safire didn't move, but Constance bent anyway, her pocketbook swinging from her wrist, and scratched his ears, rubbed his jowls. He turned and cocked his head to look at her, but then went right back to staring at his space, as if her attention had interrupted his important work. She sighed. It would be nice, she thought, to have a dog who acted like a dog—affectionate, responsive, loving. Instead, she had a dog who acted like a man—aloof, preoccupied, selfish.

She put her bag—a Hermès rip-off from eBay—down on her eighteenth-century French side table and turned. She stood there for a while. Daniel had been here, she knew. She could feel it. She went immediately to her office. Everything in its place, it seemed. The mess of papers, the books and magazines piled high. She looked behind the Inness. Nothing seemed to have been disturbed. But she put her hand into the wall to double check. The cash was still there. She walked down the hallway to her bedroom. The money remained sandwiched between mattress and box spring, tucked inside the plush bed skirt. She went to the kitchen and checked the cookie jar. Still filled. She opened the baby grand and looked at the several grand it was still holding. And finally, she went into the bathroom to check her last place—the toilet mechanism. Off with the porcelain cover, in with her arm, having pulled up her sleeve to her shoulder, and there were her wads of dough, wrapped in cellophane.

She laughed out loud. She got such a kick out of her so-called hiding spaces. Each was a cliché, been there, done before so many times that no one would ever suspect. Cash under the mattress? On one hand, you'd have to be crazy to hide what she hid there. On the other, you'd have to be crazy not to. You think the bank was safer? She could give you ten reasons why you might lose your shirt at a bank, much less than the millions that sat in her apartment. Forget the stock market, bonds, or any of the other traditional money-saving notions. Having most of her *fluidity* right here, under her nose, or rear-end (she laughed at the thought), was the safest place to save she knew.

She kept just enough in the bank and more likely places to keep the Feds off her back.

Until now. Why were they on her case now, she wondered, as she poured herself a vodka. Lots of ice, lots of soda, lots of vodka. She lit a cigarette. Smoking was a forty-year-old habit with her, a luscious vice, a delectable sin. So it kills you. You're going to die anyway and if ten years are cut from your life in order to smoke, so be it. She took a deep drag and thought of the repressive anti-smoking laws, and the loss of jobs and wages in New York City alone. Restaurants suffered, bartenders lost thousands in tips, the psyche of the city suffered. New York, once open and free, like a Paris (which she hated because it had so many French people) or a Vienna (her favorite by far) was now another Akron, Ohio. Repressed and boring, but clean. Hoboken (where she often went for dinner, drinks, and smoking) seemed a mecca of lawlessness in comparison.

Ah, to be in Europe right now, where the vodka ran like a river and the smoke filtered the light, where her friends gathered to toast the present, because the future is nothing more than a gamble.

To do that thing she so loved and at which she was so expert. To be in Frankfurt, in September. She would drink and smoke to that. If only someone young and lovely like Daniel would come with her, then all would be perfect. And of course she knew that was not in the cards, and it would make things rather messy, what with Gerard, but she savored the fantasy and felt the youthful stirrings of desire and impatience. September seemed so far away.

12

Nina had to see Daniel. She was going to take the bulls by their horns, or more aptly, the dogs by their leashes, and get his complete attention, even if she had to make a total fool of herself, which was, most assuredly, inevitable.

So she planned a special dog-walking event. Today, instead of mixing it up the way she usually did, with dogs of all kinds, she arranged to hold a little white yuppie dogfest. It took some juggling of her schedule and some finagling with Suki, another dog walker she knew from the dog run whose clientele seemed to be dogs of the cutesy, little variety and who owed Nina from that time when she went to Hawaii on a last-minute whim and asked Nina to fill in for her.

Nina could never tell the difference between these dogs unless they had unusual markings, like Stella's missing left ear, or Jedi's bald patch on his left hip. To her, they were all little white dogs, except for cockapoos, which really were cute and smart, but what else do you expect from mutts, which is what cockapoos really are. Pure-bred little white dogs tend to be owned by idiots who think of them as cute accessories, because they're tiny and you can take them on an airplane or to a restaurant. (She didn't, however, judge those who owned them because they are hypoallergenic. That was a medical reason, the only acceptable reason to own such a dog.)

But scratch any owner of a little white dog and you'll find a psychotic parent who believes that their breed is special and unique, and bore you with the difference, in detail, between a Bichon and a Maltese, about which, of course, Nina could give a shit.

But, visually speaking, as a pack, they were a sight.

She had taken them to the reservoir, hoping they'd run into Daniel. She knew he ran every morning and just the way he went. This morning it was crowded, even on the horse path that she used for the dogs. Everybody was looking at her, smiling, pointing at the adorable sight. But God forbid she use the jogging trail up at the fence. Joggers were mean motherfuckers when it came to dogs, baby strollers, walkers, or even wheelchairs, and she didn't have the energy to contend with that this morning, especially wearing these cute new sandals that were killing her.

As they neared the tunnel at the southern tip of the reservoir, a familiar dog sprang out of the darkness. It was Sid. Oh shit, thought Nina, as he bounded straight for her, here he comes. For where there was Sid, there was Daniel.

And her heart began to beat a hundred thumps a second, and a spontaneous smile found its way onto her face, as her hand went up to smooth her hair, and then pull down her shirt, wipe the sweat from her face.

Then she saw him. In a T-shirt and shorts, hair like he had just rolled out of bed, jogging with headphones and a MP3 player in his left hand, his mind clearly on the music. He ran toward her without seeing her.

Until he did. And then a smile broke out across his face, making his eyes crinkle, his cheeks dimple. She was hard to miss. She was surrounded by eleven little white dogs, the kind people tend to carry and coddle. She looked like the good witch of the north, surrounded by Bichons instead of Munchkins. And she was wearing a very short skirt instead of her usual shorts and a kind of flimsy peasanty blouse instead of her usual torn "University of" T-shirt, and god-damn uncomfortable sandals instead of her boots.

"Daniel!" She waved to him.

He headed toward her, because at that moment she wasn't going anywhere. Those little dogs were literally running circles around her. Maybe she'd fall (not that she was hoping to get hurt) and he'd have to pick her up (but this wouldn't be bad).

"Hey Nina." And as if by will, he became serious, almost stern. If she didn't know better, she would've thought he was pissed. Did he know she had been in his apartment in places she shouldn't have? As he approached her, he took his head-phones off, letting them hang around his neck. He clicked off the MP3 player.

"Like your entourage. What do you have there, ten, what

do you call them, Bichons?" asked Daniel. He smiled as he got as close to her as he could, given the surrounding forces.

"I'm impressed. But actually, I have here one Bichon, this one here, Stella. That's Zardoz, a Bichon/Yorkie mix, over there peeing on the rock. I have two Chi-poos, Sam and Dave, right there with the little pink bows, Jedi, the cockapoo, Jackie O. and John F., the two Coton de Tulears. Also, Annie, a Lhasa Apso, the dog from hell. You know what? She wears a doggie diaper when she's at home. Not kidding. And those three Malteses? That's Larry, Curly, and Moe. Eleven yuppie dogs all in a row."

"How can you tell? Who's who, I mean. They all look alike to me."

"You doggist you! And don't say 'some of your best friends are' . . ."

He laughed as he looked down. Her toenails were painted a faint pink and though her feet were a little gnarly and arched, she looked delicate and lovely compared to her usual look of biker-girl-with-dogs. He wasn't sure which look he liked better.

"No boots."

Nina was so surprised and pleased, she could barely contain herself. "You noticed. I mean—"

"No University T-shirt."

It worked, Nina thought to herself. She felt a tug on her leashes. "Stay everybody. Just stay one minute, please."

"You look nice."

Nina looked down at her toes then back up to Daniel. "Thank you. So do you. I mean . . ."

"But it's got to be hard to walk in those shoes." He looked at her feet in their strappy sandals and then at her bare legs and then into her eyes. She had seen him see her, and he blushed.

"Well, I better get these dogs walked and home." Was she a total idiot? Why did she remind him of her work? The purpose of this event was to get him to think of her *not* as her.

"That's right. You're working."

She had blown it. So she sighed and she went with it.

"I'm picking Sid up later, right?"

He nodded. "I have a meeting. So, thanks."

"Sure, it's my job." *I'd pay you to let me pick up Sid.*

Then Daniel said, "It's amazing that people like these dogs. They're cute, but they don't fetch. They're like having dolls."

"Yeah, well, people are sick," said Nina.

He straightened up and looked at her. "They are," he said, and his eyes squinted as if trying to see her closer. "They trespass."

She was taken aback. "They visit," she said, defensively.

"They snoop."

"Oh do they?" She raised her eyebrows, thinking of him at Mrs. Chandler's, of her name on his computer.

"They stalk."

"They lie," said Nina, thinking about why he, a lawyer, would be investigating Mrs. Chandler in the first place.

"They invade people's privacy."

"Exactly," Nina agreed.

They eyed each other. The dogs were getting nervous. Annie was sniffing Sid's butt and Moe was sniffing Annie's butt but Sid had no interest in sniffing anybody's butt. He just wanted to get the hell away from these little white rat-dogs as soon as possible.

"You better go," Nina said. "Sid doesn't look too happy."

Sid was baring his teeth and growling, his hackles up, his tail at a standstill.

"He's fine. Walk with me," said Daniel. "Come on."

She hesitated.

"Come on!" He was adamant.

And so they walked around the reservoir together with the dozen dogs, Daniel holding Sid with his outside hand.

"Tell me," he said. "Why do you walk dogs?"

"Why not? What should I be doing? A *real* job? Is that what you mean?"

He ignored her defensiveness. "Well, have you always been a dog walker?"

"Why, something wrong with being a dog walker?" Why did everyone assume that dog walking is what you do while failing at what you want to be doing?

"No, I'm just curious. Isn't that okay?"

"Just for about a year. Sorry. My friend, Claire, had to go to L.A. temporarily, so I took over for her, temporarily."

"Not so temporary, this year-long job. Where did you work before?"

"Random House. Copywriter."

"You gave it up for this?"

"Wasn't much to give up. Except for my mom. I took away her bragging rights."

"You're a terrible daughter."

She had to look at him to find out if he was kidding or not. He was. She smiled back at him.

"You must make some good money. Considering what I pay you, and multiply that by how many? You've got lots of dogs, right? And it's all cash, right?"

"I do okay."

"An all cash business. That's something no taxpayer should be without."

"And what about you? You're a lawy—?" She tried to stop herself but it was too late.

His eyes became thin slits and he smiled. "You can say it. It's not a bad word. Repeat after me: lawyer. Come on."

"Lawyer," she said, and they both laughed.

"How'd you know?" he asked, though he knew very well how she knew.

"Well, um, I, just a guess. You look like a lawyer. Sid is the kind of dog a lawyer would have. Your apartment, well, from what I've seen of it, looks like the kind of place where a lawyer would live."

"From what you've seen is the relevant clause of that sentence."

"Your foyer."

"Don't forget my bathroom, and the—"

"That was it. I did not see—"

"The hallway from the foyer to the bathroom, oh, and the bedroom you had to walk through to get to the bathroom."

She had to stop him. To divert him. "Yeah, it was the bathtub, shower, and toilet. They were dead giveaways. They said 'lawyer' all over them." She laughed again. "I had forgotten about the bathroom."

"Hmmm. Not me," he said, smiling.

Now up the East Side and nearing the turn to the West,

the dogs happily on their way home, Nina and Daniel had fallen into a walking groove. It was minutes before either of them spoke.

"And my trombone," said Daniel.

"What?"

"My trombone, I said."

Nina's could feel her heart beating like a drum in a jazz quartet. "You, um, play trombone?"

He looked at her for a minute, and said nothing. Then, after what seemed like hours, he asked, "You like jazz?"

"Sure, yes. I guess." Her heart had gone from snare to bass. He was either going to ask her out or find her out.

"You think you'd like to go with me to hear Slide Hampton? He's at the Vanguard and plays a strong trombone. You like trombone, don't you."

He didn't ask it as a question, so she didn't answer. "I had no idea there were star jazz trombonists."

"There are stellar trombonists, but no stars. Trumpets, saxes, of course, but trombones have never gotten their due. The trombone is the overlooked horn. Sure, French horns have classical music, tubas have marching bands, and of course trumpets and saxes everywhere, all the time. But the trombone? It's the forgotten horn, the quiet, soulful, spiritual brother of the trumpet."

She was mesmerized by his passion.

"So, you want to go hear one? Actually, five? Hampton's put together a trombone quintet. It's going to be something. And I thought since you had such an *interest*, well, you might want to come."

"Well, yeah, sure, but, I mean I don't really have . . ."

"Tonight?"

"Tonight?" She thought for a minute and remembered something. She hit herself on her hip. "Aw, no, I can't tonight." Claire was coming over and she'd never cancel a friend for a guy. Even this guy.

"Okay, how about tomorrow? They'll be around a few days. The first set is at nine. We could eat first."

Oh god. Oh jeez. Oh yes! The sun had just risen over the treetops and she could feel its warmth on her face. The dogs were happily sniffing the fresh morning air and if she didn't know better, this was the life! This was a perfect morning. Look! See! Life turns in an instant.

"Well" was all she could say.

They had reached the West Side.

"Is that a 'well, yes'?"

"Well, okay," she answered articulately.

"I'll take that for a yes. Shall I pick you up?"

She had to think fast, so wanting to avoid the usual "date" procedures that were the kiss, so to speak, of death. "Can I meet you there?"

"Sure, you know where it is? Seventh and Eleventh, north side, tiny place. Seven-thirty okay?"

"Seventh and Eleventh?" She flushed with embarrassment at not knowing the Village.

"Seventh Avenue and Eleventh Street." He smiled.

She nodded to show him she was following. "At seven-thirty," she repeated, in an excited, fearful, overwhelmed stupor.

"Good. Now I got to go. Some of us work for a living, you know." He smiled, teasing. "Just kidding." Then he touched her forearm with his hand. "See you tomorrow, right? A night of trombones."

She touched the spot he had just touched, and said, "Yeah." She had become a date-o-moron, a date-a-phobe, date-challenged. She had put the date with Daniel on the highest pedestal known to mankind, almost as high as Mount Everest, and it's hard to breathe in the thin air up there. It can even be life-threatening. One reckless step and you could find yourself falling. In love and/or to your death.

And he turned downtown with Sid and started to run and was quickly out of sight. But Nina had time enough to turn, and watch his body move in his shorts, with his muscular legs and shoulders, and take a breath in and let it out, closing her eyes, seeing him holding her and kissing her and—

But her white doggie battalion pulled her back to consciousness with all their might, and they were on their way home.

He ran like the wind, as if he hadn't already run his five miles. He felt high, though he hardly knew what that felt like; it had been in college since he partook. And he felt excited, though he hardly knew what that felt like, it had been so long since he let himself feel. And she's such a strange woman, he was thinking. But magnificent, there with those white dogs. Something about her, her strong hands, her lovely eyes, the mouth on her, the unexpected vulnerability, the openness, something knocked him out. Oh boy, this was not happening, was it? Not right now, not as Daniel, not with this nutty girl who was a veritable Peeping Tom and a tax evader to boot. He was either going to fall in love with her or have to arrest her or both. And the last time that happened—the falling in love thing, not the arresting thing—it had all ended very badly. And that was as himself. Wait until she learns, if it gets that far, who he really is and what he really does. A lawyer is bad enough. But an IRS agent? From experience he knew that knowing in advance is something that a woman could get accustomed to, but being surprised by it is something she would never get over.

And maybe she was going out with him just because she thinks he's Daniel! The Daniel in the photos, with the slick apartment, the perfect dog?

And how did she know Daniel was a lawyer, anyway? Maybe that big-mouth doorman Pete told her. Or else she had read some of his reports or mail or a number of things in the apartment that would've given it away. Good thing he was so careful to hide his real profession and identity. She had been in the closet. She had opened the trombone case. She had blown into his mouthpiece. She had bathed in his tub. Who knew what this Nina was capable of? Did she have no limits?

All he knew was that the next time, he wanted to be in that bathtub with her.

By the time Nina had walked the dogs and then gotten them home, her feet were bleeding from seven different places. Three on the right foot and four on the left. She sat on the edge of her bed, thinking what an idiot she was, while applying hydrogen peroxide and Band-Aids, as Sam dutifully licked the bottoms of her feet. Yeah, Daniel had noticed her—you'd have to be Helen Keller not to—but he knew about the bath. He knew about the trombone.

But he had actually asked her out. And she had made that happen. Now don't blow it, she told herself critically, as if she were her own mother. Referring to the date, not the trombone.

She took a deep breath in, trying to recall that T-shirt in his closet with its musky scent.

13

That night Claire came over to Nina's for dinner. They barbecued bass and peaches and corn and drank Coronas with lime. They leaned on their elbows on the brick wall as the throngs of people entered the park with blankets and dinner and wine to hear the New York Philharmonic play selections from Mozart, Schubert, and, of course, Beethoven's Fifth for the fireworks finale. They listened to the night—the helicopters flying low and loud overhead, the sirens wailing on the streets below, the extraordinary music—and enjoyed the sultry breezes of the humid night air.

"He plays trombone," said Nina.

"Really?" asked Claire. "Ugh, what happened to your feet?"

"New sandals. Found it in his closet."

"You're going to get arrested, you. And then you'll go to prison and they'll make you wear an orange jumpsuit and you'll be sodomized—"

"Really? Mmmm . . ."

Claire cracked up.

"By a sixty-year-old woman with no teeth and a tattoo on her upper arm that says 'Who's your Daddy?'"

"Tell me about your auditions."

"You have to stop," said Claire. "Seriously. It's not right."

"I know. But," Nina said, turning directly to her, "how bad is it really? So I snoop a little."

"You snoop a lot."

"So I snoop a lot. Didn't you do it as a kid when you babysat?"

"Thirteen is different from thirty-five. It was sort of expected of us then. And we didn't understand what we were looking at. You're like a grown-up version of Harriet the Spy. As a kid, snooping's cute, but as an adult, it's scary. Besides, remember all the trouble she got into."

"So I'm a little older."

"Like twenty years. That's more than a decade. That's a—"

"A bi-something."

"So let me ask you this: how would you feel if—"

"Terrible. Angry. Violated."

"There you go."

The two friends sat quietly for a few moments, listening to the strings as they rose over the trees.

"Nina, how do I put this gently . . . GET OFF YOUR BUTT and do something with your life. Go back into book publishing. You enjoyed it—"

Nina gave her a look.

"You didn't *hate* it. And it paid okay."

"Not as okay as this."

"But this is not a career. It sure ain't a life."

"I'm happy. Doesn't that count?"

"You are not happy. You're just not miserable."

Nina was getting hot, her color rising. "Is this what we're going to talk about every time we get together? My life? What about you? You don't seem to have gotten that starring role you seem to feel you deserve."

Claire glared at Nina. "That was mean of you. I'm only saying this stuff because I love you."

Nina was silent, feeling terrible about what she'd said to Claire, and so angry she was unable to apologize.

"I'm just taking this time to figure it all out. I have no intention of staying a dog walker my whole life. I have dreams. I have goals. What do you think?"

"I think you're scared."

"Me? Of what?"

"Of committing to something and going for it. Of saying 'yeah, that's what I want to do' and 'that's how I'd like my life to be.' Because you're afraid you won't get it."

Nina hesitated, so Claire continued.

"Okay, so tell me. What are those dreams and goals of yours?"

Nina whispered, "I don't know."

"Come on, you! Yes, you do. You know but you're a wuss!"

That made Nina mad. "Okay," she yelled. "I want what everybody wants—love, respect, success, kids, everything. The whole kit and caboodle."

"Nina, I love you, now and forever, you know that," said Claire.

"Oh, you. I lo—"

"But that's bullshit," continued Claire.

And Nina had to smile. This was why she loved Claire. She thought like *her*, Nina the narcissist.

"I don't know!"

"What, that it's bullshit?"

"I don't know what I want," said Nina. "Can't that be okay for awhile? Can't I bide a little time walking the dogs, being bad, really baaaad in strangers' apartments?"

"You can bide some time, but you must stop being baaaaad," Claire responded, mimicking Nina and making her crack up. "And you should start to think about your future."

"Something will come to me. I know it. My life has always happened that way. *To* me. I get a call, they need a copywriter at Random House, when I happen to be looking for a job in magazines. Soon, I'm unhappy there, but I don't decide to leave. No, *you* decide to go to L.A. Life happens *to* me. I'm not and have never been a manufacturer of my own destiny."

"That is the biggest mound of dog crap—that's Mrs. Joost's German shepherd–size crap."

"No way. It's more like the Crutchfield dachshund–size crap."

They both laughed and watched a helicopter fly overhead, while the symphony played the hell out of the Beethoven.

"What about your sculptures? They are breathtaking. Have you tried to—"

"I do them for fun! You know fun?" Nina lied.

"Well, they should be seen. I don't know much about art, but I do know they are original and magical."

"You are my friend and you love me." Nina put her head on Claire's shoulder.

"I do. But I speak the truth. So be quiet and listen to me."

Fireworks went off overhead and the two friends oohed and ahhed the rest of the night away. And Nina couldn't help thinking that her flaky friend Claire had become the grounded one and she had become the flake. When had that transition happened? When had they made the switch? Did friends always do that, compensate for the other's growth or setbacks? Well, thank god they both did it simultaneously, because two nuts would be impossible. Maybe that's why Nina and Claire were so close and would always be: they flakified and solidified in perfect harmony.

Then Claire asked, "What is it about him, anyway? I mean, he's cute all right, but that's not enough for you . . ."

"You mean Daniel?"

Claire looked at her. "No, Mahatma Gandhi."

Nina laughed.

"Yes, Daniel! I've never met him in the flesh. Tell me what's got you so interested."

Nina took a deep breath, a sip of wine. "He's not what you'd expect."

"Well, what is he?"

Nina had to think for a moment. "He's deep. And I think he's strong. He's very present, you know? Like even with that stick up his—"

Claire laughed. "Not hard to remove."

Nina nodded in agreement. "He appreciates being alive. I know that sounds . . ."

"It sounds good," said Claire with a smile.

"He's unusual," Nina said. "And those eyes."

"Yeah," agreed Claire.

"And his . . ." said Nina.

"That I haven't seen."

"Me neither. But a girl can dream, can't she?"

Claire laughed. "So that's it?"

She paused, her eyes welling with tears, recalling something missing from her past. "He looks at me. Fully, you know?" said Nina. "He seems to be . . . it's as if he gets a kick out of me or something."

Claire put her arm around her friend. "Who wouldn't, honey? Who wouldn't?"

Later, the kitchen cleaned, the grill scrubbed, Claire gone, and Sam walked one final time, Nina lay in bed and stared at the ceiling. Claire was right: Nina would have to do something else at some point. The money she was making wasn't a given; there was more competition every day, and what with the economy, people were starting to use her less and walk their dogs themselves. But the money was only part of it. She had to be honest with herself: she was ambitious. She wanted, could taste success, a bigger life. She knew she was meant for more. This dog-walking world was way too insular, the streets too narrow, the sidewalks too pedestrian, the neighborhood too parochial.

And Daniel. Tomorrow night. She replayed their few meetings over and over. What he said, what she said. Oh god, she was nervous, she was—

Just then she heard a cry from outside. She sat up, looked at the clock. It was 1:30 A.M. Sam, on the bed next to her, lifted his head, pricked up his ears. There it was again. A horrifying wail coming from the park. Sam and Nina both ran to the terrace, she bending over the wall, he with his forelegs up on its edge, unable to see over. Another howl and they were certain.

It was a dog.

Nina threw on some clothes, grabbed Sam's leash, and they were out the door and down the stairs.

The streets were almost empty. Only a car here and there and a couple people waiting for a cab on Central Park West. The crowds from the concert long gone, the park was abandoned. The night was dark, the sky covered by clouds. Only a dog's frightful howl periodically broke the quiet.

They headed down the park side of the street toward the terrified pup. Sam leapt onto one of the benches that line the stone wall that runs along the park's entire perimeter. Then he jumped onto the wall itself, something Nina had never seen him do, but it seemed he was as desperate as she to help.

The yelps were getting louder. Then Sam must've seen something because in one quick leap, he was over the wall, running into the darkness.

"Wait!" screamed Nina. "Sam, wait!"

But he was long gone. So Nina entered the park, a half block away, at the path near Ninety-third Street. The old lampposts illuminated the narrow walkway, but she couldn't make out anything beyond. Had Nina the time or inclination to think about what she was doing, she might've stopped, called a cop, gotten help. Shadows were strewn at Nina's feet, and she was afraid.

The playground rose out of the darkness. Its play structures loomed fierce inside the steel spiked fence that sur-rounded it. As she approached it, she saw the dog tied to one of the fence's steel shafts. Sam was there, too, going crazy running back and forth past the dog. When Sam saw Nina, he then ran to her and back, as if alerting her was the best he could do.

Together they approached the dog cautiously, Nina look-ing left and right and over her shoulder, in case the mad owner still lurked nearby. But Nina really knew they were safe. Like a baby left at the door of a church, this dog had been left at a children's playground in the hopes he would be found and taken in and provided for. Nina was outraged, but relieved to know she really didn't have to be afraid. Except, of course, of the dog itself, who was so frightened, he would do what he felt was necessary to protect himself. She had to be careful how she approached him.

The dog was small and mangy, with wiry hair and bright, fiery, terrified eyes. Nina thought it was some kind of terrier and poodle mix. He was pulling hard against the rope that held him by the neck. He'd pull away and was immediately snapped back to the fence. In his fear and panic, he wasn't learning, or didn't care, that the harder he pulled, the harder he'd be pulled back.

Nina could see now that his neck was rubbed raw, bleed-ing, the rope starting to cut into it, the hair matted. She tied Sam to a nearby bench, then got on her hands and knees and, from about eight feet away, she crept up to him slowly, with Sam protectively panting and pulling behind her. The dog's wails had turned into barks, as he tried to scare off Nina and whatever threat he thought she posed.

But as she got closer, he quieted down. Nina sat about three feet away from him until he grew calmer, and began to pace back and forth, as far as the rope would allow. Sam, too, had grown calmer, sensing that the abandoned dog was not going to hurt Nina. When the barking and yelping stopped, when the pacing abated and he sat, finally letting himself take a breath, Nina approached him, her hand held out, palm down, her eyes not looking into his. He waited for her and then he sniffed her hand, and licked it. She touched his head, his ears, and scratched the side of his face. She carefully got up and untied the rope from the fence and rolled it on her hand until it was a good length for a leash. Then she got Sam and took them both home.

When they arrived, Nina gave him food and water, and made him a special bed using an extra blanket she had for overnight doggie guests. She petted him and ran her hand along his back and scratched his rear, which made him wiggle with delight. Then he slumped to the floor, turned over, his four paws up in the air, waiting, begging for Nina to scratch his tummy.

Then Nina realized this he was a she. And her heart fell. Not only was she abandoned in the middle of the night, in the darkness of the park, alone, afraid, by who knows how mean or abusive an owner, but it was well over two hours after being saved that she was finally recognized for who she was. Nina cried then, and held the poor dog with both arms, her face against the dog's.

"Mimi," said Nina. "We will call you Mimi and you will always have a home here."

Sam barked at Nina, his eyes steely like that of a lion guarding his den.

"Though we may have to find you a permanent one. But not until you're up to it, of course." Nina knew that although Sam was initially proud to have saved her, there was no way in hell he was going to allow this mangy, scraggly mutt to move in on his territory. Mimi walked to Sam's bed and curled up in it, exhausted. Before they could do anything, she was asleep. Sam looked at Nina and turned around and walked out, finding the kitchen a more hospitable place to spend the night.

Nina went to the bathroom and then into bed. And all three of them didn't wake up until Nina's alarm went off the next morning.

Sam was miserable being walked with Mimi. This was his time, Nina knew he was thinking, as he ignored Mimi's attempts to befriend him. Before they'd left, Mimi had tried to play with Sam, to engage him in a game of Chase Me, Smell My Butt, but to no avail. That Sam was pissed. How long was this strange dog going to be in his space? Though Sam didn't, of course, actually voice these feelings, Nina felt she could read his mind. And please, why else would Sam take a dump on the floor under her work table? It was a first, and hopefully the last. Okay, so Nina would have to find Mimi a home. But it hadn't even been twenty-four hours yet. Nina hadn't even had time yet to completely clean the wounds on Mimi's neck. She had carefully washed her matted hair, but the skin that was rubbed raw looked like it needed something more to prevent infection. She would take Mimi to the vet later.

The Mimi Project, as Nina began to think about it, was going to take time. She had clearly been abandoned, maybe even abused, and she needed time to adjust to a loving home.

Sam would have to get used to it. To her.

14

The doorbell rang. Safire barked. There. It's him. She knew he would soon come again. Safire raced her to the buzzer at the front door. It was no contest. She reached it while Safire was still halfway down the hall.

"Hello?" she asked, waiting for his usual response.

"It's Daniel. May I speak with you?"

She buzzed the outer door, heard it open and close and then the knock. She opened the door.

By that time, Safire had made it to the door. He let out a low growl as Daniel stepped in.

"Safire, be nice!" admonished his owner, as Safire made his way back to his wall space. "I cannot *imagine* why he's not pleased to see you. That is unacceptable behavior, Safire. Always be gracious. To what do I owe this delightful visit?" She worried that her sarcasm was showing.

"I need your advice. Is this a good time?"

"As good as any," she said, unable to tell a lie. "Come, let's go into my study. May I get you a drink?"

"No thanks."

"Please. Let's at least pretend this is a social visit."

"But—"

"Vodka and soda all right with you?" And she left him in the office while she went into the kitchen.

When she returned he was sitting on the couch, his back stiff, his dark suit jacket opened. He was perusing a copy of the latest *Travel and Leisure*. It was open to her article.

"Costa Rica. I'd like to go there one day."

"It's beautiful. You must." She handed him the drink.

He sipped. "I work for the federal government."

She was surprised by his directness. "Yes, I know."

He didn't bat an eye. "I know you know. Now I need your help. Because if you don't work with me, they'll send someone else. Someone—"

"—less appealing?"

He laughed.

He was appealing, she had to admit.

"We know, of course, about your pseudonyms, your accounts, the huge amount of cash you deposit. We assume there is more, but we don't know where. This started as a tax evasion inquiry. But it's now headed to the criminal level. I know you don't want that."

She was, again, surprised. "Criminal? Ridiculous!"

"It's what we don't know that we're concerned about. Where you get this kind of cash and how much else there is we don't know about."

"My dear sir, if I wanted you to know, you'd know." She

smiled. She saw him look at her mouth, and felt a jolt of life spring through her. Her lips, her smile, had always been her strong suit, and were apparently still.

"Mrs. Chandler, I need you to work with me, so I can get these people off your back."

"Constance, please. How can we become intimate, for what is discussion about one's money if not intimate, if you insist on using that ridiculous pronoun?"

"They're going to come here, you know. They're going to search and take you to jail, if necessary, unless you help me find a way to explain your circumstances."

"What, send in police with a search warrant? Under what pretense? They need a reason. They need proof. Otherwise it's against the law."

"Trust me. They'll find a reason. If they suspect you of drug dealing—"

"I am opposed to drug use of any form, except of course, the occasional use of certain prescription drugs such as Xanax or Ambien when the need arises."

He laughed.

There it was again. That tilt of his head, those flashing teeth, the warm, natural way about him. He was so uptight, so reserved, that when he did laugh, or she imagined, felt any emotion, he couldn't hide it, it just came forth.

"I am not a drug dealer. I am opposed to drugs and would never be involved in anything I felt was unethical. Trust me on that."

"But they don't believe that, and they will come and they will do whatever it takes to prove themselves right, if only to prove themselves right."

"Up with that I will not put," she said indignantly, standing up.

He smiled. "I know. That's why I'm here."

"And how do I know I can trust you?" Though she knew she could. She sat back down.

"Because I'm all you have. And I want to help you out of this."

An uncomfortable minute or two passed in silence, as she watched him drink, cross and uncross his legs, loosen his tie.

"You're going to have to trust me."

"The last time a man said that to me . . ."

This time he raised his eyebrows and smiled, his eyes crinkling.

"Come with me." They both stood, and she took his hand, and she took him to her bedroom. They stood in the doorway, looking at her bed.

He shook his head, smiling, unable to contain himself.

"You know," she said. "You were here."

"Yes."

"You found it all?"

"I think so."

"Toilet?"

"Yes."

"Piano?"

"Yes."

"Cookie jar?"

"There too."

"The wall?"

"Yes."

"And under the bed."

"Very funny."

They sat again in her office.

"But how? This is not the earnings of a travel writer."

"Darling, this I cannot tell you, as much as I would like to. This is my secret, it is who I am, it is how I live, it is what I do, and it is private and important to me that it stays so."

He was disappointed to be left out. "Then I cannot promise protection. As long as you withhold from me, I cannot help you."

"You won't—"

"No, but I cannot stop them from coming. When they see this, they'll think drugs."

"Is that what you think?"

"It's ridiculous. No."

"So aren't there other ways a woman can earn such money? And though I am loathe to admit it, it doesn't come from selling magazine subscriptions or my body."

He hated that she wouldn't tell him. Then again, why should she? He worked for them! He had known all along she had the cash—where it came from was still the question.

He turned to leave. She grabbed his sleeve.

"I've trusted you."

"No, you haven't. We knew—and you knew we knew—that you had this money. So now I've seen it. So what. If you don't trust me enough to tell me where you get it, I can't help you."

Why was he so angry? He was lied to on every job. Every

con, every forger, every tax-evader, everyone lied. This one hurt him and he knew why.

He liked her.

As he walked out the door, he wondered what he was going to do. He turned his head to look at her, standing there in the bedroom doorway. She was proud, yet stubborn, strong and magnetic and beautiful. She was brilliant but she couldn't elude them always.

She smiled in that way that made him want to protect her forever.

15

The rap, rap, rapping on her chamber door scared Nina. She leapt out of her seat, hit the table, making it shake and messing up the pieces she had so carefully separated by size and color and texture. She hadn't expected anyone this time of day and had been sitting at her table working on a new structure. *A Little Night Music* was playing on the stereo and she had been singing "The Miller's Son" at the top of her lungs, totally off key, making the beautiful Sondheim waltz sound like an atonal something written by Stravinsky. Sam barked, having been awakened from a deep midday snore-filled sleep.

"Who the hell—?"

"Nina, open up. It's me, Isaiah."

She went to the door, looked through the peephole, and then opened it. "Who let you in the building?"

"Someone was coming out—it doesn't matter, does it? Even you don't trust me." He was angry.

"Of course I do. What's going on? Can I get you something to drink?"

"Yeah, you can get me a triple Long Island Iced Tea."

"At eleven in the morning. I don't think so."

"I was just kidding. Don't you think I have a sense of humor? What, I'm an idiot?"

This was not the Isaiah she knew. "Sit," she commanded him. "Tell me what's going on."

"This," he said. And he handed her a mauled copy of *New York* magazine.

"You're mad because one of your dogs ate it? So stop walking pit bulls."

"No, one of my 'pit bulls' as you call them, incorrectly, did not eat it. Stop being a bee-atch, and look."

She hated being called a bitch, whether cloaked in rap-ese or not. She cringed whenever she heard the word. It was from the same lexicon as "chick flick." Nina would never call herself a feminist, for she hated the label, as if every woman doesn't want equal pay for equal work, the right to choose, to be, to go. But christ almighty, if a movie isn't about fast cars, kung fu, and bare breasts, it's a chick flick. If you're a woman who's tough enough to build a multibillion dollar empire, you go to jail! And, if you're a woman with an opinion, you're a bitch or a bee-atch, which, needless to say, is the dog word for Mom.

"I'm a bee-atch and I'm proud."

"That's 'I'm black and I'm proud.'"

"Yes it is and yes you are. Though you have no right to be." Her tone, her words cut right through his hysteria.

"I'm sorry, Nina. I'm just so upset and I felt you weren't listening to me."

A moment of silence as they appreciated each other.

"Bitch," he said.

And she laughed, sat, and looked down at the article with the bold headline, "Can You Trust Your Dog Walker, or Are You Barking Up the Wrong Tree?" and hoped he didn't notice how her face had turned ashen. But Isaiah just sat there, his long body stretched out, his legs crossed at the ankles, straight out before him, his head on the rim of the seat back, his dreadlocks hanging down the back of the chair toward the floor, his eyes on the ceiling.

"Can you belie—"

"Sssshh!" Nina responded, trying to catch her breath, pretending to read.

He scratched Sam's ears. "It's just that they think dog—"

"Sssshhhh!" Nina shushed him again.

He sat up. "Would you hurry the fuck up and read the fucking article so we can fucking discuss it?"

Nina got up and walked into her bedroom with the magazine and shut the door. She could hardly breathe. There was no way Isaiah could know, but just that morning she had been inside the Quints and hit the mother lode.

It had been too long between snoops and Nina was feeling her oats. Yes, every day on every walk, she'd go a little too far, see a little too much, listen a little too closely. But she hadn't gone all the way in a while. Perhaps it was all her anxiety that created her urge—Claire's insistence that she was in denial about her life, or the date with Daniel tonight. Someone else might have had a chocolate bar. But when she dropped off King, she was drawn inside, attracted to a silver box that sat on the mantel of the living room, a gorgeous room, simple and elegant, which surprised her given how over-the-top they were about their dog. This was the dog that was fed fresh organic beef and wore a coat when the temperature dropped.

But Nina's big surprise was to come.

The morning sun hit the silver box in such a way that it seemed lit from inside. So, both Quints out at work, she took a few steps into the living room and opened it. Inside were several joints, perfectly rolled, neatly positioned, looking like sardines lying there just waiting to be eaten. Nina remembered when smoking pot was part of an alternative lifestyle. You smoked pot, you were cool. Now it had been co-opted by mass culture, gone the way of croissants—to Sara Lee. This was why there'd never be a revolution in America, Nina thought, because everything, eventually, is for everybody. Which is a good thing, democratically speaking. Except when it's not.

Well, where there's smoke, there's usually fire, so Nina's next stop was the freezer. Into the kitchen she went, and her instincts were right. There were three glass jars, the kind used for jams because they are airtight, filled to their brims with pot.

Well, where there's fire, there's usually the need for emergency treatment, so Nina went into the master bathroom. And there in the medicine cabinet was every trendy drug on the market. There was Ambien and Paxil and Xanax and Wellbutrin and Zoloft and Percocet and Prozac and Viagra and Valium and Vicodin and Ativan. They even had Clomicalm, an anti-anxiety medication for dogs.

Taking drugs was a game this whole family could play.

Suspecting more, she looked in the built-in drawers of the bedroom, in the bedside tables, and in the closets. But she found nothing else in the area of contraband. She did find a vibrator and some sex toys, but nothing to write home about. She'd seen far more wild playthings at the Kayes, who owned that crazy moon-howling, airplane-barking, UFO-hunting Lucy, who was part bearded collie, part god knows what.

So, she left.

But not before taking one of the joints from the silver box on the mantel. And now she opened her bedside table, and there it was.

She scanned the article for her name, her heart beating in fear that someone had outed her right there in *New York* magazine. Relieved that nobody had, she could relax and feel disgusted. With the magazine for having nothing more important to write about, but even more so with herself for being a thief.

She made a mental note to return the joint to the Quints the very next time she got King. She had gone too far. Looking is one thing, taking was, well, an entirely other.

By the time she came out, Isaiah was dozing out on the terrace in one of her splintered chaise lounges.

She sat down near his legs and shook him gently. "Isaiah."

He opened his eyes and when he realized where he was, who she was, he shot up and asked, "So do you know of one dog walker who does any of the bad stuff they talk about in the article? Anybody who looks in cupboards? Who has sex in the apartment? Who tries on their clothes? Anybody?"

"No, not a one, not me. I mean, do you? Every dog walker I know knows the credo—get in, get out. What kind of person would do that kind of stuff?"

"Make love on the floor! I feel guilty when I need to take a piss!"

"Yeah, me too." Her heart was beating. She was breaking a sweat.

"This is bullshit! This is libel! This is slander! What's the difference between those two anyway? Slander and libel? I don't have a goddamn clue. You?"

"All I know is they spoke to a couple of downtown dog walkers whose experiences, they assume, speak for every dog walker in New York and they wrote a cutesy article. Hey, this magazine has to resort to anything it can to get readers."

"Yeah, but even for them, this is a new low. I am sick sick sick of being belittled and disparaged because we dare do the work nobody else wants to do."

"But it's more than that. You don't see articles about housekeepers or nannies stealing stuff or sleeping on the job, or watching TV and using the phone. That wouldn't be P.C. Us, they think we're ex-cons. I think we're ex-cons!"

"I am an ex-con," said Isaiah, and they both laughed at that. "You know what?" he then said, standing up, looking over into the park. "I am going to form a union. Yeah baby, that's what I said. I am going to get all the dog walkers of New York—no, America—"

"North America, the world!"

"—to form a union to protect our wages and our rights."

Nina looked at him. She believed he would and she was ashamed of herself.

When he left about five minutes later, she went back to her construction. It would take her some time to get back in and under. That's how she thought about the process of creating. Getting her head down and in, away, apart from stuff she was ashamed of, the stuff she needed to do, the things she'd meant to say, the way Daniel looked at her that time, the little skirt she wanted to buy, the closet she needed to clean, the stolen goods she needed to return. Down and in. And into the realm of stones and glass and wire and colors and textures and feelings and reaches. Far, far from where she sat.

The phone rang. On the stereo, "Send in the Clowns."

"Hello."

"It's me." It was Claire. "Can I come over? I have something to tell you."

"Me too. I've called you a hundred times. Trying to—"

"Me first!"

"Why? Why do you get to go first?" Nina asked.

"Because I called you."

"So? Then I'm the call recipient and the polite thing to do is let me go first."

"No, I'm not listening," said Claire, and she started to sing in the phone. "*Da dada, dadada.*"

"So tell me. Okay?"

"I'm coming over."

The doorbell rang from outside.

"Hold on would you? Someone's at my door," said Nina. She put the phone down on the table and went to the buzzer. "Hell-ooo. Who is it?"

"It's me." It was Claire.

"Wait a minute—" And she looked from the phone to the buzzer, totally confused.

"Buzz me up," Claire yelled through both the intercom and the phone.

Nina buzzed her up, hung up the phone, and went to the door, waiting for the knock. She heard Claire running up the stairs. And Nina opened the door. The two friends hugged, Claire completely out of breath and in a sweat (this one actually caused by something real), then spoke almost simultaneously.

Claire whispered, "I got a callback."

And Nina whispered, "I'm going out with Daniel tonight."

Then they just looked at each other in silence before letting out screams that would've awakened the entire building if anyone had been taking a nap that hot, humid afternoon.

16

They met at the Village Vanguard that evening, down at Seventh and Eleventh in the Village, to hear Slide Hampton's trombone quintet.

It had been way too long since Nina had been to the Village and years since she'd been to the Vanguard. She was excited. So far and foreign to her, the Village seemed European and quaint compared to the suburban climes of the Upper West Side. She was surprised they let her go there without a passport. It was refreshing to be downtown. And thrilling to be with Daniel. She felt adorable and giddy and gorgeous in her high-heeled sandals—now broken in after the bloody, torturous white-doggie walk—and her little black sleeveless date dress.

"You look nice," Daniel had said when they met in front. He was there first, waiting on the sidewalk, looking unusually casual in jeans and a T-shirt. The sun was low in the sky, making it a deep blue streaked with long, wispy lavender clouds near the Hudson River to the west.

"You do too," she responded, wondering why she was such an inarticulate boob with him. Well, duh, she thought. She was nervous and this was important. Of course she'd be an inarticulate boob.

"Let's go in."

Two burgers and beers, small talk about the day's news and the dog run situation later, the music began. Five trombones accompanied by drums, guitar, and piano played a set of old standards that sounded more like dirges.

At the end of the first set, Daniel said, "Doesn't work. Very disappointing." He looked at her, concerned. "I don't want you to get the wrong idea. The trombone is an amazing instrument. But the song choices here, and the arrangements, and the five trombones at once. Well, it sucks. Let's go."

Nina looked at him sympathetically. "It isn't that bad."

"You have to hear it done right. Wait here. I'll be right back."

He went behind the stage and disappeared for a minute or so and returned carrying a trombone case so tattered and worn that it was held together with masking tape, its handle torn off, its hinges broken.

"Come on," he said. "Let's go for a walk."

"Whose . . . ?" Nina asked, gesturing to the mystery trombone.

"One of the guys. They know me. Once in a while I sit in."

"Yours is so much . . ." *Shit, be careful!* "I mean you must be a good player."

He raised one eyebrow and looked at her. "It's important to me."

The night was beautiful, balmy. A breeze floated off the river and they headed straight into it, toward the newly renovated piers that jutted into the river from the West Side Highway. It is easy to forget that the greatest city in the world is an island. Apparently the city planners forgot too, for New York City, until recently, had no waterfront to speak of. No restaurants, no parks, nothing. Well, maybe a couple in the South Street Seaport, but that was equivalent to nothing. But now, from the Village to Soho, to Tribeca and Battery Park, the city had become alive by the water, with parks, bicycle paths, and restaurants.

As they walked down Perry to the highway and then down a block to Charles, the tall buildings fell away and the sky opened up as if they were coming out of a cave after a long hibernation. The sun had just set over New Jersey—not a romantic thought, but romantic nonetheless. Lights were on up and down the Hudson, and, reflected in the river, they twinkled even brighter. The sky was an unusually dark navy blue. It was a perfect sky, Nina thought.

They crossed the highway at the light on Charles and walked to the pier. Lined with little metal tables and chairs its entire length, floored with freshly mowed lawns down its center, the pier was still in pristine condition a couple years after it first opened. Nina wondered if the vandals and graffiti artists would eventually make their marks or if they would rise to the occasion and respect this newfound oasis on the water.

Together Nina and Daniel walked to the end of the pier,

the lights of Battery Park City to her left, the highrises of the
Upper West Side to their right, the glistening embers of
light from the hills of New Jersey across the river.

"Look at that," said Daniel, almost whispering. "Isn't that
something?"

He gestured straight ahead and she followed his gaze,
though she needn't have. There, midway up the cliffs on the
Jersey side of the river, was the most magnificent sight. It
was an old railroad sign, with three grand arches in green
looming over the river, its huge letters silhouetted by the
lights around and behind it. LACKAWANNA read tall and
proud over the Hudson. A little tugboat pushed a barge in
its shadows.

Nina wondered if LACKAWANNA meant the desire for
something you don't or can't have. Or, conversely, it could
mean, she thought, to have no wants at all. You lack wants.
Ride this train and you will desire nothing more.

"It's an old Delaware word meaning 'stream that forks'."
said Daniel.

Nina smiled, her eyes on the sign, as Daniel took her
hand. Then she looked at her hand in his, feeling its size and
warmth and strength.

"Tell me," he said, breaking the silence, "what's it like to
enter people's apartments when they aren't there?"

She was caught off guard. She DINNAWANNA talk about
this. What the hell did he want to know anyway? Did he
know she had bathed in his tub? That she had smelled his
shirt, sat on his bed, touched his trombone mouthpiece to
her lips? Did he know?

"Usually I'm not alone. Luca, for example, is usually there

with her owner, Jim. Safire is almost always there with Mrs. Chandler."

"But funny things must happen when you are."

She looked at him. What was he fishing for?

"I walked in on the Quints making love."

"How'd you know? What did you do?"

"I heard Mr. Quint yell, 'Yes, you bitch!' And since the dog was waiting for me at the front door, I realized he must be talking to a woman."

Daniel laughed. "Presumably to Mrs. Quint."

Nina laughed too.

"What's it like to be a lawyer? You're in corporate law, no?"

"Yes. Not interesting enough to talk about. Believe me." He looked straight ahead at the river and the sign. "What about other apartments? Ever want to look in a cupboard? In a medicine chest? A closet?"

"Sure, but it wouldn't be right. There are unspoken rules of dog walking and one is to respect people's privacy."

"Uh-huh," he said. Then he said again what he'd said to her before: "And you must make pretty good money. All cash, too."

"I do okay." Nina felt uncomfortable with all the questions. What the hell was he after? She pulled her hand from his.

"Truth, said Heidegger, is ambiguous. Relative, actually, and conditional."

Hello. Now he's quoting Heidegger?

She was silent and so was he and they watched the lights of New Jersey reflected in the river.

And the night grew darker, until the blackness of the river merged into the blackness of the New Jersey cliffs and the sky above. Only the lights of the Lackawanna defined land from sea.

They talked a little of family and college and work and after past history of the safe and surface kind was exhausted, Daniel asked Nina, "So what, besides walking dogs, is important to you?"

First she snorted, thoughtfully, but a snort nonetheless. She was embarrassed. "I do that sometimes. I don't mean to. It just happens."

"I like it. Now tell me."

"My friend Claire, my dog, my crazy mom." She paused thinking. "My structures."

"Structures?"

"I make these weird hanging things. Hard to explain. You'll have to come over sometime and see them."

Daniel raised his eyebrows exaggeratedly, like Groucho. "Etchings? Come over and see your etchings?"

She laughed and then asked, "What about you? What else besides playing trombone?"

He grew sullen. "Not much. I used to love my job, but no more." He brightened. "But I love the trombone and I love jazz. And Sid."

"Your sister? Your parents?" Nina asked.

"Oh yeah, well, of course, my folks . . ."

"And . . ."

"And my um, my sister, um, Danielle. Yeah."

"Your sister's name is Danielle? What were your parents thinking?"

He laughed. "Yeah, silly right? Daniel, Danielle . . ."

Laughing, Nina asked, "Where does she live?"

He paused for a moment, somewhat uneasy, it seemed, to be talking about her. "Um, California. Los Angeles," he eventually said. "She's a teacher or something. Listen—"

He opened the trombone case. The brass glistened under the light of the lamps that lined the pier. Nina watched as he put the trombone pieces together. He spit into the mouthpiece and blew, pushing the slide away from his body as far as his arm would go, and then bringing it in again. It was soft and low, nothing like the five guys on stage an hour before.

"What would you like to hear?" he asked.

"Play something you love," she answered.

And so he did. He played "I've Got a Crush on You," with such sweetness. *Sweetie Pie. . . .* She swooned. Who knew a trombone could sound like this? *The world will pardon my mush, 'cause I've got a crush. . . .* Right there, on the end of the pier as it reached toward the moon . . . *my baby on you . . .* He played and she knew he was playing that particular song for her.

And then she made the connection: it was the tune she'd overheard when he was in the shower. Was he thinking of her even then?

When he finished, she leaned against him, her shoulder against his arm. He turned to her, still holding the trombone. He took her hand in his.

A few minutes later, he broke the silence.

"I haven't done this in a very long time." *I can't tell her the truth,* is what he was thinking.

"Me neither," Nina said. *And I don't know if I can go through this again.*

"I'm not sure I can." *Besides, she thinks I'm Daniel.*

"Me neither," she said again, wanting to smack herself. Though it was true.

"Maybe we should forget it." *God, I want to kiss you, to . . .*

"You're dropping me before we've even gotten started?" She made him laugh. Her stomach hurt. She pulled her hand from his.

"Somebody, in every new relationship, has to drive the train, to run the machine," said Daniel, looking out at the Lackawanna. *The last time, look what happened.*

"Well, I don't drive. I'm a New Yorker," Nina said. *Please don't do this.*

Daniel laughed. "Someone has to pursue the other. Or else you can't get to the next stop." *Fight with me!*

"Well, I'm not going to do it." *Fuck him.*

"Me neither." *Screw you!*

"So this will be the first love affair with no people," Nina said, looking down at her feet.

"A lot simpler than if it were populated." He turned to look at her. *She's only here because she thinks I'm Daniel.*

"It could last years." *Kiss me, please.*

"Or it'll go nowhere. It's not as if a new relationship can propel itself. It can simply putter out and stall on the side of the road," Daniel said, now sounding anxious. "One could get hurt."

Nina challenged him. "Well, why aren't you brave? It's not important enough to you?" *Fuck you!*

"Me? Why not you? Who said that the man has to do it? What are you, a sexist pig?" *Don't you see, it's my brother you really want?*

"Yeah. So I'd like to be pursued. So shoot me." *Kiss me!*

"I don't have to shoot you. Shoot yourself. I'm sick of having to be the one to drive the car! You know what it's like to drive the Long Island Expressway?

"Awful! That's what it's like. Trucks, old ladies with blue hair who can't see over the wheel, terrible drivers—"

"Drivers with a sense of entitlement. Feel they can cut you off, run you over simply because they're driving a Jaguar or a Hummer," Nina said.

"Hummers should be illegal. What, eight, nine miles to the gallon?"

"I totally agree!" She smiled. *He's wonderful.* She slipped her hand back into his.

"It's really a shame," *to put it mildly,* he said, squeezing her hand. "And all because we're wimps." *And because you want me to be someone I'm not.*

"Just fearful." *Why is this so hard?*

"I know." *Show me it's me you really like and not the guy in the pictures.*

"Well, this was fun." *Yeah, right.* She pulled her hand away and crossed her arms around her waist.

"I just need some time. I know that sounds . . . but can I call you?" *When I get the balls?*

"Why?" *Oh god, yes.*

"If I learn to drive?" *To come clean about who I am?*

"God yes. The minute one of us is willing or able to drive, we have to promise to call the other." *I won't do it.*

"I promise." *And you'll be disappointed.*

"Me, too." *Please.*

And they stood there for a few more minutes, in silence, leaning against each other, before heading back uptown.

Later that night, when Nina was brushing her teeth, she thought about the pier and Daniel and how, when push came to shove, she was unable to make the leap. What she had waited a year for, ever since she first went into his apartment . . . that moment on the pier was what she'd dreamt of. And she didn't fight for him. She spit into the sink and took a swig of water and gargled.

She leaned toward the mirror and spit the water right into her reflection. "You coward," she said. Then turned off the lights and went to bed.

He could not allow himself to get involved right now, not without it blowing up in his face. Sure, she was something. Sure, he couldn't stop thinking about her. Wanting her was understandable. But playing that particular song had been a huge mistake. He sure stepped in it. And it was up to his knee, Billy thought as he and Sid sat watching Conan that night. He didn't hear a word on the screen, only the echoes of her voice as she said goodbye.

17

The dog run was closed. Its gate was chained and padlocked and a sign was tied to it that said CLOSED UNTIL FURTHER NOTICE, BY ORDER OF THE MAYOR'S OFFICE.

"What's with people," Nina said, more as a statement than a question. The dog run was *closed*.

"Come," Bono said, pulling on her arm. "Come on!"

They passed the area in dispute, its trees covered with posters ravaged from rain and emotion. Corners torn, edges frayed, the words SAVE THE DOG RUN now a mere VE THE DOG on one, and SAVE THE DO on another. Christ. What's with people? Nina couldn't shake the question. To fight over doggie turf, to have allowed a few putrid, embittered humans to win, to take away from dogs and their owners the things they love most—freedom and community. It was disgusting.

"You'd think they're protesting a war, or something," said Nina.

"When it comes to dogs, it is like war," said Bono, "between those for and those against."

"When did you get so wise?" asked Nina, as she scruffed him on his head, then put her elbow around his neck and gave him a noogie.

He laughed, but for only a moment, and ducked under her arm, running off, up and into the park. He seemed blue, distracted. Not his usual self, though Nina was realizing this kid's usual self was a complex thing.

"Come on," he yelled. "Let's go to that place behind the tennis courts."

Walking the dogs with Bono was becoming an everyday event. Nina hated to think of him sitting alone (or with his so-called babysitter Melissa, which was as good as being alone) in his apartment watching TV or some inappropriate movie. Besides, she enjoyed being with him, which was more than she could say for most people. So when she went to get Che, she got Bono too. He was becoming such a regular, he knew the regimen, the rules. It did put a cramp in Nina's snooping style, but somehow, being with Bono took her mind off what might be on the inside of cabinets.

So Nina and Bono headed, with Sam and Che and Mimi—and all the other dogs—to the tennis courts in the park near Ninety-sixth. This was a change from their usual walk, so Nina had her usual trepidations.

Bono was in a foul mood. Not one joke, not one off-color comment or four-letter word, or even a line from a B movie was spoken. Che was the same. One down-in-the-dumps dog. Nina knew the minute she'd picked them up. She'd passed his mom coming down the stairs as she was going up. Mom was carrying a Prada backpack and a Tod duffel and wearing her U2 WORLD TOUR 2003 cap and she'd shouted, "See you next week! Have fun!"

Nina had seen it immediately on Bono's face. His disappointment, his sadness.

"Hey you," she had greeted him.

"Let's go," he had answered and brushed past her out the door, his hand holding so tightly to Che's leash, his knuckles were white.

As Nina and Bono walked in silence, he quiet and glum, down the block and into the park, they both knew that the morning was glorious. You couldn't miss it: there was a crystalline sky, smogless, clean, a slight breeze making the leaves shiver and the air a little cooler as well. But Nina was mature enough, she hoped, to understand that it was just a beautiful day, that's all. And not a sign of good things to come. Besides, they had taken an alternate route. And Nina knew what that meant. Probably nothing, but you never knew.

Nearing the courts, she could hear the *bunk, bunk-bunk* of balls hitting the blacktop, and the yips and barks of dogs at play. She visualized dogs playing tennis and wanted to share the joke with Bono, but he clearly wasn't in the mood. Then the courts were in view and as they approached the small building that held the administrative offices of the parks, the tiny snack bar, the even smaller tennis shop, she could see dogs running and people hanging on the other side.

Their dogs heard it too, for they started to pull, eager to

get there already to be free of their leashes, to run with the wolves.

Now they rounded the bend, passed the building, and Nina let Sam and Mimi off their leashes. And Bono did the same for Che. Then they let the others loose too and as the dogs sprang forward and ran to the grassy hill, alive with running dogs, barking dogs, sniffing booty and licking dick dogs, Nina put her hand flat on Bono's back, as if to say, "I'm here."

He turned to look at her and before shrugging her off, just as any boy his age would do, he nodded ever so slightly, but enough for her to notice that he understood.

And then he said, "Bet you ten for ten today."

"Don't even think about it. You're gonna lose. And where does a kid your age get ten bucks to just throw away?"

She looked at him. There was no answer.

"Huh?" she implored.

And then he looked up at her, with one of his wise-ass smiles.

"You're on," she said.

This was something they'd started a few weeks ago and it had become a habit with them. They would bet that they could match the dog with its owner. And this morning Bono was bullish, or so angry that he was foolish, because he was trying to bet that he could pick *ten* dogs and match all ten correctly with their owners.

"What about that one?" Nina asked, lifting her chin toward a middle-aged Birkenstocked woman with gray hair and a T-shirt that read GRANDMA AND PROUD OF IT.

"The rottweiler."

Nina laughed.

"Maybe she's just the kind of girl who lives on the edge," said Bono.

And Nina let out a roar. Heads turned their way as Nina thought, What a kid, this kid.

"And where'd you get that?"

"Stop asking me that, would you? Takes out all the spontaneity for me if I have to keep explaining and explaining and *explaining*."

"Okay, okay, *okay*. I know you're in a bad mood, but have a little patience, would you?"

The dogs were wild that morning, running up and down the hills, jumping and barking and nipping at each other. The big, powerful dogs in front, the little ones bringing up the rear, the humans in clumps of twos and threes around the edges. Lucy, the Kayes' part-bearded Collie, was going crazy because of a low-flying helicopter. She was barking loudly and getting nervous, making the entire doggie contingent anxious and rough.

"Lucy," shouted Nina, "quiet down, girl."

"Oh is that your Neardy Beardy?"

Nina turned to see the woman in Birkenstocks, who then asked her, "Isn't she part bearded collie?"

"Well, yeah." Then Nina turned to Lucy. "Lucy, it's okay."

"So she's a Neardy Beardy."

And then, in that split millisecond between the "Neardy" and the "Beardy," before Nina had enough time to think what an idiotic name that was, Nina felt something hit the back of her knee, felt her knee fold and give way, as if someone had done that stupid teenage trick of walking up behind her and bending his knee into the back of hers, making it bend. Only this time, Nina's knee bent and didn't stop. She felt bone loosen from muscle and tendons pull, leaving bones untethered, and she fell to the ground, her knee not looking like a knee at all but she didn't know what or the words just couldn't come to mind because the pain was huge, her breath hard to find, her eyes noting the blueness of the sky, the tops of the trees, and now Bono's little frantic face looking down on her. She heard her own screams of pain, and she thought, isn't that funny, she could scream. She'd always thought her voice too low, too raspy, that she could never star in a horror movie because she couldn't scream. But now she knew she could. Yes, she could scream and wail and cry out with pain with the best of them.

She heard Bono speaking softly in her ear. "You're okay. Keep breathing." And then yelling like a wild boy: "Would someone please call an ambulance? There's a hurt lady down here."

She had to know: "What happened? Oh god. What happened?"

And then there was his voice, that goddamned voice that always found her when she was down on the ground, that seemed to come out of nowhere, there to help her, sort of like Superman, in her hour of need: "A little dog jumped into the back of your knee and looks to me like he dislocated it." It was Daniel, whom she hadn't seen in the couple weeks since that night of trombones and rejection.

She could tell he was seeing the humor in this, which eluded her completely.

"Where's the fucking ambulance?" said Bono. "She's turning blue!"

"She's okay," said Daniel, and he put his hand under her head, raising it slightly off the ground.

"Is she okay?" asked the grandma in the T-shirt. "I know Jedi would never have meant to hurt her." She was holding the demon dog, the very same Lhasa Apso that started the dog fight a couple weeks back. The grandma put the crazy dog on the ground. He then licked Nina's face all over until Daniel shooed it away.

"You owe me a dollar," Nina cringed as she spoke to Bono.

"I have to admit, that ain't no rottweiler, baby," he said.

Her breathing came a little easier then, and she felt the weight of her head in Daniel's hand, and she realized how close his face was to hers and saw that he hadn't shaved yet. Boy, it hurt. To be this close and in so much pain. She laughed out loud. And followed it up with a groan in response to the pain of the laugh.

"What?" he asked, softly.

"It's you again. Why is it always you when I'm—"

"Of course it's me."

He looked straight into her. She turned her head away. It was all too much this morning, lying here on the ground, her knee unrecognizable, the pain finding its way into every artery, every muscle, every DNA strand of her body. His hand holding her head. His eyes on her. His face so close she could smell his skin, the sweat from his run. And what did he mean by that? Of course, it's me. What the hell does that mean? She felt faint.

Then she heard the sirens. Thank god.

"Thank fucking god!" said Bono. He looked at his watch. "Three minutes. Not bad for this big, dark, unforsaken city."

And then there were two big and brawny guys setting down a stretcher next to her, looking at her leg, taking her pulse.

"Wow," explained one, very scientifically. "That don't look too good."

That's reassuring, thought Nina, who would've said something sarcastic if she could have.

"Let's get her some air before she goes into shock."

Comforting, thought Nina. She grabbed Daniel's T-shirt at the neck like she was going to strangle him.

"Daniel, help Bono and the dogs get home. Please." And then to Bono she said, "Help him, would you? You know where they live."

Bono shook his head. "Okay," he said. "Sure."

"Don't worry. We'll handle it," answered Daniel. "Your key on the ring?"

She tried to shake her head no.

"My backpack. Small pocket." It was becoming very difficult to talk. "Someone has to do my walks. Or I'll lose them. Call Claire. Call Isaiah."

"Stop. We'll take care of everything," said Daniel.

She just looked at him.

"Hurts, doesn't it," said Daniel. And then: "Where doesn't it?"

"What?"

"Is there somewhere it doesn't hurt?"

She laughed. And that hurt. Where the hell were those EMS guys?

"My shoulder blade." She thought she was being funny.

But then Daniel put two fingers down the neck of her T-shirt and touched her there. He stroked her—as if he'd been there before, not necessarily down this particular T-shirt on this particular bone, but he touched her in such a way that even in her pain, she felt his fingers on her skin move with authority near her neck and back to the bone, to her shoulder, back across the bone itself and up again to the hollow at the base of neck.

She looked from his face to the sky, closed her eyes, and for a moment she was released from the pain. And then the two EMS guys arrived, one covering her mouth and nose with an oxygen mask, one strapping a board to her injured leg.

"One, two, three . . . up." And they lifted Nina onto the stretcher and loaded her into the ambulance. She hadn't had time to give instructions or say goodbye or get home safely or even thank you.

"Where are you taking her?" Daniel asked.

"To Cornell. They got a department of orthopedic surgery just in case."

As the doors closed, she heard Bono yell, "Don't worry!"

"So what do you do?" asked the EMS guy sitting in the back with her.

She could hardly breathe, but figured he was chatting to keep her awake. Or alive.

"I'm a dog walker. But I used to be in publishing." Why'd she say that, she wondered. After a year, she still felt it necessary to tell a stranger, an EMS driver, for god's sake, that she once had a real job.

"Where'd you work?"

Why was he engaging in small talk, Nina wondered. This ain't no cocktail party! No picnic either!

"Random House," she answered.

"That's funny."

She was silent, failing to get the joke.

"No, I used to be Robert Samuelson's bodyguard."

He had been the publisher of Random House when she worked there—the asshole who threw the book jacket at her.

"Small world," she said.

"Yeah, you got that right."

"Why'd he need a bodyguard?" she asked through clenched teeth, almost fainting, the ambulance having just gone over a pothole, the motion sending pain shooting directly from knee to brain and back.

"Who knows. He thought he had enemies. Publishing's a killer!" he laughed.

She had to stop herself from laughing because it made her leg hurt so much when she did, but if she had wanted to kill him—and she had—so did others. So did others.

At the hospital, she was given morphine and felt very fine very quickly. She didn't even feel it when the doctor lifted her leg and, with one hand under her calf and another holding her ankle, rearranged the bones, resetting them in place.

She was even able to mobilize her tongue and ask him in a thick voice, "Stupid, huh? A dog dislocating a person's knee?"

"Dogs and ocean waves. It happens all the time."

How fragile are we, Nina thought, which she knew was a cliché, but she couldn't help it. How defenseless. You just can't turn your back on the ocean or on a Lhasa Apso. Sure, she knew the dangers of the ocean. Like everyone else, she was taught from a young age: beware of the undertow. But being belted by a wave in such a specific way that one's knee can become dislocated? And a fuzzy ten-pound dog, with black button eyes and a little pink tongue, can hit a person with enough force, in precisely the right spot to *move bones*? Sure, it is a dog that descended from Satan, but a dog that people get because it's *nonallergenic*, for god's sake. Was it the morphine, or was it the knowledge that she'd have to sit on her butt for a week or two, or was it the way she had felt when Daniel touched her neck that made her feel desperately powerless because she had nothing on a little dog and even less on chance?

18

She's going to be okay," said Billy, putting his hand on Bono's shoulder as the ambulance drove off toward the East Side, its siren blaring, lights flashing. He watched it round the corner until it was completely out of sight.

"I know," said Bono. He was looking down at his Nikes.

Billy turned to the kid with concern. "Come on," he said, rapping the kid on his arm. "Let's get the dogs home. What do you say?"

"Yeah, okay."

And they rounded up Nina's dogs and headed toward Central Park West.

It wasn't easy getting every dog to its rightful owner. Though Bono did the best job he could trying to remember who lived where, there were maybe two or three that he couldn't immediately place. He went to a few wrong apartments and had to retrace his steps before figuring it out. Then he and Billy had to explain to each and every doorman and owner what had happened, where Nina was, why they were returning the dogs. They had to field questions about who'd walk their dogs later or the next morning, promising the job would get done.

Once everyone was delivered, except Sid, Sam, Mimi, and Che, Billy told Bono he'd get him home and then he'd take Sam and Mimi back to Nina's. Bono complained; he'd wanted to see the job through. But Billy insisted.

"I'm taking you and your dog home and then I'm taking Nina's dogs home. And that's that."

"Why can't I go? This is my job too, you know. She asked me to help, remember?"

Billy couldn't explain to him—or himself, for that matter—why it was so important that he be alone in Nina's apartment. But it was.

"And who's going to do Nina's walks this afternoon? Tonight? She's not going to be able to do this for a while, right?" Bono had a million questions upon getting to his house. "What's going to happen? Will she lose all her customers? How will she get paid? Who's going to visit her in the hospital anyway? How will she get home? Where is her family, anyway? Her mom? Is she all alone? WHAT THE HELL IS HAPPENING?"

Billy put his hand on Bono's shoulder.

"She's got to have some friends and family nearby. She mentioned Claire and um . . ."

"Isaiah," remembered Bono.

"Yeah. So I'm going to go to her apartment and check her

phone book. Worse comes to worse, she's got us. Doesn't she?"

He couldn't believe his own ears, what had just come out of his own mouth. But he meant it. She did have them.

"Yeah, she's got us," answered Bono.

Then they turned the corner onto Bono's street and walked the half block to his townhouse. Bono climbed the stairs with Che and turned around to face Billy.

"You have to—I want to know when she gets home."

"Don't worry," answered Billy and started to walk away. "I'll keep you posted. I might need your help, you know, to get the dogs walked. Okay with you?"

"Well, yeah, sure." Bono said. And as Billy started to walk down the street, Bono called after him. "Wait—my phone number. How you going to reach me? Got a pen?"

Billy turned. "Look, why don't we go to the hospital tomorrow morning? I'll pick you up at nine."

"Good," said Bono, who started to go inside, then stopped and yelled: "Eight!"

"Nine!" Billy yelled back

"Eight!" he heard from the corner.

"Nine!" he yelled again. "Tomorrow! O'clock!"

"Okay!" was yelled down the block.

Finally, it was quiet. And Billy walked quickly towards Nina's.

"BUT WHY NOT EIGHT?" he heard from around the corner, now two blocks away.

If they could've seen each other's faces at that moment, they would've known they both were smiling.

•   •   •

Billy walked on, Sid and Sam on one side and Mimi on the other. And soon he was at Nina's building. It was one of those buildings that faced the park but was entered from the side street. He wondered why, when they built this building in the 1920s, it had been designed to enter from the side, instead of the logical—and more impressive—way, from Central Park West. He'd have to get on the Net later and do a little research. Looking for her key, he fumbled through her back-pack before remembering that she had said the key was in the little pocket on the outside. Finding it, he opened the outer door and walked through the lobby to the stairs. It was nice, clean, and small, probably even elegant in its day. It felt Euro-pean, this building. With carved, curved railings and detailed moldings, with its wall sconces, the brass engraved with birds and their low bulbs, and the fact that it was walk-up, it felt kind of quirky. He imagined bohemians in the twenties living here. A perfect fit for Nina, not that he knew her well. He started up the first flight, the dogs rambling in front of him, tongues out, getting out of breath with each half flight.

There were only two apartments to a floor, he noticed, now out of breath himself as he neared the fourth, then fifth floors. Five B was hers. He unlocked the door and entered, unleashing the dogs, who loped ahead, dodging in, around, and under the furniture and corners of the tiny space.

But he just stood there for a moment, taking it all in. The tiny space, the French doors at the top of a short flight of steps on the other side of the room that led to what must be a terrace, the orange walls, the unusual table at the center of the room. The clutter, the art, the old, battered metal cabi-net that looked like it held a CD player and maybe a TV. And finally, though it was the first thing he saw, he let himself really look at the sculpture, if that's what it was, that hung from the ceiling almost to the floor. It was made of wires and stones and broken glass pieces and beads and buttons and yes, some shells, he noticed, as he moved up close to it. The wires formed a labyrinth of sorts. It wasn't simply a beaded curtain like those out of the seventies, but three-dimensional. The wires formed shapes and, strung with the beads and things, created texture and depth and a highly intricate structure. It was *wonderful*.

He took two steps and was in the tiny kitchen, which was like the bigger room—cluttered, brightly colored, and two the other way, into the bedroom. Its whiteness, its austerity, was shocking. The bed—a queen—was low. Just a mattress on a board on a frame covered in a white down comforter. It had only two pillows, also white. The sheets were white as well. The walls were white. Only a blind on the windows, nothing on the hardwood floors, except Sam's bed, which was solid brown, like the floors. One lone plain pine chest of drawers. One small bedside table. Not one bit of clutter. Or color. Billy thought the spare look was nice, but it was the juxtaposition with the rest of the place that got to him. Given the vibrancy of out there, this, in here, was the room of either a zen master, a nun, or a nut.

He stepped back into the main room and turned on the CD player, seeing there was still a CD in it, pressing play to hear whatever Nina had last listened to. He went out onto the terrace as the music began.

A man's voice, not quite operatic, more Broadway musical. Billy turned to listen.

I have dreamed that your arms are lovely . . .

He went back inside, directly to the old beat up cabinet, and found the CD cover: *The King and I*, by Richard Rodgers and Oscar Hammerstein II. Yes, of course he'd heard their music before, usually performed by jazz musicians, like Oscar Peterson or Herbie Hancock. But he'd rarely heard them sung before and he'd never heard this particular song before. He looked through all her CDs and most were musicals. Oh, she had the requisite contemporary rock stuff, but from there her collection branched in one direction only: Broadway musicals, many from the fifties and sixties. How weird for a woman of her age. What was it, he wondered. The melodies? The story? She couldn't possibly have seen actual stage productions or movies of all of them, so it had to be the songs themselves, sung by characters, so songs that told stories. The feelings of the characters who sang them: love, anger, deception, jealousy, longing. He listened again.

I have dreamed ev'ry word you'll whisper . . .

Romantic! The song was—could it be that Nina was too? For all her flip, brash posturing, she was mush, maybe even sweet. He looked again at the sculpture and he saw it differently this time. It wasn't about structure, though it was dependent on structure. Like this silly, wonderful song he was listening to, whose structure was serious and professional, the sculpture was about romance and the dream of love. He felt a tug in his chest as he looked closely at its intricate highways and byways. So complex, *so surprising.*

In these dreams I've loved you so that by now I think I know what it's like to be loved by you . . .

But he was taken out of his reverie by Sid, who licked his hand and nudged him for some attention, a pat on the head. Then Sid ran up to the terrace door and back and up to the door, begging, it seemed, to go out. Billy didn't realize it, but when he came in, he had let Sid in too but left Sam and Mimi out, and now they were clawing the door, whining to get in.

Back out onto the terrace, the dogs reunited, he listened as he took in the view, the pots of flowers, the sun-scorched furniture. He sat in what he thought was Nina's seat, with its striped and tattered pillow. He watched a helicopter rise on the other side of the park and noisily make its way to the west, passing overhead in a thunderous *wop-wop-wop*. He saw one black bird, alone, flying in the breeze. It reminded him of those crazy seagulls at the Cliff House Restaurant in San Francisco, once home of the Sutro Baths and the camera obscura, where he'd met—and lost—Elizabeth. The winds from the ocean are constant, and the gulls lift off into them, rising, elevated by the coastal velocity. Then, like a game of Russian roulette, they let down their aeronautic defenses and bet on the breezes to keep them aloft.

His hands on the chair's armrests, he thought of Nina, alone in the hospital. And he remembered why he was here. To "Shall We Dance," he got up, went inside with the dogs, and got down to work.

He had to find her address book to get Isaiah's and Claire's numbers to let them know what happened. So, first he went to her backpack, which he'd sat on the table, and took out its contents: plastic bags, Kleenex, a bottle of water, sunglasses, her house keys, her wallet (which he'd get to later), some lipstick. No Palm Pilot or address book of any kind.

So he went into her bedroom, the dogs following closely behind. There weren't too many places to look in here, except a bedside table with one drawer and that little chest. First, the bedside table, which held a funky old lamp, a phone, and a *Vanity Fair,* an *Art in America*, and a couple novels. He sat on the bed to get a better look inside the drawer. And there was her Palm Pilot. And there was a joint, perfectly rolled.

Something about being here alone in her apartment, in her bedroom, on her bed, made him want to break out of his own self-imposed boundaries and run full throttle, like mad, headlong down that slippery slope into Wonderland. He took the joint and held it between his pointer and third finger, as if smoking a cigarette, and he lay back on Nina's bed. He was not a complete bore. He could party with the best of them. He brought the joint to his lips, thinking of holding her head in his hand, her skin cold and damp, thinking of her in the hospital, of her playing his trombone, of her alone in this bed, in this white spare room.

"What the hell!" he said aloud, startling Sid and Mimi and Sam and making them bark. Then Billy sat up and again looked in her bedside table drawer. There he found some matches and he lit up, taking a deep drag on the joint. Yes, he thought, this was vaguely familiar. Then he picked up the Palm Pilot and found Isaiah's and Claire's numbers. He found her dog-walking schedule and was surprised by the number of walks she did. He found a memo about the money she expected to collect this month and August too.

Impressive, he thought. And all cash. Another time, an earlier, more dedicated time, he might have pursued this. He
took another hit of the joint and was beginning to feel its
effects, when he got a brilliant idea.

He walked, actually danced, to the boisterous strains of
"Shall We Dance?" because the singer asked him to, into
Nina's bathroom, got naked, and turned on the bathtub
faucet. Hot but not too hot. He poured in some of her bath
oil, smelling the delicious scent of the lilac, humming to the
music, and got in, careful not to wet the joint. And for the
next hour he took a bath, smoked the joint, and thought
how absurd it was to be falling in love with someone like
Nina. She was life in all its chaotic glory, full of contradic-
tions and energy. He was serious, constantly fighting disor-
der, with his one passion—his trombone—hidden deep in a
closet, and his past hurts hidden deep within his heart.

As he stared at his hand, first palm, then the back, and
palm again, he thought of the German philosophers he so
admired and what schmucks they were. "Heidegger, schmei-
degger, Schopenhauer, dopenhauer!" he said out loud and
laughed and laughed. Sure they talked about order versus
chaos and truth and relativity and Man's capacity for evil,
but what about love? What about love and getting hurt and
sex and love?

And so, from the tub, pretty stoned, he made the calls,
leaving messages on Isaiah's and Claire's machines telling
them what happened and what hospital and what she
needed help with. And then he got dressed and ready to
leave. The desire to look in her closet, in her bathroom cabinet, in her sheets was almost too much to ignore, but

ignore it Billy did, and he walked out of the bedroom, turned off the stereo, and headed toward the front door.

But first he stopped at her sculpture that glistened in the sunlight streaming in through the windows, and he touched it. He touched the smooth pieces of glass, the sharp edges of stone, the finely etched markings of shell, the flat and thinness of a button. He opened his hand and ran it up and down and up again and then around it to get a sense of the whole. He stuck his arm through, he put his head in and looked up. And only when he felt he had experienced it from nuance and detail to outright shape and overall structure, was he ready to leave.

19

"Mom, it's me."

"Honey? What's the matter?"

"What do you mean? How do you know—"

"Because I *know*. I'm your *mother*. Now tell me what's going on."

"I'm in the hospital."

"What? What happened? Are you all right? *What happened?*"

Nina put the receiver to her chest and reached for her glass on the side table. She took a sip of water. It was either her medication or her mother that made her feel as if she were dying of thirst.

"NINA! WHAT HAPPENED?" She heard her mother's muffled yell.

She picked up the receiver.

"I dislocated my knee. I'm okay."

"I'm coming. I'll be there as soon as I can. I'll have to cancel my poetry workshop and there's my Elder Hostel. Did I tell you I was going—"

"Mom, no. Don't cancel anything. I'm out of the hospital in two days and then I'll be back to work a day or two after that. Nothing broken, nothing torn. Just a pull."

"But how will you get around? Who will feed you? Can you walk? Who's walking your dogs?"

"I just wanted you to know. I don't want you to change your schedule or anything." Oh god, please don't let her come. Please just get her to say a few nice motherly words to me so I can cry and feel loved and taken care of.

"Maybe this is a good time to get your old job back."

Even now while she was drugged and sedated, a comment like that from her mother made Nina feel like a child and act worse.

So, in response, Nina asked, "Dating anyone, Mom?"

"Well, feel better, honey. How will you get home from the hospital? Can Claire pick you up?"

"Claire and Isaiah and Bono and Daniel, they're all helping and I'm going to be fine."

"Soon, I hope. Who's Bono? And Daniel? Isaiah, who's that? He sounds religious."

"My friends, Mom. They care about me." Nina couldn't believe she said that. There was a long beat before either of them spoke.

"You have a mother who cares about you too, you know."

"I know, Mom."

Then Tina, Nina's nurse, who was the size of Giants Stadium, walked in with one of those little white pleated paper cups used to carry pills.

"Time for meds!"

She had a voice as big as she was.

"Just a second," Nina whispered. "I'll be off in a minute."

"It's ten. The time to take them is NOW," she bellowed.

"Nina!" yelled her mom through the receiver.

"Can't you give me . . ."

"Now," Nurse Ratched sternly replied.

"NINA!"

"WHAT!"

"I love you."

"Oh Mom . . ."

Nina's eyes immediately filled with tears, as only chopping onions and hearing those three words could do.

This made Nurse Ratched's eyes roll to the ceiling as she stood there, bedside, holding the little cup, tapping her foot.

"I know," she answered softly, her eyes on the nurse.

"You're not in pain are you?"

She took the cup and swallowed its contents.

"Not with these drugs. I'm feeling gooo—oood."

"You call me if you need me."

I just did, Nina was thinking. Don't you know I need you? "I love you too," she said.

"Do what the doctors tell you," is what her mom answered.

"Bye Mom."

And she hung up.

•   •   •

The next morning she knew she had visitors but she was so out of it and woozy she couldn't hold a conversation. It was Daniel, she was pretty sure, and Bono, one of them carrying flowers, saying hello and how do you feel and are you in pain and do you need anything and what can we do. It was very sweet of them to come, she was thinking when she lifted her head and proceeded to throw up all over the floor. The drugs had that effect on her. Needless to say this was not something she would have preferred to do in front of Daniel, but he had quickly called the nurse and Bono had said something like "Gross! Nice way to treat visitors!" and "Looks like you had a healthy breakfast," making Daniel laugh and her feel a little less embarrassed. But she must've fallen asleep because she didn't remember seeing them leave or saying good-bye.

20

"Can't you please get closer to the curb?" Claire pleaded with the taxi driver. "How's she going to make it if you stop in the middle of the street? She's going to get killed!"

"Listen lady—"

The driver was getting pissed, Nina could feel it.

"It's okay, Claire. I'll make it."

"No way. Listen buddy. Either you move right up to the curb or you're not getting a tip. My friend here is on crutches! Can you not see that?"

"Come on, let's get out," Nina said to her overprotective buddy.

"Yeah, you better get out, or—"

"Or what?" Claire asked, raising the argument stakes. "Or you'll shoot me?"

The driver laughed. "No, you crazy woman. I'm not going

to shoot you, but I will call a cop. Now pay the fare and get the hell out, would you? Please?"

"Come on, Claire. He said 'please.' Just pay him."

Taking her wallet out of her bag, and fingering it for some cash, pulling out a ten, Claire said, "I'm not giving him a tip. Not one penny. Keep six-seventy."

The driver eyed her from his rearview mirror.

"Well, that'll show him," Nina said, and laughed as she opened her door.

"It's *something*," said Claire. "Wait," she said, "I'll come around." And she received her change, walked around the front of the cab and made a face at the driver. One of those three-year-old, bratty, tongue-out, mean faces.

The driver said, "Oy. Is she like this all the time?"

And Nina said, "You don't know the half of it."

And the driver said, "Maybe you should be taking care of *her.*"

Nina laughed. "Shoulda, woulda, coulda."

"You got that right. Now get outta here already, would you?" And he laughed.

Nina thought he was sweet in a sleazy-and-at-thirty-eight-he's-still-living-in-his-mother's-basement sort of way.

Finally they were unlocking the door to her building and walking carefully, with much effort, up Nina's stairs. She used one crutch, the railing and the support of Claire's hand on her elbow to jump one step at a time. Claire carried the other crutch plus her own bag. What seemed like an hour later, they made it to her apartment door, where a big box was waiting.

"What the hell is this?" Nina said.

"I don't know, but it's got your name on it." Then Claire used Nina's keys to open the door, got Nina in, and slid the box inside.

"Who's it from?"

"Don't know," said Claire, bending down to read the label closer. "Sharper Image."

"Ooh la la. A gift, maybe. Get scissors, okay? Let's open it."

"Let's get you settled first. Wow, this sculpture is amazing," Claire said as they entered the apartment. "It looks sort of like one of those antique birdhouses, you know, the old wooden kind from the nineteenth century, only futuristic."

"Or something," Nina teased her.

"Seriously, you have to try to get these seen and shown somewhere. When you're better. I'll help you. But for now, let's get you settled on the terrace. It's a gorgeous day."

And soon they were drinking New York City tap water, the best in the world, and sitting on Nina's old splintered wood chairs, looking out over Central Park. Claire set up a footrest, so Nina could elevate her sorry leg, and made sure she had a table next to her seat for a drink, the phone, the envelope of dog-walking keys and information for Isaiah, and a pile of magazines Claire had brought her. Out they came from her bag, every kind of magazine from rags to riches: *Us* and *Newsweek*, *Vanity Fair* and *Entertainment Weekly*, *Vogue* and *People* and *House and Garden* and *Elle Décor* and *Rolling Stone* and *Dog Fancy*, not to mention the *Globe*, the *Star* and the *Enquirer*. Nina felt lucky to have such a good friend who knew not to give flowers, which, when it comes to sick or injured people, are for the dead and dying. Of course, any other time, flowers are most welcome.

Then Claire brought out the box and handed it to Nina, resting it on her thighs. Finally, Nina knew someone who ordered something from the catalog that sold an ionic air purifier "for only $299." Claire got up and went to the kitchen and came back with a pair of scissors. She cut open the box and pulled out a gift card. She handed it to Nina, who opened it and read.

Dear Nina,

  Thought you could use this while you recuperate. Feel better.

Sincerely, Daniel

She handed the card to Claire, who read it and smiled. Then Claire pulled a big black case out of the box. She opened it and began fitting pieces together of what, apparently, was a telescope. It was large, shiny, and white, with the viewer on the side of it toward the front end. It sat on a tripod. Nina ran her hand along its glossy side.

"Wow. Nice. But 'sincerely'? It's because I projectile-vomited at the hospital. I know it. Otherwise he would've signed it 'Love, Daniel'."

"It's very thoughtful of him."

"Yeah, he thought I should spy on people."

"Well, you do."

"And I have a feeling he knows."

"Well, he's not an idiot, is he?"

"And 'sincerely'? *Sincerely?* What's that mean?"

Claire ignored her and looked through the telescope. "And why not? You here, with your leg, incapacitated, with this view. It's a little *Rear Window*, don't you think?"

"Oohhh! And I guess I'm Jimmy Stewart and you're Grace Kelly?"

"Well, I'm definitely Grace Kelly, but you are cuter than Jimmy Stewart."

"Just for once, I'd like to be Grace Kelly! Why can't I be Grace Kelly?"

"Be quiet and look," ordered Claire.

And Nina sat up and put her eye to the viewer and focused. Once she got her bearings, she realized what she was looking at. First the wall, then right into the window of that light brick building across the park on Fifth. Oh my god, thought Nina. This is like giving heroin to an addict. This was her vice, signed, sealed, and delivered to her, on a silver platter!

"I can't," she said. "It's not right."

"Oh please. This from the Queen of the Snoop," said Claire. "It's *fun*. It's something to do. And you can do it in your own home. You'll see how the week flies." She paused for a moment. "He must really like you, you know. This ain't cheap."

Nina realized how sweet a gesture it was. "I know. Or he's trying to tell me something. '*Sincerely*'? He saw me throw up."

"Worse things have happened. He could've seen you—"

"Stop!"

The two friends laughed.

"Now I simply must go," said Claire, mimicking Grace

Kelly-speak. "I have an audition. Isaiah—is that his name? He'll be here in a minute anyway. And you can complain to him why you're never Grace Kelly."

"What's the show?"

"Yet another *Law and Order* series. Cops on horseback in Central Park. They're looking for another tall blonde D.A. That would be me. At least I hope, I pray, it'll be me. God, I hope I get it."

And Nina sang. "*I really need this job, dear god I need this job . . .*"

"Shut up. You really have no business singing." Claire was gathering up her stuff, readying to go. "It really should be illegal."

"*How many people does he need? How many . . .*"

"You know, they might do a revival of *A Chorus Line*. I read that in *Variety*."

"You could play Sheila. The old one, but with a twenty-first-century twist: she shvitzes. Big. Wet. Smelly. You'd be playing Sheila who is really you. Very meta."

"Making fun of my affliction. What kind of friend are you?"

"An affliction that has made you a minor fortune."

"True, but embarrassing on a date. Trust me. And now goodbye. Call me if you need anything."

"With this baby"—she stroked the telescope in a suggestive way—"and take-out, I'll be fine. As long as Isaiah shows up and does my walks. And you come back for Sam and Mimi. And me." Only with Claire could she be so brazen about her needs.

And the buzzer from downstairs buzzed.

Nina went back to her telescope while Claire ran inside to the intercom.

"Isaiah?"

"It's me," came the answer.

And Claire buzzed him up. "Right on time."

She waited a minute and there was the knock. Claire opened the door. Isaiah walked in. Claire broke out in a sweat. Her face turned red.

"Isaiah?"

He looked at her. "You must be Claire."

"Isaiah," she said, as if she was under a spell. "I love that name."

"You're beautiful."

"You are too."

"I mean, hi."

"Me too. I mean I meant to say hi."

"You're really sweating." He touched her brow, the side of her face.

"I do that."

"I like it."

Nina yelled from the terrace. "Helloooo! Who's there? Is it Isaiah?"

"Hey Nina!" yelled back Isaiah, not moving an inch, an eye, from Claire.

"I have to go," said Claire.

"Are you sure?"

"I am. I do."

"Okay."

And she was out the door, but she stopped and turned and said, "You'll help her, right?"

"Definitely."

"Okay then."

"Will I see you again?"

"Definitely."

"Me too."

And she left. She said, "Whew" on the fifth step down.

"Wow," he answered as if he heard her.

"Isaiah, where the hell are you?" He was being called.

But he was looking at her sculpture. "Fantastic. What is it? Looks like a contraption out of a sci-fi movie, like *X-Men* or *Matrix*," he said, as he walked out onto the terrace.

"It's whatever you think it is."

"I just met Claire," he said.

"Isn't she great?"

"Yeah. Boy." He caught his breath. "So, look at you. You been beat, girl."

"That's an understatement. So, Isaiah, can you fill in for me for a week or so?"

"No problem. Just tell me who, when, and where, and I'm there."

"I'm going to want them all back when I'm ready, you know."

"Of course. I'm just helping out. You did it for me once, remember?"

Nina laughed. He had to visit his sick mom, once, for a weekend, in Atlanta. She did all his walks, and never forgot that his dogs were pit bulls, mastiffs, and rottweilers, killer dogs that scared the hell out of her.

"But don't walk my dogs with your dogs, okay? Don't mix them up."

He took it personally. "You have something against my dogs? So, my dogs are city dogs, street dogs. They've had hard, difficult lives, some of them. Just because yours are rich and coddled, let's be egalitarian, okay? A dog is a dog, whatever its upbringing, its fur color, its economic standing. You hate a whole type of dog based simply on its backround and breeding? What, you a Republican?"

"Come on! Face it," Nina answered. "You walk dogs that kill. They kill other dogs, and people too, I bet. How'd that happen? You got to wonder. Why are my dogs sweet and docile—"

"Whoa there, mama. That lab of yours ain't nothing like docile. More like *Deliverance!* I wouldn't want to be alone with him at night in the park."

"First of all Luca is a female. Second of all, yeah, well, I guess she is a little rough. But her owner is an asshole! He keeps her locked—"

"Exactly what I'm talking about! In the nature versus nurture argument, even as it pertains to the canine species, nurture wins out. Poverty, home circumstances, single master, two-hundred-fifty years of oppression. They all conspire to keep a dog behind those with more advantages. So, my dogs are ghetto dogs. Yours are rich, white, and privileged."

"Oooohhhh! What are you saying? That we should give better walks and homes to your so-called ghetto dogs to even out the playing field? Just because they're a certain breed? What if they are just killer, bad, mean dogs? Do they deserve a better place just for equity's sake? Do you know what that would do to the pool of dogs? Bring it all down."

"History shows that giving opportunities to those who've been kept down helps them to rise above the pack."

"Well just don't mix them, okay? How would I explain to Mrs. Chandler that her little fat adorable bow-legged red-eyed bulldog was chewed up and spit out by that huge rott-weiler of yours—the one with the enormous teeth, the one who drools at the sight of any dog under forty pounds? As if he hadn't eaten in a week? Imagine what he'd do to Edward and Wallis. They're British royalty."

"Colonialist oppressor pigs."

"Actually they're dachshunds."

Isaiah was fighting a smile. "Just give me the keys and the addresses and the schedule and I'm out of here."

"It's all in here." She handed him the envelope.

"Now don't you worry, Miz Nina, ma'am," Isaiah said in an exaggerated old Southern slave accent. "I be good to your white rich dogs, I promise I will. And I won't steal nuthin' from their owners. I won't! I won't!"

Nina laughed. "Oh shut up."

And then, in his normal voice, "And I'll check in with you in a couple days to see how you're doing and when you want the keys and stuff back. Seriously, you let me know if you need any help." Now slave again: "*Y'all hear?*"

"Thanks for helping me out, Isaiah."

"Thanks for throwing me the extra work. Need anything before I go?"

"Nah. Thanks."

And he turned and left the terrace. Nina heard the door open, then close.

She liked him, that Isaiah. Even if he was an ex-con. She

knew she could trust him. She hoped. She knew he was reliable. She thought. She knew she could rely on him. As much as she could rely on anybody.

She looked at her leg in its brace, stretched out before her like a huge hot dog in a bun. Shit. Shit, shit, shit. How could this have happened? There was no way she was going to be able to just sit here for an entire week! Rely on Claire for errands and walking Sam and Mimi? Rely on Isaiah for walking her client's dogs? Rely on her mom for emotional support? It wasn't that she thought they couldn't do it; she knew they were all competent at their tasks. It was that they *were* all competent, so what the hell was she needed for? What was she good for if not those things? Not to mention that for a person to fully rely on someone means they have to trust them, they have to need them. It was all too close, too intimate for Nina's comfort.

But there was Sam's face looking up at her, his tongue hanging out and throbbing as he breathed, his eyes bright and sensitive. I'm lucky, thought Nina, to have such a dog. To have people to rely on at all. I hate the relying part, but I'm lucky.

She sat forward and looked into the telescope. The day was beautiful, clear, dry—a rarity for New York City in the summer. She could see people on Fifth Avenue hanging outside the Guggenheim. She saw a woman with a toddler in a stroller ordering a pretzel from the vendor. She saw a young couple laughing and kissing. She saw two older women stroll together arm in arm, heads inclined toward each other in talk. She saw a beautiful woman waiting alone, sitting on the low stone wall that lined the museum entrance. She looked at her watch. She made a call on her cell phone. She looked at her watch again. And then she left. An elderly couple took her place on the stone wall. Each held a hot dog, and they ate. A tiny piece of bun or paper or something got in the woman's hair and the man wiped a hand with his napkin, and reached up to her hair and carefully picked it out. Not a beat was missed, not a bite. Just a quick, simple gesture between two trusting people who, obviously, take care of each other. Nina pulled away from the telescope and sat back in her chair. Amazing, she thought, how easy it is for some people to be intimate. I want that, she said to herself, I want that.

The buzzer from downstairs buzzed, making Nina jump a foot out of her chair, causing her leg some pain and the telescope to swivel three hundred and sixty degrees on its base. Nina gingerly lifted her leg with both hands and put her foot on the ground, pushed herself up using the arms of her chair, got her crutches, and went inside. Sam followed at her ankle, Mimi hurried behind him. The buzzer buzzed again.

"Hold your horses!" she said out loud. And then into the intercom: "Who is it?"

"Nina? It's Daniel."

She took in a breath. She looked at herself in the mirror. Couldn't get much worse. No shower for forty-eight hours.

"Nina?"

Oh god. "Come on up," she answered. She unlocked the door and was in the process of making her way back out to the terrace when he rang her bell.

"It's open," she yelled.

"Wait, I'll help you," he said, as he closed the door behind him, putting a brown paper bag down on her table. But she was up the three steps already and outside. As she sat, he was by her side, holding her arm, taking her crutches.

Once she was situated, he pulled up another chair and sat right next to her, like two friends on the beach, watching the waves. Or at the movies, sitting through the advertisements, waiting for movie to begin. Or in a car, watching the road ahead.

"I'm glad you came," said Nina.

"You are?"

"I wanted to thank you for getting the dogs, and Sam, home. For calling Claire and helping out. And for this fantastic gift. Thank you. Really."

"I wanted to be sure you were okay." He turned to her. "You look good."

"Oh god, I know I look like shit. And I am so sorry you had to witness me—"

He smiled. "You look good," he said, his eyes lingering on hers. And then, abruptly, he took the telescope and looked through it. "Not bad. You can see everything, can't you? Look at that apartment. They've got a Picas—this is dangerous," he said as he pushed the telescope away.

"But fun, right?"

"This is exactly what Schopenhauer was talking about. People are not to be left to their own devices. It can only lead to—"

"Schopenhauer?" she asked, remembering his computer file.

"A German philosopher who said, among other things, that the universe is not a rational place."

"Well, *duh*. What a *genius*."

"Exactly! You'd think everybody knows that. But we are eternal optimists, thinking we can control our own impulses. We invent the telescope to explore, to learn. And then it becomes another device to feed a vice."

"But look. Look through it. You can choose to look at birds—see that one flying there? What color is its beak? And look at that beautiful willow over there. You can see its leaves, the quality of its bark."

"But it's a lot more fun to look into the windows of those apartments, isn't it? There's a kid watching TV. There's a woman at a desk, on her computer. There's a guy standing naked at his window. At least I think he's naked. I can't really see him—oh yeah, he's naked." He flinched and pulled away from the telescope.

"You see? You can choose. Is it my fault you choose to look into the windows rather than at the bird?"

"That's all Schopenhauer meant. He was a real pessimist."

"So that makes two of us. And I also think the world is made up of imperfect people—assholes, really. Does that make me a Schopenist? A Schopenist Pig!"

Daniel laughed. It was maybe the first time she had seen him fully belt one out. It loosened her up. She was on a roll.

"I mean, you don't seem to be the kind of guy who'd study philosophy. You're a lawyer!"

"Uh-huh. And lawyers can't read philosophy?"

"They can. Of course, it is a free country after all." She sounded like a moron. "But come on, how many lawyers know who Schopenhauer is?"

"I took a couple philosophy classes as an undergrad, that's all."

"Interesting. I mean you are. I mean, oh hell."

"Did you study art? You're an artist, aren't you? Your sculptures."

"It's just a hobby. I walk, I pick up stuff. I think of it as a kind of recycling."

"So you do it to benefit our environment," he said with a smile.

"That too," she said, smiling back.

"Well, they are unique."

"Unique?" she asked, as if that wasn't a compliment at all.

"Outrageous unique. Wonderful unique."

She smiled. Now that was a compliment.

He turned to her and looked at her for enough time to make her feel uncomfortable. "I have to go. Before this thing becomes a habit," he said, pushing the telescope away. "Do you need anything before I—who's walking Sam and Mimi?"

"Claire's coming back for them later. Thanks, it's okay."

"Okay then. I guess I'll go. Can I come back in a day or two?"

"Well, okay, yeah. Please."

"Don't do too much of this." He put his hand on the telescope as he got up. "It can only lead to one becoming a Schopenist Pig."

Nina laughed, flattered that he had used her joke. She struggled to get up.

"What are you doing?" he asked, helping her up, his arm around her waist, her arm over his shoulder, her body leaning into his, her head almost resting on his shoulder.

She could smell him. He was delicious. And without thinking, she kissed the corner of his mouth. She couldn't *not* do it. It was out of her control.

And then he kissed her back, fully on the mouth. And then again, his mouth opening to welcome her, his other arm coming around her, holding her firmly, her good leg leaning on his, their bodies tight and connected from lip to knee. When the kiss had ended, she put her head down, embarrassed, afraid, so that his lips grazed her hair, then, as she turned her head, her ear.

"I brought you soup," he whispered.

"You did?" Though it didn't matter at all.

A kiss had never unnerved her so. This Daniel, this man who surprised her every time they were together— Schopenhauer, for god's sake!—kissed her as if the world was coming to an end, as if it were his last. And she was frantic.

"It's on the table, inside. Chicken soup."

And then the buzzer buzzed from the street.

"Who the hell?" she said.

"Wait. I'll get it," said Daniel, as he ran to the intercom inside.

She couldn't believe what had just happened. Already she was wondering if it actually had.

"It's Bono. He's on his way up. Okay?" shouted Daniel from the door.

Grand fucking Central Station, she thought. She'd never had so many visitors in one day, except perhaps on the first day she came home the last time she was in the hospital. When she was born.

"Hey man," she heard Bono say. "Wow! Check that out! What is that, anyway? Some kind of sculpture? Nina do that? Awesome. Looks like the Creature from the Black Lagoon."

And every one of them was a critic, Nina was thinking when Bono and Daniel came out onto the terrace.

"Nina! How you doing?" asked Bono.

"Hey you. Don't you ever have school?" Nina asked him back.

"It's Sunday. Remember? It's summer. Or are you in so much pain that you've lost all sense of reality? Ees eet safe?" he asked while bending over her chair, his face in hers. "EES EEET SAFE?" he yelled.

She brought her hand up, and with the palm of her hand on his face, she pushed it away. He fell back against the brick wall, laughing.

"I have to go," said Daniel. "You're—or he's—in good hands." He put his hand on Bono's shoulder.

Nina looked at Daniel and, still recovering, could only say, "You sure?"

"But I would like to come by tomorrow, if it's all right with you, of course," he said somewhat formally.

"I'll be here," she answered and laughed too loud, uncomfortably.

"Bono—you call me if she needs anything. Both of you." He looked at her once more and then he was gone.

"It's just you and me now. Think you can handle it?" asked Bono.

"Sit down and be quiet," said Nina.

So Bono sat in the chair next to Nina and they talked and laughed and looked through the telescope for the entire afternoon. They ate the soup. Nina never felt so cared for as she had that day. And that kiss. It scared the hell out of her.

21

What had he done? What was he thinking to have kissed her like that? Nothing. That's what he was thinking: nothing rational, anyway. It was as if everything Schopenhauer had said was not only right, but could be reduced to one thing: in this case, a kiss. But it was the passion that shocked him. Sometimes—and this was something he had learned about himself—he didn't know a thing about himself until it showed up in something he did. For example, he hadn't known how angry he was at Daniel that time when Daniel had used Billy's paper to get his first big job. Daniel had often relied on Billy's brains to get him through finals, but to submit Billy's Master's thesis under his own name for a job after law school was plain wrong. But Billy didn't realize how ticked off he was until that night when he belted Daniel, smack on his face, making his nose bleed, his eye black, his lip split.

First the belt, then the revelation. Now, first the kiss, then the recognition.

Sure, he knew himself well enough to know that he had been attracted to Nina. He would think about her, had caught himself wondering what she'd be doing right then, had found himself smiling when he ran into her, had felt himself a little out of breath when she looked him in the eye. But it was bigger than that. She moved him. She made him feel like he could fly. Do anything. Be himself. On the pier, that night, that was something. He actually played for her and then, like an ass, walked away from her.

And then the bath in her apartment. That was totally out of control. Those sculptures, her love of Broadway show tunes, her innate energy and warmth, the way she was with Bono, the hold she had on her dogs all seemed at odds with her suspiciousness, her sadness. The power that she didn't even know she had, hidden under a veil of vulnerability, insecurity—or the pretense of it, as if she'd been taught to recede when her natural inclination was to shine.

But none of it had added up to what he was feeling now, what the kiss had done. The standard musical clichés, to borrow Nina's references—*if I were a bell I'd be ringing,* or *the pavement always stayed beneath my feet before,* or *and suddenly that name will never be the same to me*—rang true. If he said the work "fuck," he'd say it now.

"Fuck, fuck, fuck," he said aloud, surprising himself and Sid, who barked three times in response as he followed on Billy's heels as he paced back and forth in his bedroom. "I'm sorry, boy," Billy said, bending to give Sid a pet on the head. He felt as if he were losing it, as if he were changing, as if his feelings for Nina were strong enough to open a door that once he walked through he'd never be the same.

He stood up. But she's a liar and a snoop. She doesn't pay her taxes and she's nothing but a dog walker. Not that he was ever one to be impressed by someone's job, but one had to be suspicious of someone with a job like this. A temporary job, a momentary glitch, certainly not a career or a livelihood or a valid way of life.

And she was probably only interested in him because she thinks he's . . . well, yeah. Just like what happened in San Francisco a couple years ago. He'd gone there for a few months on a special IRS assignment and had met Elizabeth. It seemed like the real thing. He thought he was in love with her. And she with him. He'd even put in for a transfer, until Daniel showed up and apparently swept her off her feet and into a long-distance relationship that had lasted a month.

That time he was aware of his feelings before he did the deed. The betrayal was huge and hard to get over. Would he never be able to shake the shadow of his perfect brother from lingering over every relationship he would ever have? He kicked Daniel out of his apartment, and vowed he'd never mix Daniel with his personal life again. He would have written him off altogether, but he was family. It took a year before Billy would even speak to him again.

So Billy vowed to wait a couple weeks before seeing Nina again, to let this thing slow down, even die down. Because the last thing he needed right now was to let himself get deeper in, only to find out that, once again, the object of his affection's object of affection was Daniel.

And then he heard his front door open, footsteps inside, and something thrown onto the floor.

Could it be Ni—? He ran out to see. It wasn't. It was . . . what the *hell?* It was as if he had conjured the asshole by thinking about him.

"Daniel," he said out loud. He noticed his duffel on the floor.

"Billy, my man."

Sid looked from one to the other and then back and spun around twice as if trying to shake the confusion.

"Sid, calm down, boy," said Billy.

"Siddhartha, I'm back," said Daniel.

The two men, who looked like bookends, who, if you didn't notice the opposite hair whorls, or if you couldn't see into their hearts, looked the same, hugged in that man way with the rapping on each other's backs and the quick pull back.

"What—?" asked Billy.

"I got tired. Missed the city. Missed work. It was time to come home," said Daniel, as he walked to the living room window and looked out.

"Some advance notice would've been good."

"No time. It was a last-minute, spontaneous decision. Something you wouldn't know much about."

Billy decided to ignore the slight.

"I'm not done here," he said.

"It's okay. I'm only here for a week or two. Then I'm off again. I have a case in San Francisco." He looked at Billy for a reaction, but there was none. "See's candy, here I come."

"But I need to be here. In this apartment. Or the whole thing will fall apart," said Billy, not quite sure if he was talking about Mrs. Chandler or Nina.

"So be here. You can sleep on the couch," Daniel said as he picked up his bag and went into the bedroom. "Right now, I need a shower and a nap. Still on Tibetan time."

"And smell."

"You got that right."

"Sort of like sheep. Who rolled in dung."

"I get the picture."

"And then dried in the sun for a week or two, so it got all caked up and hard."

Daniel turned to look at Billy to see if he was kidding. He wasn't. "You mad or something?"

"Yeah, you could say that," Billy said, surprised at his knowledge in advance of another belting, or who the hell knew what. Even his thoughts had bad words.

"Well, too goddamn bad. This is my place and I am allowed to come home."

"You should have called. You should have given me notice. You should have—"

"What? Never come back? Nice. Your brother, your twin, returns home after a long absence and you're pissed? Well, fuck you."

Billy went to the front door, turned the knob. "I'm going out. See you later."

"Don't wake me."

"Don't worry."

"Sid, come on, boy. Let's go for a walk." And Sid came loping to the door.

"Sid? Who the hell is Sid? *Siddhartha*—hey boy, you stay," commanded Daniel.

Sid looked from Daniel to Billy, confused. Then Billy walked out, leaving Sid whining at the closed door.

It had been five days since the accident with the little white stupid rat dog and Nina was busting loose. Sure, the telescope was entertaining, work on the structure keeping her busy, Claire and Isaiah and Bono visiting many times. But since the kiss, not a sign of Daniel, except a call to explain why he couldn't come by, how busy he was, et fucking cetera.

Did he regret it happened? Or worse, did he forget about it, as if it had no meaning whatsoever? Or worse still, did he not like it? Was it too wet, too sloppy, too something? Or uber worst, did he not like *her*? Did he just not want to be around her?

She was going to find out. Take the bull by the horns, or the dogs by their leashes, and go over there and find out.

She swung her leg off the chaise and stood. When one's knee is in a brace, supposedly immobilizing it, making it impossible to bend, this is not an easy feat. Of course it was the new, improved, removable kind of brace, enabling a shower which she had already taken that morning. So stand she did, and hobble on her crutches into her bedroom to get dressed.

Sam and Mimi watched. His head cocked to one side, his tongue hanging from his mouth, he looked to Nina like he was admonishing her for doing too much too soon. Mimi's little tail wagging furiously, her mouth opened to a smile, she looked as if she were saying "You go girl!" because in doggie world they don't know when a saying has become old. Or Nina was projecting. Anthropomorphizing. Or both. She took off the baggy shorts she had on, and put on some cuter ones, one sock, and one boot. She changed into a University of Pennsylvania T-shirt, just to get his attention, the one with the cut-off sleeves and neck, which reminded her of *Flashdance*, a silly movie, but one of her favorites, and brushed her hair into a ponytail. Her skin was still tawny from the summer sun, so no makeup was needed. Besides, this wasn't a seduction, for god's sake. It was a confrontation. You can't just kiss someone like that and disappear for three days.

Getting dressed was one thing. Negotiating the five flights of stairs another. She put both crutches under her left arm and held onto the banister with her right. And then she clumped her way down the stairs, one by one. It probably took about five times longer and ten times as much sweat than usual, but she eventually got there.

Once on the street, maneuvering was much easier. Though it was in the nineties, the air felt fresh, the sky was bright, and moving felt terrific. Soon she was at Daniel's building. There was Pete.

"What ho, fair maiden," he said with a flourish. "I heard about your accident. You supposed to be up and about already?"

"Well, I—"

"Would you come back to work, already? That Isaiah ain't much to—"

"Why? What happened?"

"Nothing really. He just ain't you."

Nina smiled. "Daniel home?"

"He is."

"Can you buzz up? I need to see him."

"You want it, you got it." He picked up the phone and pushed a couple buttons. "Yeah, uh, I got Nina here. She's coming up." Then, to Nina, he said, "Go on. You know where it is, now, don't you."

Nina walked through the lobby, to the elevator, which was waiting for her. As she got in, she could hear Pete yell, "Nina! Hey, wait a minute. He's—"

But the elevator closed and she was on her way. Once she got there, she knocked on his door. Daniel answered wearing only a towel around his waist.

"Nina? Good to see you, but I'm a little—" But then looking at her, her bare legs, her lean arms, he said, "Well, it's okay, come on in. Just give me a minute, will you?"

And he left her standing in the entry hall while he went back into the bathroom off his bedroom, where they had met. Sid lay curled up by the door, looking a little forlorn.

Nina bent down to scratch his ears. "What's up, Sid? Who's your favorite walker? Miss me?"

And Daniel shouted from the bathroom, "Get yourself a cold drink—there's water, diet Coke, beer. And make yourself at home. I'll be right out."

He sounded funny. Formal, polite. Weird. Or was she projecting or anthropomorphizing, given he was that strange species of male, or both?

She sat on the couch, her leg stretched out before her. Her crutches placed neatly on the floor. Sid had followed her, put his head between her legs, his muzzle resting on her crotch. The room was cool, air-conditioned by one of those postwar unseen units that almost made living in one of these apartments with cottage-cheese ceilings worth it.

"Hey beauty," she said to Sid. "What's the matter guy? Huh?"

Then he was there, in long, baggy shorts and a T-shirt. He sat down beside her.

"Your leg. How—?" he asked.

"Better. Just another day or two before I can take this thing off for good, and am walking again like a normal person. Doing the dog thing."

"Really. That was fast, wasn't it?"

"Where've you been?" She came right out with it.

"What do you mean? I was away for awhile."

"Oh! That explains it." She smiled in relief.

"What?"

"Why you didn't call or come by."

"What—?"

"You know, after we . . . I just thought . . ."

"What?"

"Nothing."

"Listen—"

"You don't have to explain anything."

"I just wanted to say that you look great. Wow. Nina!"

That seemed weird coming from him. But she said, "Well, thanks," and she saw him look at her breasts, then her legs. That seemed odd for him, too. But her heart was racing, and she liked being looked at that way, she had to admit. She knew she was attractive, cute, sexy even. But to be looked at

like a sex object! Like what she had to say didn't mean anything. She sort of liked it.

He stroked her leg.

Oh god, she thought. Is this happening? She made herself look at him. Something was different, as if he'd gone on
some far-off adventure and returned with new vigor, the
result of new places conquered, foreign people met. He
seemed confident, forward, eager.

He kissed her. It was different from the last time, but of
course it would be. That was a first kiss, spontaneous, full of
feeling. This was about foreplay, this kiss, practiced, and a
prelude to what would come next. She pulled back and
looked at him, held his cheek with her palm, put her other
hand through his hair.

But he would brook no delays, no romantic gestures. He
put his hand on her waist, at her side, then up her T-shirt, to
under her arm and then across to her breast. He stroked it
for a moment, then went under her bra and squeezed her
nipple with two fingers.

What the hell. It felt good. She was going with it.

Sid barked.

"Just a minute," said Daniel. He got up and took Sid by
the collar and put him in the bedroom, closing the door.

Nina watched him, wondering why this was all so weird.

"Okay, Nina, where were we?"

It was awkward with her leg brace, and some clumsy
moves were made. But that wasn't why it felt so wrong.

Twenty minutes later, Billy entered the building lobby.

"Hey—weren't you just upstairs?" asked Pete.

"Nah, I've been walking a couple hours. You should see the park today—it's full of—"

"I told her to go up. Thought you were there."

"Who?"

"Nina, your dog walker."

Billy's face fell, turned red. He panicked. He ran to the elevator. He had to wait for it to come down from the seventeenth floor and was about to put his fist through the wall when it finally appeared.

Daniel rolled off Nina like a log off a trailer. He was sweaty, out of breath, and exhausted. He got up, naked, and walked into the bedroom to go the bathroom, she assumed, letting Sid out, who came over to Nina and licked her face. She was on the floor, completely naked except for her panties that were hanging from her leg at the top of her knee brace. Nina stared at the ceiling, not sure what had just happened, or with whom—because it sure wasn't what she had expected. Not that it was bad. She had just been screwed—for that's what it was—and would've wanted to do it again immediately had the front door not opened and had Sid not bounded over and had Daniel not walked in—

"Whoa, wait a minute, who the hell—?" Nina screamed, and grabbed a cushion of the couch that had ended up on the floor and covered her face and body—the amount she could—with it. Her knee throbbed. Her mind was racing. Didn't Daniel just go into the bedroom?

The Daniel she had just had sex with walked in. "Oh shit," he said. "Don't you knock?" He grabbed his boxers from the couch to cover himself.

The other Daniel said, "Knock? I live here, you asshole. Nina?"

Two Daniels? Or what?

"You used to live here, you mean."

"Nina?" And then this Daniel said to the other, "Oh god, what did you do?"

"What do you mean, what did I do?" said Nina's Sex Daniel, turning around, pulling up his boxers. "We went to bed—er, to floor—and it was very nice. That's what we did, and it's really none of your business."

"Oh yes it is. It *is* my goddamn business— Nina?"

She had begun to cry, realizing, she figured, maybe, what was going on. She was confused and angry. Was Daniel not really Daniel? Then who the hell was he? Who had she just made love (a real misnomer, because all they had done was screw, which was not without its merits) to? Who had kissed her a few days ago on her terrace? Who was in the pictures? Who helped her when she hurt her leg? Who played trombone on the pier? Who lied to her? She needed to understand what was happening so she could kill one of them. Or both.

Nina held the pillow in front of her while she reached to her strewn clothes. Daniel, her sex partner, helped. She put on her bra, then her T-shirt, struggling to keep herself covered by the couch cushion. Then she put her good leg through its panty hole and pulled up her panties with some urgency because the cushion had fallen off as she tried to balance it, while keeping her braced leg on the floor. Finally, panties were on. Then shorts. While all this was going on, while tears of confusion, humiliation, and anger poured

down her face, into her mouth, off her chin, and onto the
floor, one Daniel—the one she had just, well, had walked
out, while the other Daniel stood there staring at her.

Finally he spoke. "Do you go to bed with just anybody?"

"What?"

"You don't even know this guy and you went to bed—or
to floor—with him."

"Who the hell are you?" Nina asked.

"I'm Daniel. We met in my bathroom, I helped you with
that poop-evader guy in the park, I helped you into the
ambulance, I, um, kissed you on your terrace."

She smiled at him. Then she stopped the smile, smother-
ing it like a bucket of water thrown on a bonfire.

"If you're Daniel, who's that?"

"He's not Daniel. He's Billy," said the other Daniel, now
dressed and cleaned up, and back in the room.

Daniel, or Billy, looked at him, ready to take him down.

They stood side by side and Nina looked at them. She
looked at one. Then the other. And she saw. Her Daniel, that
is, her Love Daniel, stood straighter, was thinner, his eyes
were darker, deeper, his face more lined with concern and
caring. Her Sex Daniel was looser, freer, his arms swung
when he walked, as he talked, his pants baggy, his T-shirt
ripped. His eyes were clear, his face had not a care in the
world.

She looked from one to the other and back. She could
feel the blood rush to her face, her heart start to pump
wildly, her veins pulsing to beat the band. Were they both in
on it? Was it just a disgusting, stupid, sophomoric game?
Like what she'd imagine identical twins would do in

school—pretend they were the other? Pretend they were one?

She bent to pick up her crutches and moved toward the door.

"Wait," said Love Daniel. "Wait." He grabbed her arm as she hobbled past. "Let me explain, please."

"Billy? You are Billy, right? You lied to me. And you—" she said as she turned to Sex Daniel. "You used me. You took advantage—"

"Hey, listen. You were here, you were cute, you were game. What else did I need to know. Or did you?"

"Pig," Nina said.

"Pig," Love Daniel said.

"Liar," Nina said to Love Daniel.

"I had to. For my work."

"Go to hell."

She opened the door and Sid ran up, thinking he was going to get another walk.

"Bye Sid." And as she closed the door, she said, "I won't be walking Sid anymore. Get yourself a new dog walker."

22

So Nina had sex with Daniel. *The* Daniel, the one she had first fallen for, the one she'd dreamed of, fantasized about, with whom she'd masturbated in mind. But that Daniel wasn't the one who'd whooped the guy in seersucker, who'd played that miraculous trombone for her on the pier, helped her like family when her knee was dislocated, kissed her on her terrace. That Daniel, she now knew, wasn't Daniel at all, but Billy, Daniel's identical twin brother. This Billy, the kind one, the dark one, the interesting and nerdy one, the stiff and soulful and moral one, had lied to her. For months, about everything.

And now she was in love with the lying motherfucker.

Though she just had sex with the lying motherfucker's motherfucking *brother*.

And though she felt stupid and angry and angry and stupid, she had to admit she also felt, well, young. Like when she was in college and made many, many sexual mistakes. (Though all, every time, *safely*, the only thing about sex she was strict about. Sex should thrill you, not kill you.) The difference was that then, there was no need for regret, because that's what you did then. All she was now was full of regret and rage and hurt and a terrible sadness, as if some butthead in a Hummer had cut her off, making her car swerve and hit Sam or Bono or Mimi or Claire or someone she loved dearly.

But was it the butthead in the Hummer's fault? Or her own? Hadn't she been driving too fast? Hadn't she been rubbernecking instead of focusing on the road ahead? Hadn't she been too distracted by her own shenanigans, like talking on her cell, or putting in a CD, instead of noticing the signs along the way?

She would have liked to claim no culpability in this, but she did fall for a guy for all the wrong reasons. Even though she then fell for his twin for all the right ones. Oh, it was all too damn confusing to take the blame. So much easier to be pissed and hurt. She had been lied to. She had had sex under false pretenses.

And now it was time to walk the dogs.

Well, the dogs and everyone else could just go to hell for all she cared.

She was going to stand like this, in her shower, the hot water running over her head, down her face, the tears commingling with the water, for another hour. But she couldn't, could she? She was a dog walker, there was no lying about that. There was no ruse, no cover-up, no pretense. Or was there? She was the one who you could count on to always walk the dogs. Or was she? Wasn't she supposed to be the temporary dog walker who walked the dogs *for now*, while she figured out what to do with her life? Wasn't it a lie when she said this was her life, so be it? Wasn't she being a total and complete fraud when she said she wanted nothing more from life than this?

She used to think people would find her out for being the fraud she was—find out she was really not talented, not smart, not much of anything.

But wasn't that the lie? Wasn't the real lie that she pretended not to expect much, not to have much ambition? How far scarier and threatening it was to admit her desire for greatness—and then suffer defeats and losses, or worse, to not live up to it. How much farther she would have to fall from a mountain than from a molehill. How truly brave she would be to admit her worth and talents and then go for it. Nina's big, dark secret? She was ambitious, she thought she was special, she knew she was talented, beautiful, and unique. But god forbid she ever admitted it, said it aloud, lived her life acknowledging it. Because she was a scaredy-cat. Or in her case, a scaredy-dog. Simple as that.

She was an imposter. Just like Billy/Daniel.

So she did what any depressed and angry woman would do in her shoes. She went to bed. She dried off from her shower, put on panties and her University of Hard Knocks T-shirt, pulled down the shade, and curled up under her covers.

She slept twelve hours.

She missed her morning walks. And the only reason she woke up was because Sam and Mimi were standing on the bed, almost on top of her, nudging her and licking her and whining. They had to go. Now.

So she got up, took off her cast, slipped on some shorts and her boots, and took the dogs for a perfunctory walk, allowing a pee and a poop, a little sniff and a little whiff. Her knee was somewhat stiff and wobbly but felt good being used. Then she was back inside, up the stairs, and gave the dogs fresh water, fed them, and went back to bed. Sam watched her with concern, knowing all was not right.

The first call came by nine that morning. She listened to the answering machine pick up and heard old, stupid, mean Jim Osborne screaming about Luca taking a dump on his floor, et cetera et cetera.

Nina lowered the volume on the machine and turned over, covering her head with the comforter.

The next call came about two minutes later. And the next and the next, until she got smart and put a call in to Isaiah. He wasn't home, so she left this message on the machine:

"Hey, hi, it's me, Nina, and I'm sick as a dog, so to speak. Ha ha ha. I need you to walk my dogs, okay? Would you please? Hopefully this won't last long. Maybe a couple days, I guess. I don't know. I just can't get out of bed. Or see getting out in the near future. Thanks. Will refer everyone to you. Thanks. And don't call me. I'll be sleeping, okay?"

Then she changed her answering machine recording to say this:

"Hi, it's Nina, the dog walker. I've had an emergency— nothing you should worry about—but will not be able to walk your dogs for a few days. So please call Isaiah Wallace, at 579-2120. He's good and reliable. Um, thanks. Bye."

Then she called the owners of the dogs she regularly walked and either spoke directly to them or left a message with Isaiah's number.

It all took twenty-seven minutes and she was done. If she had known how easy it was to be responsibly irresponsible, she might've done this before.

Then she went back to sleep.

When she woke it was five in the afternoon. She woke in a haze, looked at the clock, and marveled how quickly the day had passed. Sam and Mimi were at the side of the bed, staring at her, tongues hanging, tails wagging, like police dogs who'd just come upon a dead body.

"Hey guys. Mom's up."

Sam barked.

"Okay, okay," said Nina. And she threw on the same old shorts and boots and took the dogs out. Too bad she hadn't hired Isaiah to walk them, she thought, then she wouldn't have to leave the apartment at all.

When she brought them home, she undressed, ate a yogurt and a banana while standing in front of the fridge, and went back to bed.

She didn't wake until the next morning. Sam and Mimi were still asleep at the foot of the bed. It was six A.M. She shuffled into the bathroom.

Only then did she realize someone was buzzing her door from downstairs. She ignored it. Though it was difficult. *Buzz, buzz, buzz* was the continuous refrain.

She sat, pulling her panties down and T-shirt up. She wiped, flushed, pulled up her panties again, and looked at herself in the mirror. *Buzz, buzz, buzz, buzz!*

She looked like shit. She felt worse.

And there was that buzzer. *Buzzzz, buzzzz, buzzzzz.* Over and over and over.

She went to the intercom and pressed the button. "SHUT UP!" she yelled.

"Let me in," said Claire.

"Me too!" It was Isaiah's voice in the backround.

They were down there together? Was it a coincidence or what? She buzzed them up, opened her front door, and put on hot water for coffee. Though waking up fully was not what she had in mind. But she did have visitors.

She heard their footsteps climbing the stairs, then the knock and the door swinging open.

"Nina, where the hell are you?" asked Claire.

"She's right here. Look at her, would you? The girl is a mess," said Isaiah.

"Nice to see you too," said Nina, standing in the open refrigerator door. "What are you guys doing up and out so early? It's only, what, six or so?"

"We're worried about you," said Claire.

Nina paused and looked from Claire to Isaiah and Isaiah to Claire, trying to wrap her mind around this. She felt disoriented, looking from one to the other trying to figure who's who and what's what.

"You guys . . . ?"

Claire let loose a smile that seemed to span across her face, as wide and stunning as the Golden Gate Bridge. She put an arm around Isaiah's waist, and he, in turn, put his arm over her shoulders. "We are," answered Claire. Then she looked at Isaiah to cast her smile on him, and he looked at her and smiled that crazy high-wattage grin of his.

My god, these two are in love, thought Nina. She felt like puking.

But "that is wonderful!" is what she said. "Where, how, did you two . . ."

"Here," Claire said. "When you hurt your leg. I was coming in and Iz . . ."

"No you were going out and I was coming . . ."

"Iz?" asked Nina, incredulously. "You call him Iz?"

"Actually," and here Claire blushed, as she broke out in a sweat, "I call him Izzy."

"I always thought of you as a nice Jewish boy," said Nina.

Isaiah shook his dreadlocks and cracked up. "I don't mind it. She could call me shithead for all I care."

And they smiled at each other again.

"I'm going to bed," said Nina, as she turned and began to walk away.

"Whoa there, mama. Not so fast," said Isaiah.

"Don't you walk away," said Claire.

Nina turned back to them, one hand on a hip like an impatient teenager about to be grilled by her parents about her whereabouts.

"What's going on with you?" Claire asked. "You've been in bed for two days. Do you have a fever? Have you seen a doctor?"

Nina walked into her bedroom.

"I'm talking to you!" Claire yelled after her, following close behind, pulling Isaiah by the wrist. "WHAT-IS-GOING-ON?"

Nina crawled into bed and pulled the comforter up to her chin. If she was going to be talked to like a kid, by god, she'd act like one!

"I slept with Daniel," she said, not talking like one.

Claire smiled, "Oh Ni-nah! That's wonderful." She sat on the bed next to Nina, pushing her hair off her forehead. "But I don't get . . ."

"It wasn't Daniel I'm crazy about. It was his brother. His twin."

"Wha—?"

"I slept with Daniel, but not the Daniel I . . ."

"Wait a minute," said Isaiah, walking around to sit on the other side of the bed. "Do you mean Daniel has a twin brother and you slept with him?"

"Not exactly. Daniel isn't Daniel at all, but Billy, Daniel's identical twin brother. But I didn't realize it, so when Daniel came on to me, I thought it was the Billy Daniel and not Daniel Daniel, and I slept with him. But it was Daniel and not Billy, unbeknownst to me. And it is Billy I really like. Or did."

"Sounds Shakespearean," said Claire, amused by the whole thing.

Nina, failing to see the humor in any of this, just looked at her, her eyes narrowed into thin slits, like bullets.

"So, was the sex any good?" Claire asked.

"That's not the point!" Nina yelled. "And it was only so-so."

At that point, Sam and Mimi, feeling left out, jumped on the bed and settled at Nina's feet. So now there were three adults and two dogs on the bed.

"So this is why you've gone to bed, relinquished your responsibilities, stopped bathing, if I may be honest, and basically, shut out the world? Because you slept with the wrong guy? Helloooo! Haven't you done that about, oh, a hundred times?"

"She's in love with him, can't you see that?" asked Isaiah.

"Are you?" asked Claire.

"Yes," whispered Nina, closing her eyes. "Yes."

"With the one named Billy?"

"Yeah, Billy the Liar. The one who all along had said he was Daniel. All this time I thought he was the one who lived in that apartment with Sid and that he traveled and was successful and a lawyer and—"

"None of that stuff matters. Since when do you judge a book by its cover? Who am I talking to?"

"Go easy, baby," said Isaiah sweetly. "Don't forget she slept with the *brother*—the *twin*—of the guy she really likes." He was trying for something, anything, to understand Nina's stupidity.

"I'm surprised at you, Nina," said Claire.

"Oh fuck you."

"Fuck you." And then Claire said to Isaiah: "Come on. Let's go. I'm getting sick too, just being here."

"Yeah, go. Get out. And leave me alone."

"You bet I will. Maybe while you're lying there, little Miss Feeling Sorry for Yourself, you'll think about why you like that Billy so much, which obviously has nothing to do with where he lives, what kind of stupid dog he has, or what he does for a living."

"It's not about those things, per se," said Nina in the tiniest voice she could use and still be heard. "It's about the lying. I thought he was someone else."

"You did? You fell in love with him because he's a lawyer?" yelled Claire. "Ha! Ha, ha, ha!" Then she and Isaiah got up from the bed and walked out of the room.

"Ha yourself! He lied to me," yelled Nina.

"So talk to him," Claire yelled back and then slammed the apartment door.

But Sam and Mimi ran to it, yelping and crying for someone, anyone, to take them out. And in an instant Isaiah was back.

Peeking his head in, he said, "I'll take them. Come, my children." And they rushed out and down the stairs for a decent walk.

Finally alone, Nina cried herself to sleep, never hearing the two dogs come home. She didn't wake up until that afternoon.

At about three o'clock someone buzzed her from downstairs. She was in a stupor when she awoke to the midday sun's rays streaming through the window. The room was hot. She had forgotten to put on the air conditioner that morning and now she was doused with sweat. Mimi and Sam were going crazy with their need to get out, running up to Nina, nudging her with their wet noses, then running back to the door, then back to Nina again. Then standing there, staring at her, their tongues on eager display, they did a little jig, their four paws going like mad. They'd have held their crotches if they had hands to hold them with. Or crotches to hold, for that matter.

So first, Nina went to the buzzer. "What!"

"It's me, Bono. You okay? Can I come up?"

Nina's eyes rolled to the ceiling. Then she looked at her dogs and said, "I'm coming down. Give me a minute."

She went to pee, got one look at herself in the mirror, and hopped into a shower, scrubbed, washed, dried, and dressed, collared and leashed the two anxious doggies, and was downstairs in seven minutes. Part of her hoped Bono had become impatient and left.

But there he was, sitting on her front stairs, slurping an icee.

"She's alive! She's aliiiiiiive!" screamed Bono.

She wasn't amused, and though she felt like turning around and going back inside, the dogs were eager to move, and so they did, toward the park, farther than Nina had walked in days.

"So where've you been?" Bono asked her.

"What's it to you?"

"What are you, ten? 'What's it to you?' That's what idiots at school say, the bullies, the dumb ones."

"Listen, *Bon*, I'm in no mood . . ."

"You sound like my mother."

That got Nina's hackles up. Had she hair on her neck like Sam, it'd be standing straight up, her canines bared, a growl emanating from her throat. But she wasn't, so she said, "Oh shut up."

She turned around suddenly and pulled the dogs back to her apartment building. Bono had almost to run to catch up.

"It's just that I miss walking the dogs. I miss . . ."

Nina stopped in her tracks, eager to stop Bono in his.

"I am not your mother. You have a mother. Stop bothering me. Go play ball like a normal kid. Ride a bike, for god's
sake. Just leave me alone."

Bono was silent then, his face turned down toward the
sidewalk.

They had arrived back at her building. The two dogs
leapt up the front steps to the door.

Then Bono looked up at Nina. His face was red with
anger, tears drenched it and dripped from his chin. "You're
stuck in a moment and you can't get out of it!" he yelled at
Nina. "You want to know where I got that one? Go on ask
me. ASK ME."

Oh god, Nina thought. Oh god. This kid needed more
than she could ever give. But she wasn't a complete asshole
so she asked him with a sigh, "Okay, where's that line come
from?" Though, of course, she knew.

And he said, "You're not my mother. I don't have to tell
you anything. Just go home."

And she did, back up the five flights, back into her cluttered apartment, back into her zen spare bedroom and back
into bed, where there was no Billy, no Daniel, no Claire and
Isaiah, no Bono. Only two snoring dogs and her own stone
cold heart.

A couple days passed with Nina only getting out of bed for
something to eat, to use the bathroom, to walk the dogs. The
dogs were getting snippy with each other, Mimi teasing and
bothering Sam like a little sister would a big brother, Sam
growling when Mimi came near. Nobody called. Nobody
came by. Nina couldn't help but compare this shut-in situa-

tion with the one when she dislocated her knee. Then her apartment was packed with people and gifts and food. This time, though she was hurting even more, the pain deeper, this accident far more damaging, not a soul came to visit since that morning she yelled at Claire and Bono.

Why would anybody? The apartment was a mess, she undoubtedly smelled, she was beyond pissy, and in the worst feeling-sorry-for-herself state since her divorce. And for what? Because she had been lied to? Been stupid? Acted foolishly? No, it was something else, bigger, more cosmic. Something about the inevitability of her being alone, even in the unlikely event of meeting someone she could love.

And the goddamn joint she'd put in her bedside table was missing, which made her feel like she was really losing it. She remembered putting it there, but had she? She didn't remember smoking it, but maybe she had. Like losing socks in the dryer, or a twenty you know you had in your wallet, this was a case of The Mystery of the Missing Thing You Could Swear You'd Put Right There.

Or, maybe, while she was in the hospital, someone came into her apartment, and . . . maybe she'd become the snoopee, rather than the snooper! And someone had stolen her joint, which had originally been stolen by her, so she couldn't really complain. Perhaps, just as life is cyclical, so too breaking and entering and theft.

So Nina did what she usually did at times like these, as if she hadn't learned a thing from the times before.

She called her mom.

"Mom, it's me, Nina, your daughter."

"Hi honey, it's me, Mom, your mother."

"I'm not feeling so good," she said.

"You sick, sweetheart? Have you seen a doctor?"

"Nah. I'll be okay."

"You have all those nice friends to take care of you."

"Yeah, sure. They're great."

There was a pause.

"You sound blue, honey. Anything wrong?"

"Nah, I'm okay."

"What happened. You can tell me."

"Nothing."

"Nothing? Then why the long face? I can't see you, but I know you have a long face. I'm your mother. We know these things."

"You're amazing," said Nina, trying not to sound sarcastic.

"So tell me."

There was another pause, as Nina thought about what to say.

"I'm in love, Mom."

"Aw, honey, that's wonderful."

Nina started to cry.

"But it's supposed to make you happy."

That made Nina laugh. "Yeah. I know."

"Well, dear, try not to screw it up this time."

There it was: the smack, the whack on the side of the head, the sock in the labonza. When would she stop asking for it and learn the limits of this relationship? Not all mothers could bear the disappointments of their daughters.

"Hey thanks, Mom, for your support. I'll talk to you soon."

"I didn't mean . . ." Nina heard her mom say as she hung up the phone.

That would be the last time for a long time Nina told her mom anything but good news, which was, in fact, miraculously, to come.

23

Why was he surprised, Billy wondered, as he unpacked his ugly bags, hanging his dumb dark suits back up in his one tiny closet, in his old apartment down on funky old West Forty-ninth Street in the very skuzzy, but "up and coming," according to the *New York Times* (yeah, and he was Slide Hampton), area of Hell's Kitchen. This had happened before and most likely—unless man's propensity for chaos and stupidity were to end, and the only way *that* would happen is if the earth flew off its axis, spun around the sun a couple times, and landed in a gosh darn, no, a *goddamn* crater on Jupiter—to happen again. There was no getting away from it, from him, from their inevitable, symbiotic relationship. They were the ultimate in codependents. They were brothers, and everything that implied. Since the dawn of mankind, brothers were competitive, jealous, and resentful. Billy and Daniel, walking proudly in the shoes of Cain and Abel.

Okay, he had to face it, there was no hiding it: he was pissed. Nothing had ever made him this angry. Not when Daniel had taken credit for his paper, not when Daniel had stolen Elizabeth, not when Daniel left, or when he came back. Billy loved his brother, always had. And he knew Daniel loved him. They were *brothers—twins—*and that's what twin brothers do: they love each other, protect each other. Screw each other's girlfriends. Want to kill each other. Rip each other's throats out and never see each other again.

The sweat poured off Billy like Niagara Falls in the springtime. The left side of his face was the Canadian side, the right, the good old US of A. He rubbed his right finger into his left palm: have to go to Niagara next spring. Ride a Maid of the Mist. Eat at IHOP. It was the kind of place that would have an IHOP, wasn't it?

He missed Sid. Christ, now he'd have to get a dog. But he'd never buy one, like that jerk of his sibling did, not when so many went homeless at the ASPCA and Bide-A-Wee and other animal shelters everywhere. He'd go, as soon as he could, and get a mutt who needed some TLC. God knows he did. They could help each other out. Not that he didn't love that Sid. He did.

And he missed her. It had only been a week or so. Specifically, it had been four days, seven hours, and thirty-six minutes since he'd found Nina in bed, or on floor, with Daniel. Sure, she had pleaded, she had screamed, she thought Daniel was him, but how would he know for sure that she didn't sleep with Daniel because he was Daniel and had that thing, that je-ne-sais-fucking-quoi that made women fucking swoon?

There. He had now descended into the arms of the devil, his language, at least in his fucking idiot head, in hell.

He took out his trombone. He put it together. He licked the mouthpiece, blew into it. Thinking about her. Her lips had been here. Her lips. Her face. Her laugh. That kiss.

First, he played some angry blues. He wailed, he jammed, he blasted. Then he stopped for air, putting the trombone facing down, between his legs, and saw Nina's face streaming with tears, in shock, when she knew the truth, the hurt and anger melding to contort her beautiful face into something other. That was a look he'd do anything to prevent in the future. He would do anything to never hurt her again, to prevent anyone from hurting her ever ever again. This was a woman who deserved to laugh and be loved.

He picked up his trombone and he played.

He played for her, a song that he knew she must know, must adore. He played "All I Need Is the Girl," from *Gypsy*, slow, deep and blue, from his heart. And though he didn't know the words, when he saw Nina's face now, as the melody dipped and soared, her mouth was moving to the music.

24

Everyone has her limit for self-pity. Nina's was four days, seven hours, and thirty-six minutes. By then she was sick of herself, sick of her bed, just plain sick. She needed a snack and there were none. She got a gander of herself in the mirror and it scared her. Her dog, Sam, wouldn't talk to her and that she expected him to scared her even more. She hadn't listened to one musical and was worried she would forget the words forever.

So, with all the verve and passion of her old self, she said, "Fuck this shit!" and got up out of bed, stripped it, and remade it with fresh white sheets. Then she took a shower, got dressed, put on a little makeup, and walked Sam and Mimi. She brought them home and went to the grocery store for eggs and juice and bread and pasta and vegetables and fruit and some cookies. One cannot live too long without cookies.

It was almost September, the summer having sped by like a runaway train. This one realizes only once the train has come to a complete stop. While on the train, no matter how fast it's going, it seems to be excrutiatingly slow. So, too, summer for Nina. Each hot day had melted into the next, languidly, slowly, but by the time it was over, she wondered where the hell it had gone.

And lying in bed worked wonders. It gave Nina the time and place, the opportunity, to cry, to wallow in her sadness and hurt, which was something she wouldn't usually allow herself to do. It proved beneficial.

What really bugged her about what happened with Daniel and not with Billy was how she must've hurt *him*. Billy, that is. She couldn't begin to imagine how he must've felt to find her naked with Daniel, his *twin*. Whatever he said to her that was a lie couldn't compare to what she did to him by doing that.

She loved him, all right. She was crazy about him. The thought that she hurt him hurt her. So he had lied. There had to be a reason for impersonating your brother. So he wasn't those things she thought he was, but he was so many more. How could she not be in love with him? He wasn't her wish list but you know what you can do with lists? Shove them up your ass.

And there was more. She missed Bono. His jokes, his movie lines, his ridiculous haircut, just about everything about him.

She missed Claire. Her best friend with whom she hadn't had a heart-to-heart in too long. She even missed Isaiah— who she loved because he loved Claire.

And Sam. She had been neglectful. He was obviously
unhappy about Mimi, and she had ignored it completely. Now,
he hardly got out of his doggie bed. He'd lie there, prick up
his ears when he'd hear a noise, look for Mimi, and upon seeing her dancing about, put his head right back down, sadly,
on his front paws. Nina's wonderful, intelligent, and spry
cohort had turned into a pathetic creature of the canine kind.

All this from lying in bed for four days and seven hours
and thirty-six minutes. She had a lot to do, but looking at
Sam curled up, depressed, on his bed, she knew what had to
be done first. She picked up Mimi and walked out.

Mrs. Chandler came to the door with a drink in hand and
quickly offered Nina one.

"No, thanks. Could use an upper rather than a depres-
sant."

She smiled at the little dog Nina had with her on a leash
and raised her brows. "And why is that? What's the matter,
dear?" She scratched the little dog's head and then closed
the door and gestured to Nina—and the mutt—to follow
her into her study.

Nina saw Safire standing in his usual spot, staring at the
wall. She looked at Mrs. Chandler, with her vodka, living in
this big house all by herself with this dog who gave her
nothing. Then she looked at Mimi.

"You know," she said to Mrs. Chandler, "you might be
happier with a more responsive dog. One who is affectionate and attentive. Who would make a nice companion."

"In lieu of a man, you mean, don't you, darling."

"No, better than a man. Dogs don't lie. They never pretend to be someone they're not. They are true and loyal and completely honest animals."

Mrs. Chandler laughed. "I can't have two dogs. Safire would not allow it." She turned to look at the clueless canine. "No, I'm stuck with him. If he were a man, well, I have five exes, so that tells you what I'd do."

"Five husbands," said Nina full of awe. "Wow. I've only had one. And he was a mistake. I can't choose a comforter for my bed, so what makes me think I could choose the right husband?"

"Sit, my dear," Mrs. Chandler said, patting the cushion next to hers. "I'm very insightful when it comes to marriage and relationships. I'm not very good at it myself, but I have had much experience."

Nina sat down on the cushy couch and noticed how beautiful Constance Chandler was. If there was a poster girl—or woman—for middle-age babehood, she was it.

"Choosing a man is much like buying a couch."

Nina laughed. "Tell me," she said.

"Everyone wants the same thing in a couch," she said, stroking the beautifully soft leather of hers. "Comfort and beauty. A couch that's both good to look at and feels good to be with. Sometimes you select one that's too stylish for your own good, that won't stand the test of time. The shoddy workmanship makes its life a short one. The sun, the shade, who knows? It can fade after the first rush of excitement.

"Sometimes if you don't invest the time and effort to find the perfect couch, you end up buying the wrong one. It's chintz when you wanted stripes, it's silk when you wanted mohair. Beware of the rebound sofa.

"Then you come upon a used couch on the sidewalk. You pay a few strapping high school boys ten bucks each to bring it up, you have it reupholstered, and it's perfect. The best couch you never bought."

Mrs. Chandler threw her head back, laughing. "Sometimes, the thing most valued is the thing that is underappreciated by someone else. Perhaps this is why you have not found the man who is right for you. You are searching for the perfect couch."

"And it doesn't exist, does it?" said Nina.

"Ah, but it does. You're just seduced by the red leather and not seeing the interior construction, my dear. It just might need a little reupholstery. I'm not suggesting a simple slipcover. I'm talking the kind of work that affects the springs, the frame, the heart of the couch itself."

"But I have found that couch."

"Billy."

Nina was surprised. "You know his name is Billy?"

Mrs. Chandler nodded. "He's very special, you know. He's the couch that's been thrown away, unappreciated, that someone with an eye discovers on the sidewalk, takes home, and cleans up a little. With a little muscle, a little imagination, a little love, the couch opens to reveal the sofa bed inside, the comfort, the surprise. Perfection for the right person. Listen to me. I, the pragmatist, have gotten sentimental. But it is true about Billy, nevertheless."

She paused, offered a cigarette to Nina, and then when turned down, lit one for herself and sipped her vodka and soda.

Nina thought about the ways Billy had surprised her. "He is unusual, don't you think?"

"Even more unusual for a treasury agent."

Nina's mouth opened wide in total disbelief.

"IRS, to be specific."

"I thought he was a lawyer."

"Daniel, his brother, I'm fairly certain, is the attorney of the family."

Now Nina lost it. "But, IRS, for god's sake? What's he been doing? Why is he living in Daniel's apartment? Why was he pretending to be Daniel? Wait a minute—he thinks I'm not paying my taxes. I bet that's it. He's been snooping on me."

"Let's not jump to conclusions, my dear. Take a breath."

Nina did as she was told.

Mrs. Chandler continued. "Billy has been after *me*, I'm afraid. He's not the first and he won't be the last. They think I'm, well, they think I'm—dear god—a drug dealer! Can you imagine? The only drugs I have experience with are of the prescription variety that induce sleep." She started to laugh. "Or they believe that I import some sort of contraband." Now she couldn't stop laughing. "Why yes! I have a closet full of imitation Kelly bags. Arrest me, please! Or that I launder money. The only laundry I know is the Chinese one at the corner, which picks up and delivers, by the way," she said, as if sharing some neighborly advice.

Now Nina was laughing too.

"They simply lack the intelligence and imagination to come up with anything else a woman of, well, a certain age, might do to acquire lots of cash."

Nina was silent, hoping Mrs. Chandler would elaborate.

"They just would never suspect that a woman could be a, well, an excellent . . ."

Nina was silent again, waiting. No such luck. Still, she was impressed. To have enough cash to elicit interest and determination from the United States Treasury. But she was pissed. Billy was not only not Billy, he was not a lawyer, which she was kind of relieved about. But an IRS agent? A civil servant?

It all started to make sense now: the dark suits, the goofy shoes, the uptight walk, every cliché about the IRS—except for everything that Billy was.

"They will never leave me alone," Mrs. Chandler said sadly, interrupting Nina's revelation. "I am destined to be hounded, searched, and stalked my entire life, which is not looking very long at this point. You know they sent two men in black suits to *Town and Country* magazine carrying guns and a search warrant to check the files? Compared to that, Billy has been a delight. But it won't be Billy forever. They'll replace him with a by-the-book paper pusher, a suit. This I know."

Safire had wobbled over perhaps to get Nina to take him out, but he stood staring at Mimi, who yipped at him. He reacted by turning to stare at the couch.

"That's my kind of girl," said Mrs. Chandler with a laugh. "She's awfully feisty, that little Mimi, is she?"

"She is. Very."

Nina then picked up Mimi and held her out to Mrs. Chandler.

Mrs. Chandler took the scruffy little Brillo pad of a mutt and held her nose to muzzle. It was a stare-down. Neither would blink nor look away. Then Mimi licked Mrs. Chandler's face. Put her paw on Mrs. Chandler's cheek. Mrs. Chandler, Nina could swear, had love in her eyes, as she kissed Mimi's face, first on one cheek, then the other. This was a match made in . . . well, New York City.

"I'd like to make a deal with you," said Nina.

"Music to my ears," answered Mrs. Chandler.

"Let me have Safire. I know just the place for him."

"Not the pound!"

"No . . ."

"Not a cemetery!" Mrs. Chandler looked at her suspiciously.

"No, no! A home, the perfect one. With a master who wants a dog—he doesn't know he wants it, but oh, he does—just like Safire."

"And to make it 'a deal,' I then get something in return, I presume?"

"You're holding her. You get Mimi."

Mrs. Chandler held out Mimi at arm's length and considered the proposition—and the mutt—before her.

She smiled. "Yes," she said. "You have made yourself a deal." And she hugged Mimi to her and Mimi yelped, Nina assumed, with joy.

Nina and Safire left. Her next stop was to pick up Che—and get Bono to come along for the ride.

As she approached his building, she saw him hanging outside, under the green awning in the shade with his doorman. He looked bedraggled, hands in his pockets, head down, kicking a can around on the sidewalk.

"Bono, hey!" Nina called from a few doors away.

The kid lifted his head and looked at her, and turned away. But she could tell from the upturn of the corners of his mouth, that he was pleased to see her, even if he wasn't going to show it.

"Whatcha doing, kid? Want to take a walk?"

"Can't."

"Why not? You don't look busy."

"My mom said never go anywhere with a stranger."

"I am not a stranger."

"You are too."

"Am not. Come on, Bono," she said, kneeling down, her face right in his. "I'm sorry. I know I was horrible, but I was . . ."

"A bitch."

"Yes. I was. Now please forgive me. Come on, let's take a walk . . ."

"But you're not my mother."

"No, I sure am not."

"So I don't have to."

"No, you do not *have* to. But it would be fun if you did. Where's Che?"

"Inside. With Mom."

"She's back. That's good." His mom had been away since before they last saw each other, following U2 on the last leg of their summer tour.

"But she's leaving today again." He looked down again, hands in his pockets.

"I thought—"

"Extended. Another two weeks. Bono sucks."

She put her hand gently, carefully, on the back of his

head. "He doesn't mean to. I'm sure, if he knew, he'd be very . . ."

"I hate that we have the same name. I hate that. He's the main Bono, and I'm Bono the Second. I hate my mom too."

Nina then put her arm around Bono's shoulder and looked up at the sky, today a hazy brown, and let out a deep breath and said, "Let's go in and talk to her."

"We can't. She's resting. She's packing. It's exhausting, you know, all this traveling back and forth. She ought to just stay back."

"Come on," said Nina, and nudged his short stocky body into the townhouse foyer, and up the stairs.

It was dark in the house. The hum of air conditioners was all that could be heard.

"It's quiet. Too quiet," said Bono in a scary movie voice.

"Where—?"

"In her bedroom."

"You wait here. I mean it. And not a word. Watch TV or something."

"I'm bored with TV," he whined.

Nina scruffed his hair. "That's a good sign. Sit there with Che"—who was asleep on the floor, hadn't even heard they were there—"and keep an eye on Safire, though he ain't going anywhere. Read a book, or something. I'll only be a minute."

"And then I can come with you to walk the dogs?"

"Promise."

"Pinky."

"You got it." She extended her right pinky to him.

"Double pinky."

And the two friends each crossed their wrists, fingers folded in, pinkies out and hooked onto each other's opposite pinkies, and shook hard three times.

"If you break that—"

"I won't. I will never ever break a promise to you, and I will try to never say anything hurtful to you ever again."

"Deal."

"But I'm only human, though, not perfect, though I like to think I'm as close to perfec—"

"Okay, already!" Bono smiled. And sat next to Che on the floor, and pet him while he slept.

Down the dark hall, lined with photos of Mrs. Armstrong at U2 concerts from California to New Jersey to Paris and Munich, with Bono, with the band, Nina saw the light coming from under the far door. She approached it and knocked lightly.

"I'm resting, Bon. Please leave Mommy alone."

"It's me, Mrs. Armstrong, Nina, the dog walker. Can we talk for a minute?"

"Nina, didn't Bono tell you I am unavailable? I—"

Nina opened the door. Mrs. Armstrong, who had been lying in bed, sat up and glared at her with the kind of selfish, recriminating eyes that reminded Nina of her own at times.

"What is it? Is something wrong with Che? What could be so important . . ."

"Bono—your son Bono, not your obsession Bono—that's who's important. Or have you forgotten you have a son?"

"And who the hell are you to talk to me—"

"A concerned citizen. A friend of your son's. He's hurting, Mrs. Armstrong. He needs you."

"What do you know about—"

"Nothing. I just know he is a sad kid. I know he's had nothing to do all summer because you failed to put him in camp or get him lessons or set up play dates or do anything with him. He takes care of his sick dog—"

"Che is sick?"

"He's old, he's deaf, he has a hard time walking."

"And besides, Bono didn't want to do any—"

"Like any kid, he wants, he *needs* to have friends, be active. For god's sake, he sits in front of the TV all day, every day. Unless he's with me, walking my dogs. He is lonely, Phyllis."

"He has a babysitter. She takes him places."

"You know what your babysitter does all day? She reads. And she complains and she eats and she talks on her cell phone. She is no companion for your child, who, in case you aren't aware, is bright, and funny, and interesting, and deep, and wonderful. I'll take him if you don't want him."

At that, Mrs. Phyllis Armstrong stood up and came frighteningly close to Nina, her right arm raised high, her hips swaggering, her eyes as cold and mean as one of Isaiah's pit bulls.

"Get out. Get out of my house. Who the hell are you to come in here and lecture me about my child? I love my child," she screamed. "I love Bono, my son Bono, I mean, not the other Bono, more than anything in the world."

Nina whispered now, perhaps in reaction to the volume, "Then show him. He needs you. He needs a life. He needs your attention. He needs you home."

Bono-the-kid's mom ran down the hall, Nina following.

There he was, sitting there on the floor right where Nina had left him, stroking Che, waiting to hear how all this would end.

Mrs. Armstrong was crying now, as she got on the floor and took Bono in her arms. "Is what Nina's saying true?"

"What, that an asteroid is about to smash into Earth and life will cease to exist as we know it? Nah, it's not true."

"I'm not joking, honey. Do you really feel . . . ?"

He shook his head. "Yeah, I guess."

"I'm sorry. I didn't realize . . . Wait . . ." She had come up with something.

He brightened. "What?" he asked.

"I know! Why don't you come with me?"

Bono looked skeptical.

"Yeah, come with me, Bono. You'll love it. The music, the crowds. I'll get you a backstage pass. You can meet him. He's very nice, honey. And he does such important work. Come with me."

The look of disappointment that flushed across his face was heartbreaking. Didn't she get it? Bono looked down and started to cry. Nina's eyes welled with tears. The stupid, selfish bitch!

Tears come too easily to many people, but they can be strong medicine for those to whom they don't.

"Oh sweetheart," said kid Bono's mother. "I didn't know. I'm sorry, but I didn't know." And then she started to cry too, so that all three people sitting on the floor of the dark hallway were crying about a lonely boy's need for his mom. She put her arms around her son and held him tight. At first he tried to wriggle away, but then he let himself go and collapsed into her fierce hug.

And then Bono looked at Nina and smiled through his tears. She would never ever forget that moment, his look, his face. That's all the kid wanted. Basic, simple. His mom, to be loved by her, to have her full attention. To be her number one Bono. For her to be his number one fan. To have her home.

"But Mom," he then said, "would you please stop calling me Bono?"

His mom pulled back from him to get a better look at his face. "Oh honey. Sure, of course. What do you want to be called? We could use your middle name, Van."

"No, I don't want to be named after anyone. I want my own name. A simple, regular name."

"Okay, sweetheart, like what?"

"Like Bob."

"Is Bobby okay?"

He smiled. "Yeah, it's perfect." And he hugged his mom tight.

"You coming, *Bob?*" Nina asked him as she got up to leave. She showed him her pinkies, referring to the promise they'd just made.

"Nah, you go," he said, wiping his tears and burying his head on his mother's shoulder.

Nina was on a roll. As with the Snoop, which took on a life of its own, the Intervention seemed to be an organic, living thing. It's difficult, almost impossible, to do the first brave thing, but once accomplished, the next brave act is easier and then easier still until bravery becomes a thing in and of itself. Like snooping. Only better, because there's no guilt and you don't have to worry about getting thrown in jail.

So when Nina and Safire and Che got to Jim Osborne's apartment and found Luca crying at the back baby gate, going crazy lonely in her three-by-three space while Jim was meeting with some TV types in his living room, she did what she always did: she got her leash from its hook, hooked it to her collar, said a nice "Hey girl, wanna go for a walk?" and took her out the door.

Then she took a deep breath. And put Safire in Jim Osborne's apartment. She unhooked his leash, hung it on the leash hook, and Safire, seeing the tiny space behind the office, the baby gate, sensing the owner who would pay no attention to him, seemed at home immediately. For once, Safire looked straight at Nina. He blinked at her, then turned to stare through the gate into the apartment. She couldn't be sure, of course, but she thought he was saying *Yes*.

While waiting for the elevator, she heard "What the fuck! WHERE'S MY DOG?" being yelled from inside the apartment. Oh god, she thought, where's the elevator? Come on, come on! She braced herself, expecting Jim's door to open, for him to accost her, but then the elevator was there. As she jumped in, she held its door open for a second, realizing all was quiet in the apartment. And she smiled, knowing Safire had blinked at Jim too, and even Jim couldn't escape the truth: Safire was the dog he'd always wanted.

Then she took Luca and Che back to Bobby's. This kid needed an active, fun-loving, booda-bone-playing, ball-chasing dog. Che would die soon and Bobby so needed a dog who would take his place. Well, now he had one. He needed the exercise and the responsibility, the dog needed a kid who played with him, would cherish and adore him. If people can't choose the right dog for themselves, by god, she would do it for them. Who better than she could match the right dog to the right person? She had much experience with the needs of dogs, the habits of people, and who belonged with whom. She laughed out loud, as she rode the elevator down to the lobby. She was a goddamn matchmaker. Move over match.com! Here comes Nina! She began to sing "Matchmaker, Matchmaker" from *Fiddler on the Roof.*

> *Matchmaker, matchmaker, make me a match,*
> *Find me a canine, catch me a catch!*

The word "canine" was hers, of course.

Then she went to her apartment to get Sam. He noticed she was Mimi-less. He barked and jumped, delighted, grateful. And now they were going for a walk, just the two of them.

Nina went to bed that night, with Sam at her side, feeling almost perfect. Except for the gigantic hole that was left when Billy had walked out of her life. And the anger she still felt at Daniel for taking advantage of her.

As she fell asleep, Nina was thinking about true bravery. Sure, it was brave to acknowledge your desire to achieve, to find that thing that makes one special. To go after it, even braver. It was brave to get a dog the right home, especially in the face of opposition. It was brave to play trombone. It was brave to audition for any part. It was brave to stand up for yourself and demand rights that you know are legally and rightfully yours. Everyone around her was brave. But no one more than those who were brave enough to love—Bono,

Bob, that is, and his mom, Mrs. Chandler, even, and Claire and Isaiah. To love someone takes the most open-hearted, huge, exceptional kind of bravery.

Nina fell asleep, by the light of the August moon, hoping she would discover that kind of bravery in herself. She would see Billy tomorrow and find out.

25

But first she had to wrap up some loose ends with Daniel. She could not just let it go. She was not a let-it-go kind of girl and never had been. Here was a man who was so self-assured, so shallow and manipulative, he needed a little lesson in the treatment of human beings. And who better than Nina to give such a lesson. She was, after all, the Captain of the Poop Police.

So, first thing in the morning, at about five-thirty, when she knew he'd still be in bed, she went to Daniel's place, giving Pete a warm hello and using her key to get into the apartment, which wasn't easy because Sid was asleep right against the door. But she gave it a couple small shoves and Sid was up. The second she got in, Sid leaned his head against her hip, his tail wagging like a metronome to some joyful tune, he was so happy to see Nina. He wasn't sleeping in the bedroom anymore, but by the front door, perhaps waiting for Billy's return. Nina scratched behind his ears and kissed his muzzle.

"Don't worry boy. You've spent your last night in this apartment," Nina said to Sid. And as if he understood, he sat quietly by the door, waiting.

Nina heard snoring from the bedroom, and laughed to herself that even he, prince among men that he was, was about as refined as a moose.

A second later, she was standing next to Daniel's bed and Sid was on Daniel's bed, sitting on Daniel's chest, and Daniel was screaming, "Sid, what are you doing? Get the hell off me. Get out of here." But Sid didn't budge. The seventy-five pounds of him weighed heavily on Daniel.

And Nina, very very quietly asked, "What's Billy's address?"

"Oh," Daniel smiled. "It's you. Miss me?"

And then she said, "I'd like Billy's address, please."

Sid hadn't moved and Daniel was having trouble breathing. So he gave it to her.

Then Nina said, "Sid will be coming with me. Say bye-bye."

And she could hear Daniel screaming as she walked out, "You fucking insane dog walker! Get the hell out of my house."

Standing outside Billy's apartment door with Sid, Nina listened. Oh god, she thought she might blow it completely by opening her mouth and singing along. That would clinch it. Her singing was about as bad as Billy's playing was good. And his playing was wonderful. She leaned her back against the door, letting her muscles go, her body slip to the floor. Nina sat, then, listening to every note, every mournful wail and blow. She had never heard this song played this way before, as a dreamy, sad story of loss. Sid sat too, his head cocked, his ears high, listening, recognizing, knowing who was on the other side of the door. He panted in excitement.

Nina sang along, silently, to the tune: *We'll take this big town for a whirl, All I really need is the girl* . . . But she was here. Right outside. She knew, though, that once they were face to face, her feelings of desire and love would turn into anger and uproar.

But she had to try.

Billy heard a knock on his door. Putting the trombone down on his bed, he walked over and asked, "Yeah? Who is it?"

But he knew. As sure as the earth will keep spinning on its axis, he was sure it was her.

"It's me. Nina."

He opened the door and Sid sprang forward, his paws up onto Billy's chest, forcing Billy to take a couple steps back to keep his balance. He scruffed his head, he gave him a kiss, and Sid romped away to check out the apartment.

And there she was. Though logic should dictate that he recognize her, he was struck by her face as if he had never seen it before. Those dark eyes, the brows that rose expressively when she spoke, the dimple on her left cheek when she smiled, which she did now, but just for a nanosecond. This was a face about which he'd never be complacent.

"So, you live here," Nina said.

"How'd you find me? Sid, how you doing, guy?"

"Well, I . . ." And she smiled, and there was that dimple. "I know your brother."

Billy just looked at her. Then away.

"Can I come in, or what?"

"Sure. Why not." And he stepped aside, opening the door, letting Nina walk through, then closing it behind her.

She stood, taking it all in. The clutter of books, piles of them, and magazines too, and sheet music over there on the coffee table. The music posters—one of Jazz at Lincoln Center, one of a huge golden trombone against an ink-blue background with the word PLAY in big red letters, another with the word JAZZ big and bold and black on a white background, all by itself. And more. CDs from floor to ceiling. Black-and-white photos of musicians with their instruments and some others too from maybe the thirties or forties, she thought. This was an apartment to live in. How could she have fallen for Daniel's shallow bachelor modern Bauhaus?

"Thanks for bringing Sid for a visit."

"Not to visit. He's yours."

Billy's eyes brightened. "You went to . . . you got . . . how'd . . . ?"

"That brother of yours doesn't know much about any-thing. But he does know when he's number two. And to Sid, you are Alpha."

Billy was pleased. "You want something to drink?"

She hadn't realized until then how hot it was in the apartment. "No air-conditioning?"

"Broken. Thought I'd go this afternoon to get a new one."

"I'll come with you. Let's go."

"Now?" he asked. "Wait." And he poured Sid a bowlful of cold water.

"Come on. Let's go somewhere else to argue," said Nina, as she pulled Billy by the wrist to the door.

"Is that what we're going to do?" Billy locked the door behind him.

"Don't you think we should?"

"I suppose we can't avoid it."

"You lied to me," said Nina.

"You slept with my *brother*,"said Billy.

"About everything!"

"Do you know how that feels? When someone you really, well, care about, maybe, you think you might, actually goes to bed with your own brother?" He turned to her, and with his arms out to the sides, asked, "Can you even begin to imagine that?"

"No, I can't. But what about when you find out that someone you can't stop thinking about, who you've trusted, has been lying to you about everything he ever said?"

"Not everything."

"And I thought he was you," she yelled.

"You thought I was *him*," he yelled back. He turned away to his window. And then he turned to her. "And you have lied too. About plenty."

"Wha—? God, it's too goddamn hot. Can we get some air-conditioning?"

And they left. Sid found a comfortable spot under the window where some air found its way in and he lay there the entire afternoon, happy to be home.

•   •   •

On the street, Billy flagged a cab, and the two of them climbed in. It was nice and cool inside. This would've been a good place to talk. But they rode in silence. It was as if they needed the rhythm of the world around them—the honking of horns, the drilling of blacktop, the screech of a subway coming to a stop, the cry of a baby in need of a bottle, the roar of a jet, the bark of a dog, the slam of a door—to accompany the He-Lied-to-Me-and-She-Shtupped-My-Brother Blues they were dying to sing together.

But once they got to The Wiz, the band got rocking. Perhaps it was the feeling of safety in numbers (they were having a buy-one-get-fifty-percent-off-the-second sale, so it was packed) or maybe they both were turned on by public displays of disaffection.

It began the minute they reached the air conditioners, which were right inside the front door.

"You aren't only *not* Daniel, you're *not* a lawyer." Nina had to yell to be heard over the buzz of TVs, stereos, and all things electronic.

"How do you know? Snooping at my apartment? Going through my things? On my computer? Playing my trombone?"

"You're IRS!"

"Now how the hel—" But he stopped himself. "How do you know that?"

"Mrs. Chandler told me."

He let out a loud, "Hah! *Et tu Brute!*" He was pissed and felt doubly betrayed. Sure, he had been after her, but respectfully so. Hadn't they forged a bond? Wasn't he biding his time while he came up with a plan? Didn't Mrs.

Chandler know that? Why would she talk to Nina about him?

"I was only doing my job, which was why I lied to you. I couldn't tell you. It would've blown my cover."

"Which was blown on its own."

A salesperson approached. "Do you need any help, folks?"

"Yeah," Billy said. "I'll take this one and this one too. Can you deliver today?"

"For an extra fifty bucks."

"Done."

"I guess we are," said Nina.

"Wait," said Billy, grabbing her wrist.

"If I hadn't come to your apartment, I was never going to hear from you, was I? You were going to let me go, weren't you?"

"No. I mean yes. I mean . . ."

"That'll be five-hundred and sixty-seven dollars and eighty cents," said the sales guy.

Nina pulled her arm free of Billy's grasp.

"You were willing to never see me again, just because I made a mistake. Which I only made because you lied to me. Ach. This is so boring." She turned to leave.

But now he grabbed her arm, and pulled her to him so his face was in hers. "Did you? Was it a mistake or hasn't it been Daniel you've wanted all along? The guy who skis, the lawyer, the fun one, the wild one. I'm Billy. Know me? I'm the dork."

"Well, yes, at first, but no, not . . . you're the one." She began to cry. She pleaded with him. "Billy, you have to know that it's you."

He let her go and turned away. "So what do I owe you?" he asked the cashier.

"Nothing. You owe me absolutely nothing," answered Nina, her face wet with tears as she ran out the door, into the white-hot sun of the day.

And he was left at the register signing the receipt.

26

Mrs. Chandler, let's finish this," said Billy as he walked through her door.

"I'm fine and how are you?" Mrs. Chandler responded.

"I've got a deal to make with you."

"That's the second offer that's come my way in so many days."

"I'm sorry," said Daniel, flustered. "I'm well, thank you. Nice to see you. How've you been?"

"All right, let's drop the small talk. What's the deal you intend to offer me?"

"I want to make an investment with your money. In lieu of prison."

"You don't have anything on me that would send me to prison." Mrs. Chandler laughed loudly, unusual for her.

Billy thought she was nervous. He continued, taking full advantage. "I don't report your, um, so-called hidden assets, and I close the books on you so you will never be investigated again."

"Interesting. That's quite an offer. How do I know you can do that? What happens when you're gone—and you will be, this I know—and they send some low-class individual in your place who thinks he can use me to make his name?"

"You will never have to open your door, or your files, or anything, to one of us again. I promise you this."

"I take a promise quite seriously."

"Trust me."

"That's what Brutus said to Caesar."

Billy laughed. "Exactly! The investigation of Mrs. Constance Chandler will be complete, the file closed, certain information 'lost' in the shuffle."

"And what, my dear Billy, must I do in return?"

"You will donate half of the cash in this apartment to a charity of my choice."

Mrs. Chandler let out a throaty, gleeful laugh. A deal like this made her giddy with excitement.

"Hmm, a third."

"Two-thirds."

"You said half."

"Okay, half. Do we have a deal?"

"And to what charity am I making this astronomic donation, if I may ask?"

"It doesn't have a name yet."

"Sounds fascinating." She rolled her eyes. "It's not the

Billy Maguire personal retirement fund, is it? I haven't mis-read you, have I? This isn't funding for you to run off with Nina to Tahiti, is it?"

Billy's cheeks, normally flushed with color, turned crimson with embarrassment. "Nina? Why would you—?"

"I saw her. We spoke of . . . *upholstery*. But I sensed that you two might be in for a wonderful life togeth—"

He cut her off. "It's for trombone playing."

"Excuse me?"

"You will be funding a program for New York City public schools to encourage and teach kids of all ages how to play trombone."

"Trombone. How many children want to learn trombone?"

"It is the most underappreciated musical instrument in existence."

"One could argue on behalf of the accordion."

"It's about exposure. Once the kids are exposed to it and learn to play, they'll be converts."

"Well, I appreciate your trombone evangelism, but one should give the children a choice in the matter, don't you think? Or you won't be able to *pay* someone to *take* my money."

"All right, then. We'll encourage the trombone, but any other instrument they might choose will be okay. And we'll teach jazz. And we'll offer classes in every school within the five boroughs. We can call it the Constance Chandler Horn Blower Program."

"Or something else a little more, ah, lyrical. If, of course, that is all right with you. And never with my name. I prefer my anonymity, especially when it involves philanthropy and blowing, shall we say, *horns*."

Billy smiled. "Sure."

"And I assume, I get to continue my line of . . . work?"

"As long as it doesn't involve drugs, as long as it doesn't harm children or animals, as long as it hurts no one, yes."

She put her hand to her chest, protesting too much. "Please sir, you do mistake me."

Billy smiled. "Good."

"And how would you like it? Check or cash? Perhaps money order?"

Billy smiled. "I'll take the cash. How about on Monday? Gives me a few days to close my side of the deal."

"For this, I cannot wait."

Billy knew she was being sarcastic but he couldn't wait either. *A wonderful life,* she had told him.

The next day Billy was at his computer screen reading the Constance Chandler file and filing his last report. When he was finished, he clicked the tiny box on his screen marked CASE REPORT FILED and then the next one that appeared, CASE CLOSED. He knew no one would question his judgment, that it was his judgment they were waiting for. But for finality's sake, to be sure that all's well that ends completely, he pressed DELETE, and the entire file, except his final report, of course, no longer existed.

All he wanted to do was to call Nina, to tell her what he had done, how excited he was to make an impact, change some kids' lives, change his own. But he couldn't do it, not yet, maybe not ever. He just could not get the image of her, on the floor, with *him,* out of his mind.

A month later Billy was at home reading the newspaper that contained the article about the new music and performing arts program donated to the New York City public schools that would start in October. It would be run by one Billy Maguire, jazz maven, trombone aficionado, ex-government employee. Of the anonymous donor all that was known was that she was of considerable means from an unnamed source.

Mrs. Chandler was sitting in first class on her way from JFK to Frankfurt reading the newspaper when she came upon the same article. A tall glass of vodka was on the table at her side, and a broad smile swept across her face. She was proud of being part of the music program, and had committed to funding it for the next ten years.

She took another piece of nicotine gum from her bag. Disgusting, she thought. One should never, except in dire circumstances, chew gum. But a six-hour flight is dire. As she chewed she heard a yip from the Louis Vuitton carry-on case on the seat next to hers. She opened its mesh door, stuck her hand inside, and said, "Not too much longer, Mimi, my love." Then she zipped the case closed and thought about the coming two weeks in Frankfurt, where she would be the only woman in attendance at the very private, extremely exclusive annual poker game in the Schopenhauer Suite at the Frankfurterhof Hotel. She'd see all her poker cronies, including Manuel Alvarez and Tommy Rozzano, Jim Susskind and Earl Hochschober. And, of course, she'd see her dear, Gerard, a gorgeous French banker, her lover and best friend, who adored her so that even after fourteen years, he still sent her winnings in U.S. funds, two packets at a time, to her P.O. box number in Hoboken. And for all this, he still only asked for ten percent.

27

Claire and Isaiah were coming to dinner. Nina's first attempt at a dinner party—albeit a small one—in she didn't know how long. Getting them over was not easy, not after their last visit. But she whined and begged and pleaded and apologized and swore she had showered. So they accepted. And were about to arrive.

Nina had set a small table out on the terrace. The one she normally used for her mess of pots with flowers and herbs. Those now sat on the terrace floor and the table was set with a pretty cloth, candles, plates, and napkins. It looked festive and when cluttered with the BBQ'd steak and the corn and the salad, it certainly qualified for a make-up meal. The special kind of meal one serves to make up for all sorts of mistakes.

Her indoor living space had become inundated with her structures. In the last few days she had been so productive, as if making up for lost time spent in bed. She had been infused with a wild new energy from her dog match-ups and her Bono intervention. So much so that an entire new structure had been completed and two others had been reworked to Nina's liking and finished. She was admiring them, cascading in sparkling colors and complex textures from the ceiling, when the intercom buzzer buzzed.

"Claire?" Nina asked.

"It's us!" she answered and was buzzed in.

And then they were there, carrying wine and flowers, just like people do when they go to a real dinner party, thought Nina, accepting the gifts graciously. Claire looked beautiful and Nina told her so.

"She is gorgeous, isn't she?" agreed Isaiah.

Claire beamed at him and then back to Nina. "You are too, Ni-nah. You're glowing, in fact."

"Especially compared to the last time we saw you," joked Isaiah.

"Ha, ha, ha," laughed Nina, poking him with her elbow.

Then Claire turned to the structures. "God, these are something," she said. "You're going to have to show them to somebody."

"I know," said Nina. "I will."

"I mean seriously. They're fantastic."

"I plan to, really. I have a few other things I have to get done and then I will."

"Speaking of which, have you heard from him?"

"Not since our air-conditioner shopping outing. Come, let's go outside. Who wants a glass of wine?"

Claire's face was full of concern for her friend, but she

followed the crowd as it headed outdoors. Then the wine
was opened, the food was cooked and served. Claire finally
revealed to her best friend that she had gotten the part she
had been auditioning for, the new *Law and Order*, filmed in
New York City, thank god, so she'd be staying right here for
a long time. Then Isaiah told her that he'd started a new
Union, Local K-9, for dog walkers, sitters and groomers and
trainers. They'd had their first meeting, and it was okay that
there were only three people in attendance, because there
were sure to be more in the future. And the first thing the
union was going to do was get that dog run open again.

They screamed and whooped and toasted each other and
marveled at the warm Indian summer night. Claire and Isaiah took turns looking through the telescope, oohing and
aahing at the stars and the interiors of apartments across
the park.

But when they offered Nina a look, she turned them
down.

"Nah, I'm not really doing that anymore."

"Doing what?" asked Isaiah.

"I'm not into the spying thing. I, uh, well . . ." Her voiced
faded off.

But Claire picked up where she'd left off. She put her arm
around Nina and said, "Good. It's not really nice, is it?
You're right."

Then, Nina dropped her bombshell.

"Besides, I have news too," she began innocuously.

Claire and Isaiah looked at her hopefully. Perhaps this
had to do with Billy.

"I'm not going to be walking dogs anymore," she said.

Nina could see down the throats and almost into the lungs of her two friends, their mouths were open so wide.

"I assume, Isaiah, that you'll keep my dogs and Claire's for yourself, since Claire here is going to be a star and too busy to take them back. And I, well . . ."

"I may have to farm them out, since the union's taking up so much of my time, but they'll be taken care of. I promise."

Very quietly and cautiously, Claire looked at Nina and asked, "So, what is it, you? What are you going to be doing? Not back to copy writing for those publishing ass . . ."

But Nina stopped her with a smile that beamed full and strong, as if finally finding her thing in life lit her up like a planet reflecting the sun. She handed each of them a business card that she'd pulled from a jean pocket.

LOVE ME, LOVE MY DOG, was what the card read. A HUMAN-CANINE MATCHMAKING SERVICE. There was a little illustration of a person holding a dog by its paw.

"Brilliant," said Claire. "I love it." She gave the card to Isaiah who looked at it and, throwing his head back, laughed. And then Claire did the very thing Nina knew, if she knew her friend Claire at all, she would do. She sang. She got up on her chair, which made Nina uneasy, given they were on a terrace, and sang at the top of her Broadway show tune lungs:

Matchmaker, matchmaker, make me a match . . .

Nina gave her a look, which stopped the singing, though not her humming the remainder of the song. But Nina couldn't blame her; she had done the same thing herself when she first thought of this business, had she not?

"I've already gotten a dozen clients. It's out of control. It's as if people are finally able to come out of the closet on their ignorance about dogs. The nice family who gets a rottweiler because they've read the Carl books and only later realize a rottweiler would eat their child if it could. The older woman who can't control her cute standard poodle. The teenager who thinks he looks cool with a mastiff that weighs more than he does. The corporate exec with a stupid setter. It's as if people don't have a clue who is really right for them."

"You got that right," said Isaiah. "They choose a dog for all the wrong reasons."

Claire laughed. "They choose *each other* for all the wrong reasons. Why would they do any better when it comes to a dog?"

That made Nina laugh too, and then she looked at Sam and said, "But the right dog with the right owner is everything."

"Want to join a union? We could expand to have dog matchmakers," offered Isaiah. "We are considering allowing doggie shrinks."

"If a dog needs a shrink, its human needs shock therapy." Claire laughed again.

Nina did too. "It's just glorified dog training anyway. It's like calling dog walking Canine Physical Therapy. Hello."

"I heard about a feng shui specialist for dogs. She calls it 'Fang Shui,'" said Isaiah.

Nina laughed. "No way."

"Hey, if the market demands it . . ."

"My capitalist pig," said Claire, giving Isaiah a kiss on the cheek.

That remark reminded Nina of Billy and the whole Schopenist Pig thing and she lost her breath for a moment and felt as if she may have lost him forever.

"You know what?" said Nina, "I'm going to hold off on the union thing."

"Yeah," said Claire, admonishing him. "Why join a union when you're making millions as the boss?"

And that's just what Nina did. She eventually went national and appeared on talk shows and magazine covers and made contributions to the pound and shelters and the Animal Hospital and pet charities of all kinds.

But that was later. Now she had to serve dessert, kiss her friends goodnight, give Sam a good chest scratching, and marvel at the magic of unconditional love.

After they left, she put on the original Broadway cast version of *Gypsy*, skipped all the blowhard bullshit of Ethel Merman, and listened to his song, that song, the song she had overlooked in this show until he played it that night. "All I Need is the Girl." What a song it was, it is, she thought. Sure, it was hopeful and fun and lovely, but more than anything, it was his, it was hers.

Not that night, but one soon thereafter, Billy was on the stage of PS 87's auditorium introducing a group of legendary jazz musicians. They had agreed to perform to help entice kids to pick up an instrument, preferably trombone, of course, and join Billy's new public school jazz program. The place was noisy, packed with television cameras and reporters, with kids and their parents, all excited about the concert.

But when Billy started to play a wild rendition of the "Star Spangled Banner" to open the program, the entire room became silent. From there they did several jazz standards, but there was nothing standard about this night. For there, on the drums, was Billy's idol, Max Roach. It was if Billy were in a dream, here on stage, hundreds of kids listening, riveted, he playing with Max.

When they played a duet, Billy had to hold back his tears, for this wasn't a dream at all. It was life, *his* life, as Billy, challenging and promising and exciting. It was right then that he knew he was ready for Nina. In fact, he couldn't live happily another day without her.

28

Nina thought that she'd never see Billy again. Now that she wasn't walking his dog, now that he wasn't even in the neighborhood, now that he was so angry and unforgiving, unable after all these weeks to call her, she was sure he was out of her life for good. Had he seen her mentioned in the *Observer?* Had he seen her picture in the Metro section of the *Times?* Her matchmaking clients had blabbed and gossiped and spread the word, and her new career was burgeoning. Her apartment had to be rearranged to hold the files of press materials, of brochures, of clients to be matched and clients who'd been. She had joyfully taken over her bedroom for Love Me, Love My Dog files.

Her structures would always have a place and the table was still dedicated to their creation. She had even showed them to the owner of an outsider art gallery in Chelsea and he was considering including one in a holiday show in December.

But where was Billy?

She missed walking dogs. Sure, she still saw Bobby almost every morning when they walked Luca and Sam together in the park. Che had died soon after she brought Luca to live with them. And at first Nina blamed herself, thinking Luca's arrival had killed him. But Bobby swore he had died happily, knowing Bobby was in good hands—or paws—with Luca. It was as if Che had been waiting for something—or someone—to enable him to go. And Luca was it.

But she missed the dogs, she missed the having to get up and out, she missed the park culture she had so hated. She got a taste of it walking Sam, but it wasn't the same from the layperson's point of view. Walking in that park with a dozen dogs gives you a certain perspective, a particular entitlement, which you don't get from walking just one.

She didn't really miss the snooping aspect of her dog-walking career. It had transmuted into a secret of her past. Like an old affair. She remembered the excitement of it, the revelations, the sexy, breathless quality of it, but it was over and done. In the past. Something she could recall as an adventure of an earlier life.

For there was to be life before Billy and life with.

One evening in early October, while she sipped wine and worked on her laptop on the terrace (the planning of appropriate matches took much time and research), she let out an occasional sigh in recognition of the beginning of fall. The air had begun to cool, the leaves to turn, and the sky to darken earlier. It was sweater weather, her favorite kind. Sam was enjoying it too. He held his head up, his nose eagerly twitching as he tried to catch the smells of the autumn night. A breeze brushed a strand of hair across Nina's face and as she caught it and put it back behind her ear, someone buzzed her from below. She looked at Sam and he at her and she went to the intercom, her heart beating overtime, as it did every time the phone rang or the buzzer buzzed.

"Yes?" she asked.

"It's me."

Yes, she thought. *Finally.* She let out a long breath as if she had been holding it in for weeks.

"Can I come up?"

She buzzed him in. She wasn't sure how she'd greet him. She had played this scene over and over again in her mind a hundred different ways. But when she heard him on the stairs, she didn't think, she didn't measure or consider. She ran down two flights and into his arms, Sid running past her right up into the apartment to hang with Sam.

"I was afraid . . ." she said, between kisses. "I so love you." *There,* she said it.

He stroked her hair. "And I . . . well, I just . . ."

"I know. You don't drive."

He laughed quietly. "Do now. Like a demon."

And he kissed her again, hard and passionately.

"Don't you see," he said, "I love *you.* I've loved you from the moment I saw you in my—*his* bathroom. I just had to make some stops along the way, to sort of fuel up, take a side road." He kissed her again, and held his palm against her cheek. "To find you on my own, as me."

"I thought I'd lost you for good," Nina said, and then the tears came. "I lose people, you know, people who mean a lot to me. But losing you was the most devast—"

"You'll never lose me. I'm like a dog. Loyal and . . ."

They looked at the two dogs. Sam was licking his balls and Sid was rolling on his back, his four legs high in the air.

"Not really," Nina said. And they both laughed, Nina trying to wipe her eyes, but it was no use.

And later, after more tears and apologies, they sat on her terrace under the stars, the two dogs chasing moths.

"Use the telescope much?" Billy asked.

"You like having Sid."

Billy looked at that dog with love in his eyes. "Daniel never really loved him. Besides, he moved to San Francisco."

Nina smiled.

"So what about the telescope?"

"Never use it. Know someone who'd like it?"

"I'd say let's trash it, let's rip it apart, and formally once and for all bury our spy habits forever. But I can't help myself, now that I'm involved. We'll donate it to one of my schools. For astronomy classes."

"Good idea."

"Now that we've transformed."

"Our days of spying and lying are over."

They sighed together and sipped their wine, looking out over the darkness of the park to the lights of the East Side and beyond.

"You know," said Billy, "sitting here reminds me of that time when we . . ."

"Went on a cruise?"

Billy looked at Nina like she'd gone mad. "We never . . ."

"You're right. We'd never go on a cruise. When we were in Tahiti?"

His eyes crinkled and he smiled and thought about that. "Maybe, but not what I was thinking."

"Were in Venice?"

She smiled and he went with it, though he had been referring to the night on the pier.

"Yes, that's right. Our trip to Venice. That was great."

"We stayed at the Gritti."

"We stayed at the Cipriani," insisted Billy.

"Oh, I loved that place!"

"It was perfect. We drank Prosecco."

"You got drunk. I remember . . ." said Nina.

"A little . . ."

"No, a lot! I had to carry you across the Piazza San Marco on my back!"

"You have a terrible memory. I was a little wrecked—we both were a little wrecked—and you and I made love in a gondola."

"Well, no wonder I forgot. I get seasick."

"Not that night. Trust me. It was the best lovemaking of your life."

Nina smiled, teasingly. "Really? I'm not remembering the details . . . Perhaps . . ."

"How about now?"

"Well, that would be fine."

And they both put their wine glasses down, got up, and went to Nina's room, closing the door on Sid and Sam, who barked and whined a couple times until they found some good floor space, scratched at it with their claws, turned around three times, and hunkered down for the night. The light of the moon streamed in through the terrace doors, making Nina's structures twinkle like the stars that hung in the New York City sky on this most amazing night.

Acknowledgments

When you write your first novel after a long career on the other side of the fence, you feel grateful to so many people. Actually to everyone you've ever met. So, to everyone I have ever met, thank you.

But a very special thanks to Helen Schulman who helped get this book started in the right direction and to Dr. Robert B. Shapiro without whom it wouldn't have been started at all.

For their wisdom and insights, for reading and rereading, thanks to Ellen Kaye, Corinne T. Netzer, Liz Perle, and Tom Spain. Also thanks to Patty Dann, James W. Hall, Craig Holden, Erica Jong, Galt Neiderhoffer, Christopher Reich, Dani Shapiro, Harry Stein, and RD Zimmerman for things you said to me during the writing of this book that were more helpful than you could ever know. And also things like: "Now you know what it is like to be on the other side," and "I bet you'll never talk to writers the same way again."

Thank you thank you thank you to Judith Curr, Greer Hendricks, and Karen Mender, and everyone at Atria Books, for taking the shot, for everything. What would I have done without the wisdom, instinct, and brilliance of Greer, my editor, who pushed me to places I was afraid to go. Also, much appreciation to Audra Boltion, Suzanne O'Neill, Paolo Pepe, and everyone at Atria Books who worked so hard on my behalf. And thanks to Sandi Mendelson of HMI East.

To Richard Pine, the agent with soul, who had faith in me and this book long before there was any reason to do so, thank you for your guidance, ideas, and encouragement. Thanks to Lori Andiman, whose good spirit is so appreciated. And thank you, Arthur Pine, for you taught me that when one door closes, another door opens.

Thanks to Amy Schiffman and David List, my West Coast team who were there for me so very early on.

I am lucky to have wonderful friends who provided me with much support and encouragement during the writing of this book. Though I made fun of some of your dogs, I love them, I do, though you might consider training for them and/or therapy for yourselves. Thank you all from the bottom of my heart.

To my wild family, the Schnur pack in California— Myrna, my mom; Milton, my dad, and Louise; my three brothers and their families, Alan, Julie, Adam, and Zach; Jeff, Ellen, Danielle, and Jake; and Ken, Denise, Emma, and Noah—thank you for your love, inspiration, and insane humor. Mom and Dad, please know this is a novel, which means it is fiction, which means I made it up.

And a million thanks to my co-conspirator and husband, Jerry "Keep Your Eye on the Ball" Butler, for his inspiration and patience and love and patience and wisdom and good humor and patience. Did I mention patience? Thank you with all my heart, always.

THE
DOG WALKER

LESLIE SCHNUR

READERS CLUB
GUIDE

ABOUT THIS READING GUIDE

The suggested questions are intended to help your
reading group find new and interesting angles and topics for
discussion for Leslie Schnur's *The Dog Walker*. We hope
that these ideas will enrich your conversation and increase
your enjoyment of the book.

Many fine books from Washington Square Press feature
Readers Club Guides. For a complete listing, or to read the
Guides online, visit http://www.BookClubReader.com

A Conversation with Leslie Schnur

Q: You worked in the publishing world for many years in both marketing and editorial roles. What is it like to experience publishing from the author's point of view?

A: It's terrifying! I know what actually goes on behind those closed doors where decisions about the cover, publicity plans, and marketing budgets are made. So the hardest thing for me has been to trust my publisher, to relinquish control. And you know what? So far, so great! I thought I knew everything. But my publisher has proven that there is more than one way to do something—and they do it so well.

Q: How is it different to write a novel than it is to edit it? Did your experiences as an editor help you with this novel?

A: You'd think after ten years as an editor I would've learned a thing or two about writing. Well I didn't. It's very different to be on this side of the editorial table. Being an editor—choosing what books to publish, helping writers do their very best possible work, making sure the book is published well—is not an easy job. You have to first trust your own instincts and then stand by them. And though the hands-on editing itself can be creative and challenging work, it doesn't compare to writing original material from scratch—making a story, creating characters, and writing compellingly where there was once a blank page.

Nothing could have prepared me for how hard it is to be a writer. There is nothing as difficult, except maybe hiking the Himalayas, as sitting down and facing that empty screen, and then relying on the voices in your head to fill it. But most importantly, I learned that rewriting is where the real work lies and that with every rewrite, magic can happen. Every writer needs an editor. My novel is much richer because of mine.

Q: Do you think everyone struggles with some of the issues that prevent Nina and Billy from connecting at first?
A: Yes, I think it's difficult for people to allow themselves to reach out and make real connections because they are so afraid of being hurt. If you've had any experience with falling in love, you know what it means to have a broken heart. People become guarded so that they'll never have to feel that kind of pain again. Of course, we all know there's only one way to find love—to put oneself out there in an open and vulnerable way. You need to be open to allow yourself to love and that very openness will get you killed. Sounds fun, doesn't it?

Q: As a writer, who are your role models? What did you learn from them? Could you recommend any other books for us?
A: I am a huge fan of Nick Hornby because his books are full of humor and music and depth and an unexpected sweetness.

He writes about love and angst with wit and his characters are rich and layered. And he tells his story straight, without unnecessary embellishments or pretentions. I loved *Middlesex* by Jeffrey Eugenides. It was my favorite book of last year. What a family, and told from the point of view of a fascinating, heartbreaking character. I thoroughly enjoyed Zoë Heller's *What Was She Thinking? (Notes on a Scandal)* and Tom Perrotta's *Little Children*. They both deal with gray moral areas—the kind we grapple with every day as humans on this planet. And both have humor and heart. I guess I like books that move me. Well-written, of course, but simply and unself-consciously told. Books that are both funny and deep. They're hard to find, but they're out there.

Q: What, if anything, do you think a snoop would learn about you from your apartment?
A: Oh my god, I'd want to clean up first before anybody snooped here. With two kids who seem to think the entire apartment is their playroom, and a husband who never learned to put his clothes in drawers (what a radical thought, right?) the place is usually a mess. A snoop would learn that our kids rule the roost. Like most parents, we don't throw one piece of art or writing away. That I like paper napkins, the kooky, cute ones with bright colors and designs and I buy them whenever they're on sale. I could have a cocktail party for millions. That I have a lot of stuff but nothing really valuable stashed away, nothing illegal, or secret, or very interesting. A snoop would learn that we don't always put the DVDs back in their boxes, and the CDs are not organized. We

do have some interesting stuff on our computer. That's where our secret stash is. Highly provocative stuff, like ideas for vacations, lists of things we need to do, new material I'm working on, and what we've bought on eBay.

Q: Regarding Nina and Isaiah's mock argument about nature vs. nurture and how it might be applied to dogs, do you think dogs naturally have a certain temperament, or do you think their characters are developed by their owners?
A: I certainly believe that nobody should own a pit bull. Period. I don't care about the argument that they're really sweet if you treat them nicely. It is a fact that pit bulls are born with the propensity to be aggressive and violent. And look at yappy chihauhuas. They yap. A lot. No matter what. As do a lot of other small dogs. Probably because they're small and want to be noticed. I can understand that; I just wouldn't want to live with it. Many dogs are born with characteristics specific to their breed and no matter how hard you try, how good the training, a Lab is always going to be a Lab. That's why we love them.

However, I think there are many neurotic owners who make their dogs nuts. People who spoil their dogs, people who anthropomorphize their dogs. Any dog who wears a raincoat and boots is probably going to become vicious at some point in his life. We have friends who take their dog everywhere—to parties, to restaurants, to our place—because they feel badly leaving her at home. Hello. The dog would rather be at home asleep on the cool floor than running around a stranger's house chased by a bunch of kids. No wonder that dog always leaves us a personal gift of the stinky, dirty variety every time she visits.

Q: What inspired you to write *The Dog Walker*? Have you met anyone like Nina or Billy? Where did the idea for this story come from?
A: The idea for this novel was, at first, visual. I was riding in a cab up Park Avenue, and saw a guy walking at least a dozen dogs. What a sight. But he looked like an ex-con and I began to imagine all the things this guy, or anybody who has access, does in an apartment when the owners are out. I remembered snooping as a kid when I would baby-sit. And then I thought about the moral issues of opening a closet you shouldn't, or reading someone else's email or letter, and I realized these are issues facing us daily. One thought and then another and it stuck with me, and the idea was born.

I have never met anyone like Nina. Oh, except me, of course. She is insecure and romantic, like me. She likes musicals and dogs and art, like me, and she's worked in book publishing, like me. But she's also different. I've never been a dog walker. And I've never snooped. Well, hardly ever. Like any writer, I took what I know as the basis for Nina but then used my imagination to create a character who I hope readers will find vital and universal. Billy is somewhat like my husband—the sweet, practical, and unassuming part—but again, that's where the comparison ends. Billy's a combination of a few men of my past, as well as of my mind.

Q: Did you have a particular audience in mind as you wrote *The Dog Walker*? **Is there a particular theme or idea that you would like your readers to be thinking about?**

A: I was writing for women from twenty to eighty. I guess I assume since I love movies and pop culture, since I'm a mom and a wife and have worked most of my life, my concerns are many people's concerns. This is a book for women who are romantic and love love love life and have a sense of humor and appreciate dogs, of course. The themes that are most important to me, I think, have to do with the moral issues. Is it right to take a bath in someone else's apartment when they don't know you're doing it? To read someone else's mail or computer or anything? Is it right to pretend to be something you are not? To lie—even for the larger good? Or to not be true to yourself? When does desire become an obstacle to getting what you really desire? That is, how do we hurt ourselves by coveting what our neighbor has? When is what we have and who we are enough? And just right?

Q: *The Dog Walker* **has been optioned for film. Who would you like to see play Nina? How about Billy?**

A: Reese Witherspoon, whose production company has optioned the film rights, with Universal, is perfect. And Billy? John Cusack or Matt Damon would be terrific. Just thinking about who should play what character from a book I've written is thrilling in itself!

Questions and Topics for Discussion

1. After reading the first chapter, what have you learned about Nina? What does she care about? What are her weaknesses? After you'd read a few pages, did you feel like you knew her, or that she was someone you'd get along with? Did the end of the chapter surprise you? After you found out she was trespassing, did your opinion of her change?

2. Both Nina and Billy like to snoop. The author describes the urge by saying, "It was like eating one of those See's candies. You know it's bad for you, but the force to do it, to reach, to eat, is so much stronger than the force to stop and think and consider the fat and cholesterol content, or, in this case, weighing the moral issues" (133). Nina and Billy devote a lot of thought to weighing the moral issues after the fact (and sometimes even mid-snoop). What conclusions do they come to? Do their ideas differ significantly? How do their experiences with each other change their snooping habits?

3. Do Billy and Nina learn anything valuable about each other while snooping that they might not have learned by talking to

each other? Think about Nina's discovery of Billy's trombone, and Billy's discovery of Nina's sculpture and her obsession with old musicals. Do you think either of them would have revealed these secrets on their own? How does snooping circumvent their natural tendencies to protect themselves? Does it help them develop intimacy?

4. Nina thinks she's in love with Billy because she was in love with what she knew of "his" apartment. Billy is aware of Nina's preconceived notions, and he's afraid that Nina really is in love with his brother. How much does Nina really know about the inhabitant of Daniel's apartment? Is there a difference between her infatuation with Daniel and her love for Billy? Is it reasonable for Billy to be afraid that Nina is really in love with his brother?

5. Claire, Billy, and Bono all respond to Nina's sculptures. "And," as Nina says, "every one of them was a critic" (232). Compare Claire's response to Nina's sculptures with Billy's. What does she think Nina ought to do with them (see page 218), and how does her opinion reflect her wishes for Nina in general? How does Daniel respond to the sculpture (see page 211)? How does his relationship with it reflect his desired relationship with Nina?

6. Nina's relationship with her mom seems strained and unsatisfying. What does Nina want from her that she's not getting? When Nina is in the hospital, do you think anything changes for them during their phone conversation? Later, when Nina

tells her mom that she's in love, and her mom tells her not to screw it up, Nina asks herself, "When would she stop asking for it and learn the limits of this relationship? Not all mothers could bear the disappointments of their daughters" (261). By recognizing this, will Nina improve her relationship with her mother? How else might she build on their relationship?

7. Why do both Nina's mom and Claire make it a point to push Nina toward finding another profession? Nina finds this annoying and avoids admitting to either of them that she agrees. Do you think their prodding is useful, or does it encourage Nina to resist change? Is their advice a form of caring, or is it just meddlesome? What is it that finally allows Nina to develop her career?

8. On page 159, Nina says to Claire, "I'm not and have never been a manufacturer of my own destiny." But by the end of the book, Nina is not only mistress of her own fate, she's helping others as well. What changes in her make it possible for her to be so proactive? How does her newfound confidence contribute to her happiness and the happiness of others?

9. Along the same lines, Nina's relationship with Billy almost becomes "the first love affair with no people" (188) because neither wants to be the one to pursue the other and risk being vulnerable. Both have their reasons for being reticent. Are Nina's reasons more valid than Billy's, or vice versa? After Nina's brief entanglement with Daniel, she pursues Billy and tries to heal their rift. What enabled her to be able to do that?

Do you think Billy would have gone looking for her if she hadn't beaten him to it? Had he changed as well?

10. Did Billy handle his work with Mrs. Chandler ethically? Professionally? Why was he so upset when she refused to tell him how she made her money (see page 171), and why didn't he turn her in? To some, Billy's deal with Mrs. Chandler might seem like a reasonable compromise; to others, it might seem like a shake down. How did Billy's arrangement with Mrs. Chandler allow him to reconcile his professional responsibilities with his ethics?

11. What did you make of Daniel's behavior regarding Nina and his brother? Billy described his relationship with his brother by saying, "Since the dawn of mankind, brothers were competitive, jealous, and resentful. Billy and Daniel, walking proudly in the shoes of Cain and Abel" (263). Nina, on the other hand, doesn't regard Daniel's behavior so philosophically: she demands retribution in the form of Daniel's dog, Sid. Were their responses commensurate with his behavior?

12. After her successful matchmaking, Nina decides to start her own business linking up dogs and owners. As Claire says, "[People] choose *each other* for all the wrong reasons. Why would they do any better when it comes to a dog?" (301) How does that observation describe the complications in the relationship between Nina and Billy? Think about Nina's conversation with Mrs. Chandler about sofas. How does it help her to understand why she wants to be with Billy?